PATRICIA DIXON

BLOODHOUND
— BOOKS —

AUTHOR FOREWORD

What you are about to read is based on a series of true events.

From behind the safety barrier of fiction, shielded by characters I created, I'm going to share them with you.

There are many types of victim, male and female, who suffer in different ways at the hands of others. They carry the burden of their memories, pain, fear, shame, injustice, and so much more.

The first step to freedom is finding courage, coming forward and speaking out.

The second step is belief. All victims want to be heard and have their words believed. That is why I wrote this book. It's for every type of victim.

You see, I am one of them, I know all of them. I have walked in their shoes, felt their pain and my own.

As you read this story, please remember, it happened to me, too.

PROLOGUE

Strangeways Prison

Dear Billie,

I am praying that this letter has reached you so, please, if it has, don't throw it in the bin. I beg you, just give me a chance. I tried to disguise my writing on the envelope because your mum will probably tear it into pieces if she realises it's from me. Who would blame her? I just hope she hasn't twigged and you get to read these words. I wanted to ring you, but my credit would run out before I even started. That's why I've gone old school and put pen to paper, because at least this way I can get everything out without someone earwigging or you slamming the phone down on me.

Before I begin, I just want you to know that I swear on my mum and our Darren's life, that the words I'm going to write are true and that my feelings for you are the same. They always will be. I'll regret losing you till the end of my days. So will you please give me a chance to explain? Read this to the end and if by some miracle you believe me, I'm begging you, please come home. Please come and see me. I need your help, Billie. I need to see your face. I need a shred of hope.

I am going to lay myself bare on these pages and tell you step by step what happened and how I've ended up here. You might not like some of what you read, but it's the only way to make you see that I was manipulated, fooled, and looking back, I think I lost my mind. One night ruined my life. I have no life now. The one I had with you, that I threw away and should have clung onto with all my might, is a distant dream.

I wish I could turn back the clock and that I'd chased you to the airport, begged forgiveness and boarded that plane with you. I should have seen how much you were struggling and needed my help. I was selfish. I was a coward. I was a cheat. And I am sorry, more than you will ever know. So here goes, this is my version of events, the one nobody believed.

It's the truth, the whole truth and nothing but the truth. Please believe me.

Stan x

1

Billie looked up at the sodden, towering walls of the prison and shuddered. The minute she spotted Strangeways looming on the horizon, its unmistakeable tower looking out over the city, touching the grey Manchester sky, her stomach swirled and fear gripped her heart. The place always freaked her out, even as a child. She remembered coming to Cheetham Hill on a Sunday with her dad to buy cheap T-shirts and trainers from the rows and rows of tatty shops that were piled high with fake merchandise. Curiosity always got the better of her so she'd snatch a glance at the ominous building, then avert her eyes quickly, knowing that bad men were inside and could be looking straight at her.

Today, Billie had parked her mum's car in one of the side streets that bordered the prison, a few metres away from the Salford Van Hire yard that teemed with activity. That was precisely why she chose the spot to gather her thoughts and calm jangling nerves. Wagons came and went, and she could see the security men at the gate, signs of life, free people who worked in the shadow of the oppressive Victorian prison. Only feet away, somewhere behind those red brick walls that seemed to slope slightly inwards like cupped hands, keeping thousands of men captive, was her Stan. That's how she still thought of him, even now, after everything that had happened.

But going down that road would be a fool's errand. So Billie shook away that thought and leaned back against the headrest. She couldn't bear to take even a glance at the barred windows that peered out like dark, all-seeing eyes belonging to hollow souls. They were like voyeurs, watching malevolently, preying on the citizens of Manchester below, and despising the liberty of passers-by whilst lamenting their own fate. Instead, Billie focused on the yard and free jolly people, like the chap eating a pasty from Greggs. The familiar white and blue wrapper was clasped tightly in his hand while in the other, a steaming plastic cup jiggled as he laughed with the yellow-coated security men.

Billie had kept the engine running just in case she was asked to move on. Her overactive mind had convinced itself that she'd been spotted on the security cameras that were dotted along the wall that bore signs saying 'No Drone Zone.' Maybe they were watching her right now, from a control room, taking her car reg and suspecting her of staking the place out, plotting an escape. *Stop it! Just stop it,* Billie told herself. This wasn't helping, not one bit. She had to get a grip and decide if she was going to do this, if she was actually going to use the visiting order and go inside.

It was all too weird, even looking at his proper name on the order, not Stan, the nickname he'd insisted on since he was a child and everyone, even his family, used. She imagined the judge saying it out loud as he passed sentence, his voice echoing words of doom. 'Daniel Ernest Stanley, you have been found guilty of...' Billie couldn't even contemplate the effect of the shockwaves as they reverberated around the courtroom.

Swallowing down nerves, Billie took the creased letter from her bag and unfolded it slowly, knowing exactly what the words said because she'd read it over and over again, until she almost remembered it line for line. Still, one more time wouldn't hurt, just to reaffirm that she was doing the right thing, to give her the strength she needed to face Stan.

Another deluge began. Huge globules of rain pounded the windscreen, while a thousand fingers drummed on the roof, obscuring the prison from sight and for the first time in her life Billie was grateful for the Manchester weather. Taking the first page of Stan's letter she placed it at the back of the pile then started with the second, focusing on the words written meticulously in blue biro. Words she prayed were the truth.

2

I wasn't that into Kelly when I met her. It was more or less one month after you left and I was still reeling from the shock and trying to get used to living on my own. I'd managed to avoid the trauma of Valentine's Day and life basically consisted of going through the motions. It was the 3rd of March, thanks to my party-trick photographic memory, I can see the date on my desk calendar, written in red with a stupid quote for the day: 'Surrender to what is, let go of what was, have faith in what will be'. Do you reckon that was an omen, or just a freaky coincidence?

Let's get back to devil-woman. Now I come to think of it she was too full-on, not in a common or gobby way, more quietly controlling. Or perhaps you'd describe her as calm but firm, like a sensible teacher who knows just how to keep her class in check and get the best out of them.

I spotted her at the gym. She was on the bike next to me, all sweaty and focused on her spinning and I never gave her a moment's thought really, not until we bumped into each other later in the foyer by which time she had scrubbed up and looked completely different. I was on my phone and didn't see her coming so when we collided and *all of her belongings ended up scattered across the floor, I silently helped her pick them up. After I apologised and she went on her way I finished my call, collected my own bag and headed for my car, just as the heavens opened.*

I wish it had been a sunny day, or just hadn't rained because then, when I saw her getting soaked at the bus stop, I wouldn't have asked if she needed a lift and I wouldn't have ended up here. That's how it began.

Billie paused and imagined the scene. It would have been a day like this, grey and dismal. She could see Kelly standing at the bus stop, battling to control her inside-out brolly as cars splashed the pavement. One of them slowed, the driver pressed the button on his door to lower the window, asked the damsel in distress a simple question and bam, his life changed forever.

She knew exactly what blue-eyed Kelly looked like, with her highlighted hair styled in a messy bob that framed her stupid face that she airbrushed with Snapchat filters. The cute bunny ears and nose didn't make Billie smile, because while Kelly was pissing about on social media, smiling coyly into the camera, Stan was banged up. It had been shockingly easy to find the proverbial Manchester bunny-boiler. She wasn't shy and from the looks of things enjoyed splashing her face and story all over Facebook and Twitter. No, it seemed like Kelly had recovered from her ordeal and was making a thoroughly good job out of a bad situation.

Inhaling deeply to trap the bubbling rage that was rising in her chest, Billie held her breath then exhaled slowly. It did the trick, that and turning down the heater – it was getting too hot inside the car which did nothing for her temper. Then Billie got on with the letter. She was far too early and had no desire to queue up with the other visitors, so instead concentrated on Stan's words.

Kelly and I chatted easily on the way to her flat which was about two miles from the gym. There was a nice pub on the corner and I'd been in a few times, so when she asked if I fancied a drink I said yes. I didn't intend to stay so long, or end up in her bed but I did. Like I said, I wasn't that fussed about seeing her again but she pursued me. It was easy sex, no relationship required, or so I thought. But things changed. It was like she eased herself into my life, with stealth. That's the best way to describe it.

I would find her bits and bobs in my house, like a marker reminding me of her existence, I suppose. She'd be waiting on the drive when I got home with a bag of ingredients to cook dinner, or turn up at the yard for impromptu lunchtime picnics at my desk. Me-time gym sessions turned into her being my training buddy and then, before I knew it, she'd met Mum and Darren. That was genuinely a fluke because no way had I even entertained the idea of introducing her, but she was in the car when Mum rang to say the shower was leaking and water was coming through the kitchen ceiling, so I shot straight round. Before I knew it, Kelly had added both of them on Facebook and when she miraculously bumped into Mum in town, they ended up having lunch.

The thing was, on the face of it, she seemed like a nice girl. She had a good job as a dental nurse, a rented flat of her own, a newish car and yes, she was good-looking with a great body and, at first, a great sense of humour. Gradually, she began to grow on me and I let her into my life bit by bit. I remembered that I liked being with someone, waking up next to a warm body in the morning. I wasn't in love with her or anything like that, but she made it so easy to like her when, in fact, that was probably all part of her game. I thought I was so clever, playing along, filling my boots in every way possible.

Up until this point I really believed I could keep her at arm's length, feeding her titbits of what seemed to make her happy, occupying a few hours in the evening and at weekends with sex and a shit chick-flick. At the same time, she kept me well fed, did the odd load of washing, changed the sheets and looked good when we went out. You might think that was shallow, but I swear she did all the running and what red-blooded bloke would refuse a three-course meal and sex on tap?

Sorry, that might seem like too much information, but I have to tell it how it was so you understand.

It was the rugby thing that really pissed me off, like she'd crossed an invisible line. I'd told her not to come to the match on Sunday because as you know, just like training night, it was a religion that afterwards all the lads hit the pub. It never bothered you. You loved your Sunday lie-ins and who wants to stand in the freezing cold and watch their boyfriend get covered in mud?

So when she turned up on the sideline, I saw red. No way was I going to let her muscle her way in and when I told her afterwards I'd give her a call in the week, she stormed off in a sulk. Not that I was bothered, I was glad. But when I got home later that evening she was waiting on the step, crying her eyes out. She looked a right state, panda eyes and black stuff running down her cheeks. I did feel a bit tight, so I took her inside and let's just say that once I assured her that I didn't mean to sound harsh and she wasn't dumped, we made up.

Thinking back, that's when the erratic behaviour began. It was like a switch would go off in her head because one minute she'd be fine and then boom! The smallest thing would set her off. Totally inconsequential comments turned into a bloody parliamentary inquiry and I know women are touchy about the size of their arse but Christ, saying your pants look tight doesn't warrant a meltdown and the skinny jeans being torn into shreds.

You could see the darkness arrive. It started in her eyes and then *washed across her face. I knew from the set of her jaw and the thin line of her lips that the anger was building and a monster was about to be unleashed.*

I was about six months in by this stage. Maybe I was getting complacent or used to her sulks that more often than not would be blamed on hormones and her dad, because she seemed to have real issues with him. From the bits she fed me, he was a narcissist and she'd struggled with self-esteem throughout her childhood as a result of his behaviour towards her and her mum. I bought it hook, line, and sinker. Why wouldn't I believe her? I never actually met him so didn't get the opportunity to see for myself. But I wasn't arsed. I didn't want to be around a bloke like that.

Billie sighed and shook her head. Typical Stan. Typical bloke. This was him all over, too easy going, very easily pleased and sex mad. She would've laughed if it didn't hurt so much, if she wasn't so angry with him but sad at the same time. Billie didn't want to imagine Kelly cooking dinner in the kitchen she'd once painted cranberry-crunch red, then hated it and spent days going over it in magnolia.

Dragging her mind away from other tortuous scenarios she focused on the beautifully formed handwriting before her. There was something about it that screamed intelligence and Billie was sure that a graphologist would confirm this and many other personality traits, none of them bad.

Stan doesn't have it in him, she thought. He could be a prize pillock, a bit vain, body obsessed, couldn't tell a joke to save his life, was a prankster, a total scruff around the house, and had the natural ability to spend money like it was going out of fashion. But he worked and played hard and could afford it after building up his businesses, so who cared? Most of all, Stan was kind to his family. He adored them, and was a good mate to those in his circle. That's why it was so incredible to be sitting outside a prison reading the words of a convicted rapist.

~

Anyway, after the trouser-tearing tantrum came the jealousy. I'm not going to detail every single instance, but I was considering getting one of those collar things they give you at hospital for whiplash, because that would've kept my head still and stopped my roving eyes supposedly ogling other women! Seriously, Billie, it was beyond a joke and I was scared of being too polite to waitresses or anyone under the age of thirty. Actually, that's wrong, because she even accused me of fancying been-round-the-block-twice Tracey. You remember her, the landlady at the Dog and Duck? She's addicted to leopard-skin and miniskirts and must be well past fifty!

I never lock my phone. There's no need: I have no secrets. But I caught her a few times reading through my texts and emails. She made light of it, saying she was checking she was the only girl in my life, which is why I was so bloody careful to delete your messages, or so I thought. I'll come back to that later, because I reckon that when you got in touch it was the catalyst that sent her completely doolally. You popping up out of the blue sealed my fate.

At the beginning, when she asked about ex-girlfriends I mentioned your name but didn't go into details, I just told her we'd lived together, it didn't work out and you'd gone abroad. I know she will have tried to find you on Facebook because she freely admitted she'd checked out all my female friends, so it must have pissed her off that she couldn't snoop on you. Your dislike of social media served you well, and to this day I'd be surprised if she knows what you look like because the only photo I kept of you was the mermaid one. Do you remember it? I took it in Acapulco. You'd been swimming and fell asleep on the sand. Your hair was almost waist-length (you loved those extensions that cost me a bloody fortune) and it was wrapped around your body so it looked like you were naked. I kept it in the back of my wallet. It's my favourite photo of you ever and I said you were my sleeping mermaid. After you left, I'd look at it now and then and wish you'd swim back to me, across the Mediterranean, along the Atlantic coast, then brave the Celtic and Irish Seas until you reached Liverpool. Then you'd swim up the Mersey, then the ship canal to Manchester and when you reached Salford Quays I'd be waiting with a big net and drag you ashore, then keep you in the bath forever. Sorry, I'm letting my imagination run riot, but there's plenty of time for that in here.

You're probably wondering what happened to the other photos of you. Please don't get upset when I tell you this because you have to understand it was a form of self-protection. It was the only way to deal with our break-up once I knew you really had left. It wasn't done in a rage or out of spite, more a sensible choice. You see, I removed you from every single device I had. I just couldn't bear to see your face even by accident. I stored them on a memory stick and put them with the framed pictures of us together. They are in the loft. Right at the back, buried under the stuff that Mum insisted I took from my old bedroom when I bought the house.

I told her to do the same and remove any photos of you that were dotted around her house. It pissed her off because there were some great ones of us all together, but I insisted. It killed me, seeing you smiling from the window ledge or to be reminded of Christmases at Mum's as I passed the photo on the landing wall. Mum's house is like a sodding gallery and everywhere I looked, there you were, reminding me what a total dick I was. Anyway, back to the psycho.

Billie looked up from the letter and rubbed her eyes, realising also that she was frowning and would probably have deep crease marks between her eyebrows. As she turned to her right she spotted the security guard from the yard speaking into his radio and paranoia kicked in. Feeling uncomfortable, Billie placed the letter on the passenger seat and started the engine.

She was probably being stupid and the bloke could have been chatting to anyone, nevertheless Billie felt the urge to relocate, out of sight of the cameras and other suspicious eyes. She drove towards the main road to find a side street to wait in, and then she could finish reading Stan's letter.

3

Billie's new parking spot was much more secluded, tucked away in the corner of a litter-strewn makeshift car park on some wasteland behind the rows of shops that lined the main road. She couldn't even see the prison which was a relief. Making sure her doors were locked, Billie shivered. The whole area was dingy and borderline seedy. Next time – if there was one – no way would she get here so early, her nerves wouldn't take it. Trying to take her mind off her surroundings Billie went back to Stan's letter.

Most of the time, Kelly behaved like a normal person and I'd got used to her jealousy. Maybe I was flattered that she liked me so much. It was an ego boost, especially after being wiped out when you left. I'm not making excuses here. It's just a way of fathoming out where the hell my head was and why I didn't run a mile when I could.

We were jogging on nicely and there'd been no major incidents for a while then out of nowhere, you texted me. I nearly cried when I saw your name on the screen and then lost my bottle. I had this premonition that you were going to say you'd met some Greek millionaire and were getting married, not that you were coming home and wanted to meet up. My imagination went crazy, concocting scenes where I met you at the airport and you flew into my arms, saying you forgave me and you wanted to make a go of it. I know exactly how many texts you sent and what they said, every word, because I memorised each one before I deleted them. My photographic memory came in handy once again.

I was in a right dilemma, though, because I'd ascertained you were still single, that your dad had been really ill and your mum was still a cow. I was pleased to hear you loved working at the shop and had settled in well with Marissa, but what I really wanted to read was that you missed me and were prepared to give me another chance. I clung on to that hope and realised that if I was with Kelly when you came back, the chance of reconciliation was zero. That's why I never mentioned her to you. I knew there and then that she had to go.

It wasn't like I needed much encouragement and was willing to throw Kelly under the bus for you, not literally, obviously. Christ, I'm in enough trouble without adding murder to my list of offences. So when the body-art performance occurred, she played right into my hands.

We were going for a meal – her treat she said – and I think I was well and truly getting on her nerves because I was easing myself into the 'can't be arsed' phase of my grand plan to dump her. I began by ignoring her texts, sounding bored when she rang me at work and vague when she tried to make arrangements to meet up. I faked a pulled muscle so I couldn't go to the gym and caught a nasty forty-eight-hour stomach bug. I thought I was being so clever.

Anyway, she'd bought a new lipstick – it was an orangey-pink colour – and when she came downstairs I just burst out laughing and asked if she'd been Tangoed. That was it! She went insane, pulling at her hair, screeching that I was trying to humiliate her and make her feel ugly. Apparently, I wasn't funny, I was a narcissist and my insults were a form of control. When she ran back upstairs, I didn't follow and knowing we wouldn't be going anywhere, I opened a beer and settled in front of the telly. No way was I running after her. I actually hoped she'd piss off home in a huff but I wasn't that lucky.

After a while, curiosity got the better of me but I went to the bathroom first, which is where I found her. I nearly shit myself when I saw her, sitting on the floor in the dark and when I turned on the light it was like a scene from a film set in a mental asylum. She was naked and had drawn all over the walls in the lipstick. Bad Girl, Ugly Girl, Fat Girl, Nasty Girl. And she'd drawn all over herself too, the word Ugly across her forehead and arms and legs. What could I do apart from try to comfort her? She sobbed and said she was sorry, telling me over and over it was Daddy's fault, Daddy hated her, Daddy said she was ugly and fat and it made her nasty. By the time I'd put her in the shower and then to bed, cleaned the bloody bathroom walls and calmed down myself, she'd fallen asleep. When I woke up the next morning she was gone and I admit I was glad, but it was short-lived because it was only to the supermarket to buy breakfast.

While we ate, she explained more about her estranged father who was a bona fide wife-beating narcissist and had made Kelly's life a misery, which was why she felt worthless and reacted so badly to criticism. I listened and nodded in all the right places, but I didn't feel sorry for her, and do you know why? Because I didn't believe her. I didn't even want to believe her and even if I had, I didn't care, not one fucking bit. I had no time for some screwed-up woman in my life and I had no intention of being the bloke who fixed her. Even less so with your imminent return at the forefront of my mind.

I bet you think I'm a hard-hearted bastard for saying that but there was just something – intuition, bloody-mindedness, not-giving-a-shitsville – that told me that she was faking it and deep down, nothing more than a drama queen. No, a raving lunatic! Sorry, but that's the truth and I did promise it to you.

When she cleared off home later that day, I swore I was going to end it, get rid of her once and for all. I fobbed her off for two days, saying I was rushed off my feet at work because one of the lads was on the sick, so I had to cover for him. On the third night she turned up at the yard. She said she wanted some air and fancied a walk, which was fair enough because it's not that far from hers and it was one of those warm September nights. Just to make the point though, I didn't lock up and go home with her. Instead, I got stuck into paperwork that I'd supposedly got behind on, during which time she pissed about on her phone and generally got on my nerves.

It was 9pm by the time I finally gave in to hunger and we stopped at the chippy. I bought her pie and chips, I had a kebab. I had no intention of taking her to mine so said I'd run her home but she suggested we stopped by the Quays and eat it in the car before it went cold. That's when it all turned sour. I think she knew I was cooling off and I sort of expected her to turn on the charm, but instead she went the other way. She came right out and asked if I was going to dump her.

Despite what you might think, I'm not completely heartless and said that I thought we should cool it for a while, take a break and see how we felt about each other. I told her I didn't want to get serious with anyone, not right then and I hoped she would understand it wasn't that I didn't like her, I just had to focus on work and had no time for real commitments. There's no way I can describe the next bit accurately so I will just say it was like being trapped in a car with a feral dog, because she totally lost it. She was like a savage.

First, she threw her pie and chips at me, then she hit me in the face with the kebab carton which exploded everywhere. I thought afterwards that if anyone had looked out of their flat window they'd have seen a car shaking from side to side, the windows splattered with kebab meat and hot sauce while a banshee went mental inside. I never knew girls could hit so hard, and the language was ripe. Once she'd called me a user, a liar, a scumbag piece of shit... etc etc, she grabbed her bag, opened the door, booted the passenger door, then stormed off along the quay saying she never wanted to see me again and was well rid. I would have laughed at the irony but I had hot sauce in my eye and the car stank and cost me a bloody fortune to have cleaned.

Maybe she thought I'd chase after her, but instead I started the engine and drove in the opposite direction and went home. I was bruised, half blind and covered in all sorts, but I was elated. I truly thought that was it. I didn't hear a peep out of her and no way was I getting in touch. I'd confidently stuffed all her bits and bobs into a bag for life, like I was packing her away. I put the bag out of sight in the wardrobe, and intended dropping it off at the gym or her works when I got round to it.

Four days passed and then she texted me. It was a very brief conversation. Kelly asked if she could pop round to collect her stuff after work, she needed the make-up apparently. I said I'd have it ready and that was it. Although I was dreading seeing her again, I decided to get it over with.

It was a Friday night and once I'd passed Kelly her stuff, I was looking forward to a takeaway, a few beers and continuing the text conversation I'd been having with you. I felt like we were reconnecting slowly. I didn't want to come over as pushy or desperate, even though deep down I was. I sensed you were purposely keeping things light, making no promises or giving me false hope. I remember you'd been describing the parade that had passed through your village the day before and the huge feast in the market square. We had to stop chatting because you were due to start your shift in the shop but promised to continue later. I'd told you I missed you and was counting sleeps till you got back. You replied with 'Lol' and five snoring emojis. That was the final text I got from you, before the shit hit the fan and my life imploded. It was the last time I can remember being happy.

I'd picked up a takeaway, plus extra for the freezer like always, then drove home and parked on the drive. When I got there I expected the house to be in complete darkness. I noticed a light on in the front bedroom, though I thought nothing of it. I presumed I'd forgotten to switch it off that morning. I let myself in and switched on the hall

*light. Then I heard footsteps overhead, heels tapping on the wooden
floor, and knew instantly who was in the house. I froze for a second,
totally shocked.*

*When I recovered I took the stairs two at a time and found Kelly
lying on the bed, the sheets pulled back and let's say she wasn't
wearing a lot apart from a sickly sweet smile on her face. Then she
said, 'Surprise'.*

Too right!

*I know you are probably screaming at me right now 'why didn't
you just throw her out?' but my head was mashed. It wasn't working
properly. For a start I wanted to know how the hell she'd got in. Later
on, I worked it out. At some point she'd had a key cut from my spare
set because NO WAY had I ever offered her one. She denied it in court,
amongst other things, like having a twat for a dad and being a second-
generation psycho herself.*

*I could tell she was enjoying getting one over on me, you know,
being in my home, mooching about. She must have parked her car
further along the road and then snuck in and waited. It was dark
outside and there were no witnesses to her arriving. You know what
the garden is like, all those bloody bushes are great for privacy but
also hide nutters lurking in the shadows. The next few minutes of
madness will haunt me forever. It's like Groundhog Day or a never-
ending nightmare. Please try not to hate me when you read the next
bit because the hatred I have for myself is swallowing me alive.*

Here goes, this is what happened next.

Billie looked up from the letter and began to fold the pages.
She knew exactly what the blue biro said and had no desire to
read it again. Glancing at the dashboard clock she saw it was
time to go. You had to register forty-five minutes before visiting
time which meant being in the godforsaken place even longer.
Would everyone know where she was going? Would people
driving past in their cars stare and point at the woman making
her way towards the prison? Before she'd even gone inside Billie

felt the stigma and may as well have worn a fluorescent high-vis vest, emblazoned with the words 'Visiting a Con'.

Placing the letter inside the envelope Billie slipped it into her bag. There was no point stalling any longer, so ignoring the free folk who were going about their business on the streets of Salford, she focused her mind on the captive who was waiting behind the walls of the prison across the road. He'd be counting down the minutes until they were reunited and that thought alone wiped away any doubt. But it was replaced by a wave of anxiety. She just wanted to get inside, see his face and somehow try to make things right.

Riddled with guilt, that's what she was. Billie felt so ashamed that until she received his letter, she'd actually considered the notion that Stan was guilty. *How could I have?* she wondered. Billie knew from her own experience that the law was an ass, and that it sometimes didn't protect those who needed it the most and even when it did, the system was eating itself and you had to fight for help or justice, or both.

It was down to Billie now, to put things right if she could and not just for Stan. There was more at stake. Once inside, if she had the bottle and could find the words, if the time was right, Billie was going to give him a tiny shred of hope. Something to cling onto.

4

Stan's mouth was bone dry and his hands were sweaty. He had to keep wiping them on his joggers as he lined up with the other inmates who were waiting to be let into the visiting hall. His heart was pounding as he focused on the officer up ahead, watching for movement. At least it kept him occupied otherwise he'd be counting down the minutes again, in sixty-second bursts.

He'd woken at 5am, too wired to sleep. It was almost impossible to eat. Nerves were whipping up acid in his stomach, causing it to swirl but he knew he'd be starving later so swallowed down his ridiculously small portion of cereal and warmish milk that had been stashed in his locker. There was no way of keeping it cold because they gave it to you at teatime to keep in your cell until the following morning. Stan actually looked forward to breakfast. It was *the* crappiest cereal in the world, but at least it spared him the trauma of mealtimes with the other inmates and broke the monotony of spending twenty-three hours in a cell watching daytime telly. That was when he was in the most danger, as prisoners from different wings crossed paths on their way to or from collecting food from the canteen. Everybody hated the men in Stan's queue.

After breakfast he'd spent the whole morning looking at photos and keeping an eye on the clock. He swore the hands moved in slow motion just to torment him. One image in particular had kept him mesmerised, his mermaid photo. He'd already committed to memory the slope of Billie's nose, perfect full lips, long lashes closed over pale-brown eyes, the line of her collarbone and slender arms that were wrapped around her waist. Stan had copied the original photo and packed it with the rest of his meagre belongings before the trial. His mum had said he'd be coming home and wouldn't need them because she knew he was innocent and so would the jury. Pity the twelve men and women, good and true, didn't agree.

There was movement up ahead and then the sound of a metal door opening and everyone began to shuffle forward causing Stan's heart to flip. Swallowing down nervous bile he wished they would get a move on because he was desperate to see Billie. As he stepped into the white-walled room dotted with blue plastic chairs separated by Formica tables, he began to search for his blonde mermaid, expecting her to stand out a mile amongst the pale insignificant faces and bodies in front of him. His first sweep produced nothing and then the light dawned. She'd changed her mind.

And then it started, the slow creep of a panic attack. Stan knew the signs because he'd been suffering them since he was arrested and once he was charged they became a regular occurrence. It began with a rush of heat, sweeping through his body and setting his face on fire. Then his heart would start to pound followed by a choking sensation, invisible hands around his throat. Once the attack took a firm hold, Stan's only thoughts would be of escape, fresh air, somewhere to breathe. The thing was, in prison there was no way out.

He became aware of bodies passing him by, nudging him out of the way just as the familiar trembling began and a current of pain made its way across his chest. Stan was becoming disconnected. This was another familiar occurrence and he knew he had to go back to his cell otherwise he'd make a fool of himself. By the time his metamorphosis was complete, he'd be a sweaty gibbering wreck with jelly legs and chattering teeth. Just as he turned to go his attention was drawn to someone standing tall above those already sitting. A waving hand attached to long arms led to a face he recognised, but it wasn't swathed in mermaid locks; it was topped by short, pale-pink hair. In that second Stan almost cried out with relief and on shaking legs, made his way towards Billie, sucking in deep breaths with every step.

When he reached the table he couldn't speak, especially when she wrapped her arms around him for the briefest of hugs that gave him a few seconds to gain composure and reattach himself to the here and now. His arms enveloped Billie, his hands clung on tight but there was no time to relish the feel of her body, the softness of her mohair jumper or even consider the skin that lay beneath. Within seconds they were detached, only their eyes connected them, locked on.

There followed a moment of awkward silence where neither he nor Billie seemed to know what to do. Aware that the guard was eyeing them and not wanting to draw attention, Stan found his voice as he lowered his body onto the chair. 'I can't believe you're here. Thanks for coming, Bill. For a second I thought you'd changed your mind. I actually didn't spot you at first. You've changed your hair. You look great by the way.' Stan was talking too fast, nerves were getting the better of him but he was just so relieved. She was here, in front of him and he couldn't stop staring at her.

'I should have told you about my hair... bit radical I know

but I started hacking away at it because it's so hot over there and it was getting on my nerves. In the end I chopped it all off. The pink is new though.' Billie touched her hair that was cropped close in an elfin style, with a barely-there fringe swept to the side.

'And the piercings. I bet your mum had something to say about those.' Stan was taking it all in. The diamond nose ring and the three matching studs on each lobe, and a tiny one on the floppy bit. 'Did that not hurt, what's it called anyway, that part of your ear?' He pointed as he studied closely every part of Billie.

'Tragus, it did sting a bit and yep, mothership had plenty to say but, as usual, I just ignored her.' Billie rolled her eyes and smiled.

'I'm just glad she passed on my letter. Did she know it was from me?' Stan had always been wary of Claudia who was best described as a 'pushy mum'. She was also Billie's worse critic, in fact everyone's, and had thought both her daughter and Stan were a pair of all-round let-downs. In the end they proved her wrong, both did well and made a go of it. But then in a way, when it all fell apart, they proved her right again. Dragging his thoughts away from Claudia, Stan concentrated on what Billie was saying.

'It was Dad that posted it on, not Mum. She didn't even get to see it because he suspected it was from you so hid it. Hardly any of my post goes to theirs, never mind a handwritten letter. You were lucky she was in the garden when the postman came otherwise she might have binned it. You know what a cow she can be.'

Stan could only nod in agreement. He could never understand why Mike had ended up with such a control freak of a wife, but maybe that was how she snared him... he knew the feeling well. 'Will you thank your dad for me? He's a decent bloke, always was. To be honest I was beginning to give up hope and then I got your reply. Hopefully, I can use the email service soon but you have to earn that privilege and I haven't even been assigned a job yet. But then again it's safer if I stay in my cell. People like me are the lowest of the low in here, apart from the paedos.' Stan had to swallow down a wave of shame and anger, followed closely by desperation.

'Is it bad, Stan? Are you safe?'

'For now. I just keep my head down, get my food and go straight back to the cell. I dread going to the shower. I try not to get into conversation with anyone apart from my roommate. I'm on a vulnerable persons unit where, for various reasons, prisoners are segregated. It's for our own safety but I don't trust anyone especially when I'm labelled as a sex offender, cos that's what they all believe I am.'

The minute he said the words he regretted them because Billie's eyes were wide and even beneath her suntan he could see she'd paled. Then again, the whole point of the exercise was to get her to help him, so perhaps honesty really was the best policy, for now. He omitted the night terrors, when it was almost impossible to sleep because of the screams that escaped from the cells of tortured minds, and some men cried or shouted obscenities. It was mental torture, just listening to it. And he'd overheard horror stories while he queued for food, of faces slashed by razor blades, of biros rammed into flesh and eyes, and of punishment beatings.

'God, Stan, I can't bear to imagine what it's like for you. Seeing you in here is bad enough never mind actually having to live in this place. You look like you've lost weight. I don't think I've ever seen you this thin, apart from when you were a spotty teenager.' Billie smiled and pushed her hands closer to Stan's so that their fingertips touched.

He appreciated the attempt at mirth but the nod to the past

stirred up memories and he felt his eyes begin to burn. He couldn't go there, back to the beginning, to a time when a gang of unruly teenagers held court on the park and spent half their time trying to get adults to buy them cans of lager and cigarettes from the offie. 'I'm not surprised I've lost weight. I'm bloody starving most of the time and the food is shite. I stock up on snacks from the shop but it's not the same as proper meals. By the time I get out of here I'll have reverted to spotty Stan the Man, the wheelie king and teenage gang boss.'

This time levity didn't work and neither of them smiled. Referring to his old nickname and the past was like dabbing TCP on a cut.

Billie sighed then spoke, jabbing her fingertips against his as if to jolt him out of his gloom. 'Hey, I'll remind you that I actually fell for spotty Stan the Man even though he didn't know I existed until I was twenty-one... but I forgive you, even for the time you kicked me in the head from the rope swing. I think I still have a trainer imprint on my forehead, see.' Billie pushed her face closer and pointed to where the imaginary mark lay. It was then that he caught a hint of her perfume – roses – and spotted the tattoo.

'Well, amongst my huge list of regrets that's right up there on the list, us not getting together sooner, and the kick in the head, obviously.'

'Stan, we all have regrets, me too, but if we sit here going over them all it'll drive us mad and anyway, we need to talk about you and the here and now. There's things I need to say. For a start, before you tell me how your mum and Darren are doing and we discuss the contents of your letter, there's something I have to ask you otherwise I'll feel like I'm being fake.'

Stan's heart lurched. He'd been expecting this. 'Okay, ask away but I think I know what you're going to say.'

When Billie pulled her hands away and folded them across

her chest, Stan felt the dynamic shift. She had gone from jovial and concerned to defence mode. She was also fixing him with her 'I mean business' stare.

'Why didn't you tell me the truth, Stan? That's all I want to know. I've always hated liars, you know that. I asked you during one of our text exchanges if you were dating or if there was anyone in your life and you said no. I kind of worked out that you wanted to come across as single and why; but you should have been honest. It was really important to me that you told the truth and you didn't.'

'I know, I know. It was a fucking stupid thing to do and you're right, I should have been honest but Bill you can't imagine how elated I was to get your message so I just panicked... the letter explains the rest.' Stan knew how much Billie hated being lied to even about the smallest of things and he'd made a huge error so now he had to put it right. And he only had forty-five minutes to do it.

'Jesus, Stan. You really do know how to mess with my head, don't you? I expected you to be with someone. It's not like you've got a great track record for keeping your zip up, is it? All you had to say was that you were seeing someone but it wasn't serious. I'm a big girl. I'd have dealt with it.'

'Don't you think I wish I could change that? It was just one more stupid mistake that I'm paying for along with the rest. I knew that's why you shut me off when I was arrested, plus I'd been accused of rape. I swear, Billie, I thought I was going mad, I didn't know which way to turn not to mention being scared shit-less. I did consider texting you and explaining but I had to focus on saving my skin and staying sane.' Stan hated talking about that time, his starring role in a horror movie.

The anger in him was building and he had to suppress it, smother the flames of hate that could be whipped up even by the merest hint of the past. He focused on Billie, her eyes, her nose ring, her lips as she spoke and like someone turning down a pan of bubbling water, the heat began to subside.

'I feel like such a bitch, turning my back on you like that but I panicked and went into meltdown when I got the message from our Debbie saying you'd been arrested and what for. You know what she's like, the family Facebook detective who loves a bit of gossip. I nearly passed out with the shock but didn't believe it, not for one minute. I presumed straight away it was a mistake. I even concocted all sorts of drunken, nightclub scenarios in my head where a one-night stand went wrong. I was already making excuses for you. As usual Debbie only had half a story so I tried to ring you but couldn't get through which is why I rang your mum to see what was going on. She told me the police took your phone and other stuff. I swear that when she told me you'd been going out with Kelly for six months I thought I really was going to faint. That's when I saw red because you'd lied to me. I just couldn't deal with it. My head was a mess at the time and I just snapped.'

'It's okay, I understand.' Stan noticed that Billie was blushing and couldn't meet his eyes which told him she really did feel bad.

'Well it was wrong, I see that now and I'm sorry because the last thing you needed was me turning my back or doubting you for even a minute, and that's what I did and I feel like a bitch.'

'Honest, Bill, it's okay. I swear I understand and at least you read the letter and gave me a second chance. You came today and that's what counts. Seriously, I was such a mess that you couldn't have helped me. In the end nobody could, not even Mum who has been dragged through the shit with all this, and our Darren.' Stan leant against the back of his chair. His whole body was rigid and he needed to ease the tension that had taken hold.

When he saw Billie smile and then replace her hands on the

table, slender fingers spread wide, adorned with silver rings, Stan relaxed slightly.

When she spoke her voice seemed lighter and had lost its edge. 'I'm glad we got that out of the way though... it's been eating me up.'

'Let's just forget about it and move on, but I've got a couple of questions for you, seeing as we're being honest.' Stan saw Billie's eyebrows raise before she smiled, which gave him courage to continue.

'Go on... but before you ask I'm not going to send you naked photos of me or talk dirty on the phone, just so we know where we stand. I've heard that's what goes on in these places.'

They both laughed. It felt good. Stan couldn't remember the last time he'd smiled, which then made him feel sad. Pushing the thought away he asked his questions. 'So, question number one is why did you decide to come home? You never actually said and from the sound of it you were settled on the island. And question number two is, what's with the tattoos? I noticed the one on the inside of your arm. What does it mean?'

For Stan the first answer was really important. The second would merely satisfy his curiosity so he held his breath and waited for Billie to explain.

'Dad's not been well and is having tests on his lungs and you know what Mum is like, bombastic and not the most soothing person in the world so I thought I should come home and be there for him. You know, lighten the mood and keep her off his back. And the tattoo is one of three. I've got one on my foot and a small one on my hip. One of my friends has a tattoo shop in town and after I had the first one done I was hooked.'

Stan felt slightly deflated now he knew the reason for Billie's return wasn't to reunite, but he wanted to see where the land lay and to know if this was a flying visit. And she hadn't said what the Greek writing on her inner arm meant. Not only that, she had blushed when he asked and he now suspected it was a man's name.

'So are you living with your mum and dad?'

'Yes, for the time being. The holiday season is over in Greece so I'll hang around for a while and spend time with Dad, and Mum wants me here for Christmas. If I go back it will be around March.'

Stan's heart had lifted on hearing the word 'if'. 'Does that mean you might stay permanently?'

'I honestly don't know. Dad's got early stage COPD and he's probably going to slowly get worse. His lungs are knackered and he has terrible flare-ups where he coughs so badly with an infection that it wipes him out. I think I should be here in case he needs me, so I'm in a dilemma. Not just that, it depends on how much Mum does my head in. Up to now she's been bearable, just.'

Despite the relief, Stan felt bad for Mike. 'I'm sorry about your dad. But I bet having you home has cheered him up. What did he say about the tattoos? You didn't say what that one means.' No way was he giving up, he had to know.

'Loosely translated it means "colours of the rainbow".'

'Ah, so that explains the hair and the change of style... have you gone all hippy on us?'

'You could say that. Living on an island amongst a close community definitely rubbed off on me. It's so peaceful there and it helped me get my head together. The pace of life is slower, though it can be busy when a tourist boat comes in. I'd describe it as a place full of colour, bright, I suppose. It lifted my spirits and got rid of some of my demons. But never mind Greece and my tattoos. Tell me what it's like in here. Is your cellmate okay?'

Stan grimaced. 'Well that's one way to ruin a conversation... please describe in one sentence your life as a prisoner. Here you go then: this place is infested with rats, and cockroaches and it's freezing and draughty. The food is disgusting. It's totally depressing, scary as fuck and completely and utterly shite.'

The second he said the words Stan regretted them because for the first time during the visit, Billie looked like she was about to cry.

5

Billie was repeating the words 'don't cry, don't cry' over and over again to prevent herself from falling apart in front of skinny Stan the Man. She had been so naive and hadn't equated her training and meagre years of service in the police to visiting the man she used to love – still loved – in prison. It hadn't prepared her for this, nothing could.

Stan looked so changed. His almost black, unruly curls were definitely peppered with grey at the sides and Billie knew he'd hate that. He'd always taken pride in his looks, especially his hair that used to be groomed and tamed but was now far too long. No matter how many times he pushed it away as he spoke it refused to remain swept off his face, flopping over brown eyes that looked tired and puffy. His skin – what she could see of it – was sallow, the rest was covered by his beard that was longer than she'd ever seen it and needed a bloody good trim. Where had her burly, fresh-faced rugby player gone?

It was as though he'd shrunk, shrivelled, and her rabbiting on about a paradise island was borderline cruel especially when he looked in need of sun on his skin and some fresh air. She could've kicked herself for speaking of Votsi, the village where she lived on the small Greek island of Alonissos. The pastel-painted houses, the golden orb that shone from the cloudless blue sky that was reflected in the Aegean Sea, on which bobbed fishing boats and tourists with their multi-coloured lilos. There was no darkness there because even at night the heavens were illuminated with crystal stars while the coastline was dotted with fairy lights and the glow from seafront tavernas and restaurants. Alonissos was all the colours of the rainbow and it had brought her back to life.

For a while it had also taken away the nightmares and cured her of the crippling disorder that had taken over everything. It was so easy to describe the idyll of living in Votsi because the place and people had soothed her soul, invaded it, actually, and she was already missing the sand beneath her toes and the sun on her face.

Billie had run away to Greece, after her oldest school friend Marissa offered her a bed and a job for as long as she wanted. Marissa had fallen in love with an islander when she went back to visit her grandmother and now worked for her husband's family doing a bit of this and that. Billie had fitted right in. After a month-long rest, Billie started work at the beginning of the holiday season in March. It wasn't hard graft, cleaning holiday lets or serving in the little tourist shop that sold the usual holiday knick-knacks. She kept herself busy and partied hard, embracing a bohemian, carefree way of life while trying to wipe Stan from her mind. She really thought she'd cracked it, had found her place and then boom, everything changed.

Now she was back in rainy Manchester, prison visiting. The contrast was stark. But no matter how much she yearned for that heavenly life, mentioning Votsi, and bloody Christmas was cruel and insensitive and akin to torment when you were trapped in hell. Billie made a note to watch her tongue and think before she spoke, and to be brave.

It was no use though, a tear leaked from her right eye so she had no option other than to swipe it away and divert Stan from the mundane and hideous to something positive, a ledge to cling onto. That's if she could find the words, pick her moment. 'Stan, I'm sorry, that was a stupid question. I wish I hadn't asked.' Billie pushed her fingers closer and felt him do the same.

Stan sighed. 'No, I'm sorry, I didn't mean to upset you but honest, Bill, there's nothing I can say about being in here that will cheer you up. I'm on a wing full of nonces which means everyone classes me the same. I share a cell. We have a telly with Freeview channels, oh and a radio. It's a really long, boring day but on the other hand, there's nowt I can't tell you about antiques and how to renovate a shagged-out house.'

Billie tried to picture it in her head but had to rely on what she'd seen online. A stupid mistake and she'd wished afterwards she'd not taken to Google and looked. 'What's he like, the bloke you share with?'

'Doog. He's okay. In for revenge porn. Can you believe that? I didn't even know what it was. Turns out it's not actually a sexual offence but it will be soon so they chucked him in with the pervs, weirdos and me. He got six months but will probably be out in three because they need the space. Apparently, there's no shortage of freaks to fill up cells, so fuck knows who I'll end up with next.'

'But do you get on? It must be a strain living in a confined space.'

'Yeah, he's fine and from what I can tell no danger to me or anyone really, just a bit of a pillock, I suppose. Apart from sharing explicit photos to the world of his ex who cheated on him, his main occupation is a doorman at night and in the day selling snide clothing and basically any knock-off he can get his hands on. He's a character, reckons he knows some handy lads on the outside. He's built like a brick shithouse and up to now has kept me out of harm's way.'

Billie forced a smile. She couldn't manage a laugh. 'Is your cellmate here? Which one is he?'

Stan shook his head and stared, warning her of some hidden danger with his eyes. 'Don't be looking about, just focus on me. It's best not to draw attention or make eye contact. I don't like the idea of them gawping at you. Fuck knows what is going on in their heads. I told Mum the same when she first came. You know what she's like, wants to be everyone's best friend and say hello.'

'How is your mum, and Darren? I was going to go round and see them this week, if that's okay? I haven't had time and it's rained ever since the plane landed two days ago. Mum has this thing about me driving over the pass when it's wet but I over-ruled her today, which as you know takes some guts.' Once again Billie wanted to bite her own tongue off because she spotted instantly Stan's intake of breath and tears welling in his eyes. She knew it was the mention of his family that had affected him and he was trying to control his feelings.

Ignoring Stan's advice and glancing to her side Billie noticed that all the other couples were holding hands. She'd read the many rules that were posted in the waiting area and minimal contact was allowed so she folded her fingers around his and felt him grab on tightly. They sat in silence for a few moments while Stan gathered himself. Billie surmised that crying wasn't a good look and would show weakness to other eagle-eyed prisoners.

His voice when he found it held a hint of anger. 'Will you go and see her, Bill? She's in a bad way and so is our Darren. All this has ruined their lives because mud sticks and they are paying the price for me being a dickhead.'

'What do you mean? What's happened?' Billie squeezed his hands and tried to force some comfort into Stan.

'I mean that people judge and whisper and one by one, apart

from Hilary next door, all Mum's friends and that lot from the church turned their back on her. She loved going to the coffee mornings and book club and, as you know, she never missed a Sunday service. From what our Darren has told me she's not been to church since I was sent down. They didn't openly blame her or tell her to piss off, but they gave her the cold shoulder and she knew they were gossiping behind her back. Everyone in the avenue knows her son is in prison and why. At the corner shop it was on those board things outside, written in big black letters, "local man found guilty of rape". It destroyed her.

'And that's another thing. *She* received anonymity throughout the trial but as for me, my name was plastered all over the news, on the radio and sodding Facebook. What happened to innocent until proven guilty? Mum and Darren ended up being found guilty by association and it makes my blood boil.'

'Oh God, Stan, that's awful. How can people be so cruel? And what about Darren? What's happened to him?' Billie was starting to get it, the drip-drip effect of imprisonment.

Stan huffed his exasperation. 'After I was arrested he fell apart and started missing school because of the whispers and nasty comments. Basically, he was getting bullied and I think it all got too much. He turned into a bit of a snapper and got into a couple of fights, which is out of character. He just couldn't take it, the usual stuff, name-calling, notes stuck inside his locker, text messages and then it was all over Facebook. His girlfriend dumped him when her parents stuck their oar in, and when it came to his GCSEs the only way Mum could get him to go was by dropping him off at the door. He'd aced his mocks but his actual results were a disaster so instead of going into sixth form like he wanted, he's moved schools and has to resit them all. Because of me he's always going to be a year behind and to make things worse he lost his mates. They've all got on with their lives while he's had to start a new one without me there to help him.'

Billie was stunned and angry and sad. It then occurred to her if she felt this way then Stan would be riddled with the same feelings, only magnified a million times. 'Well I'm here now and I'll go and see them tomorrow. I promise. And I'll do whatever I can to help. I love them both to bits, always have and always will. Nothing's changed.' Billie meant it with all her heart. Splitting up with Stan had hurt even more because it meant losing Sue and Darren too. Hopefully that was going to change.

'Thanks, Billie. It will set my mind at rest if you do. They've both been in to visit but the first time Mum just cried all the way through and Darren looked like he was in shock. It was bad enough waiting for nearly a year to go to trial and the strain was unbearable for all of us, especially because they both believed I was innocent. So this...' Stan flicked his head to the side. 'It's almost finished them off.'

'Well, I'll work out a rota with your mum so that we both get to see you. Or maybe we can all come together if that's what you want. It says you can have up to three visitors at a time so we can all squeeze in.' Finally, Billie felt she'd found something positive to say and hoped the idea of a happy group chat around the Formica table would lift him. Maybe now was the time to say more but Stan's next comment interrupted her train of thought. Or was it just another excuse?

'That'd be nice. Whatever's best and it might give Mum and Darren a break if they know you are going to visit. I can't imagine they enjoy coming here. I try not to think about what happens before they get to see me because it just makes me want to scream.'

'It's not too bad, don't worry, and I'm sure they think it's worth it to see you. I did.' Billie gave him a wink and hoped once again it would hide her feelings because she hadn't enjoyed one bit being searched by the stony-faced prison officer or sniffed by the drugs-dog. You couldn't even compare it to the rigmarole at the airport because at least there, you knew you were only a few steps away from your holidays and the checks kept you safe from suicide bombers; whereas here, it was a few steps towards misery.

Billie looked up at the clock and saw they only had thirty-five minutes left. The time had flown by.

Stan spoke next. 'Do you want a brew or anything? I can't go to the tea bar but you can.'

'No, I'm fine. Shit, do you want something? Let me go and get you some snacks and you can eat them while we talk. I feel awful now. You should've said.' Billie could've kicked herself. She needed to focus and pack as much into the visit as she could. Not waste it daydreaming and as usual, avoiding the issue.

Stan shook his head. 'No, I'm fine and anyway I want to spend every second with you so it'll just waste time.'

Time... there it was again, a reminder that she needed to come clean, get this over with so Stan knew exactly where he stood. Taking a deep breath Billie opened her mouth but Stan was quicker and spoke first.

'Listen, Bill, there's something I need to ask you... tell you... well both really. We haven't got long so I'll try to be quick.'

Billie felt Stan's fingers move from beneath hers then wrap around them. Whatever he had to say she had the feeling it wasn't going to be something uplifting so braced herself, wishing she had a poker face, or a mask, anything that would hide how worried she was.

6

Billie was mildly comforted that Stan didn't seem to have noticed how his words affected her so maybe she should take up poker after all. She was still holding on tightly to his hand as he continued.

'Look, I've had to be practical and make a few decisions and set things in motion. You might think I'm being hasty with some of them and a bit morbid with others so bear with me.'

'Okay, go on, but the morbid bit has got me worried. What do you mean by that?'

Stan took a moment before he answered. 'Well, for a start I made a will–'

'For God's sake, Stan, is that necessary... why did you do that?'

'Like I said for now, my room-mate is okay but that could change at any time. If it does, I could be a target. Look, I'm not going to go into details but shit happens in here. You must've heard about it on the news and when you were a *you know what*.' Stan had lowered his voice considerably and Billie knew why so just nodded and listened.

'Anyway, I thought it wise to make a will so Mum and

Darren will be okay. Eddie's taken over the plumbing side of the business because he's been general manager for so long and knows the job inside out and Kenny is just carrying on as normal with the self-store facility. Hopefully everything should keep ticking over. At least being in here hasn't affected trade – not so far anyway – and the mud hasn't stuck to the lads. I was worried at first that it would, especially as they go into people's homes. If I lose Dad's business that will finish me off, I swear.'

'Surely people aren't stupid enough to think that. But your arrangements sound sensible and I'm sure everyone at work is behind you and if not, you should sack them.' Billie was starting to get irritated by fickle gossipers and would have plenty to say to anyone who said a word against Stan. That's how sure of him she was. Now.

Stan gave a wry laugh. 'You'd be surprised. When I was arrested I felt like I had a contagious disease and when I was charged I may as well have had the full-blown plague.'

'Well I suppose you found out who your friends were. Out of interest, who stood by you?' Billie could feel anger rising in anticipation of Stan's answer.

'Just Pete and Todd, really. Pete's away on the oil rigs most of the time so more or less out of the equation but he believed me and keeps in touch. Todd did too, but he was one of the reasons I left the rugby club as soon as I was charged. I didn't want him defending me and getting into lumber because you know what a hothead he is. I'd ruined Mum and Darren's life so I stepped back and left Todd to it because he loves playing for the team. As for everyone else, I got the impression that even those who were prepared to give me the benefit of the doubt were under pressure from their other halves, who wanted nothing to do with me. Like you said, I found out who my friends were and I'll never forget.'

'Well I hope I don't bump into any of them because I'll give them what for.'

Stan laughed. 'I wouldn't bother because I'm in here and that's all they need to know. The jury found me guilty. End of!'

Silence settled and the truth of Stan's words had a sobering effect on Billie, throwing cold water on her vehement defence of him. Rallying herself, she tried to steer the conversation away from false friends. 'So, what are you doing about the house?'

'It's up for sale. My solicitor suggested I let it but I just want it gone and the money in the bank. I moved in with Mum after I was arrested and have no intention of stepping foot in mine ever again, for the obvious reasons. But I'm keeping my car for now and I wondered if you wanted to use it? It's taxed and insured so you may as well get the benefit of it. Save you borrowing your mum's.'

Billie was taken aback. It was a kind gesture and now her parents had retired and downsized they shared a car, so Stan's would come in handy and save her feeling beholden to her mum, especially. But would it send out the wrong message to a desperate man? Then again, hadn't coming here done just that? Billie's head was all over the place, never mind her heart that had been melting with every minute that passed. Who was she kidding? She was in it for the long haul now so why dither? Stan needed her and Billie was going to be there for him.

'Okay, if you're sure. It'll save me getting the bus and having to share with Mum and Dad. But I'll put some towards the insurance and tax. I'm not having you paying for it all.'

'Nope, no deal. It's an hour journey through traffic from your mum's and if you are staying through the winter I want you to have a safe car to travel in. For once in my life I agree with Claudia and if you are going over the pass in all weathers, my car is perfect. So, do we have a deal?'

Billie rolled her eyes and sighed. 'Okay, we have a deal.'

'Great. I'll let Mum know and you can pick the keys up from hers when you go. It'll make me happy knowing you're driving it about. Right, now that's sorted, I have one more thing to tell you.'

Billie raised her eyebrows and got the feeling this was going to be the biggie. 'Go on.'

Stan leaned in closer and Billie copied. Obviously this was something Stan really wanted to keep under wraps. 'Okay, this is a long shot but I've got some news about my conviction. I asked my solicitor to lodge an appeal. The wheels are already in motion and I should hear soon. It has to be done within twenty-eight days of sentencing so we have to be on the ball. The downside is if they agree to an appeal but it fails, I could get time added on, or start my sentence from scratch.'

'Oh God, Stan, it all sounds a bit risky... do you think there's a chance? What did your solicitor say? Have you got new evidence?' Billie's heart had skipped a beat.

'He's paid to do as he's told and I think it's worth a try. I don't care about the risks because I have to get out of here. I can withdraw the appeal at any time so if the barrister thinks it's a waste of time, so be it but until then we crack on. It's my only option. The law turned its back on me. And you know what else drives me crazy, apart from being in here?'

Billie shook her head.

'The fact that I've got no voice. I never gave any thought to what it must be like to be at the receiving end of injustice, how it feels when nobody believes you and nobody listens. Well now I do because it's happened to me too.'

'Oh Stan...'

'Ssh, it's okay. I don't mean to upset you but I do want you to understand. And there's something else, and this is really important. I've not told Mum because I don't want to get her hopes up so don't say anything, but I hired a private investigator. He's ex-police and costs a bloody fortune but it's paying off already. He's found a few interesting things about Kelly that contradict some of her evidence and also, she's made complaints of a sexual nature before, but never to the police.'

'Shit... but can that be used in evidence? You're going to have to have hard facts, surely.'

'Yeah I know. It's going to be tough to prove. But I'm going to ring the detective – his name's Aiden – and tell him to give you access to what he's found out. I want you to see, just so that you know she's a liar and I'm telling the truth. Is that okay?'

'Stan, I already believe you and you don't have to prove anything to me. I swear. I don't give a toss about the jury because I know you're not like that. You've never been violent. Even when we were kids I can't remember you getting in a fight or throwing your weight about and certainly never with me. When I read your letter, especially her account of that night or how she says you behaved before, it doesn't fit with the Stan I know and that's all there is to it. I know a lot of people will say I'm naive and shit like that, but I don't care. I'll stand by you and if it makes you feel better I'll go and see Aiden and read the file.'

'Really? I can't tell you what it means to hear you say that. The only thing that's got me through the past four weeks is thinking of you and I even started praying. Bet you never thought you'd hear me say that but I was desperate.'

Billie glanced up at the clock and saw they only had minutes left. 'No, I didn't but I get the desperation bit. Look, you need to stay positive. Hopefully Aiden can dig up more dirt on *her* and in the meantime you can ring me anytime you want, okay. I saw that we can email and they print it off for you, so shall I write or do you prefer to speak on the phone?'

'Both, or just phone calls. Whatever is best for you.'

'Do you need me to send anything, or is there anything I can bring next time I come?'

'I'll let you know but there's not much I need really...'

Stan stopped mid-sentence and just held Billie's stare which she returned, their eyes locked. She wished she knew what he was thinking. Or maybe it was better if she didn't.

It was then that Billie felt the grip of panic. Or was it desperation because she didn't want to leave him behind? There was so much more she wanted to say but it wasn't the right time. She could see that Stan was fighting a tremendous battle to maintain his composure and throughout their conversation there had been moments when she'd seen his lips wobble and tears well. There was plenty of time for her to tell him what was really on her mind but not today, in front of all these strangers. She realised that now. Christ, that really was the stupid understatement of the year. Stan had six whole years stretching in front of him. But he had enough to deal with and what she had to tell him could make being trapped in here a zillion times worse. Billie had to get it right for everyone's sake.

The bell signalling visiting time was at an end made Billie jump and she saw Stan slump, then he straightened and the brave face returned. Others in the room were getting to their feet and embracing so she did the same. Billie knew the rules: it had to be quick, no lingering kisses. But when Stan's arms wrapped around her body she wanted so badly to stay there forever. Now it was her turn to hold it all in.

Mid-embrace, Billie's eye's rested briefly on another prisoner. A bona fide meathead with a bald, shiny scalp and tribal tattoo along the length of his neck. His blue eyes stared her out and he walked past just a bit too close for comfort. She'd spotted him earlier as she waited for Stan and again during the visit. He'd been checking her out and now he was definitely giving her evils and it made her shudder. Billie averted her eyes and pulled away from Stan before they got into trouble from one of the officers who were herding inmates from the room. It was clear he couldn't speak so she did it for them both, just.

'Right, I'll ring your mum as soon as I get outside and, don't worry, I'll be positive when I speak to her. I'll make arrangements to go over tomorrow if she's up to it, and I'll get in touch with Aiden too. I'll see you in a fortnight, okay?' Billie could hear the crack in her throat and she knew she had to go before she lost it, so hugged him quickly one more time and kissed him firmly on the lips.

It lasted for a second but it was enough to break Stan and she heard him catch a sob then hold it in. As she watched him abruptly turn away and head towards the officer, Billie prayed he wasn't crying. She was, and as she followed the rest of the visitors towards the exit, tears streamed unchecked down her face.

7

At the door of the community centre on a forlorn and forgotten estate in Openshaw, a bedraggled, rain-soaked woman took shelter under the corrugated roof and pretended to search for something inside her bag, thus averting her eyes from the much drier woman in the pink puffa jacket who was making her way up the steps.

Once Pink Puffa passed and folded down her umbrella, shaking the residue onto the floor, the woman zipped up her bag and listened as she pushed the buzzer. When a voice said 'hello', Pink Puffa spoke into the intercom system. 'I'm here for the women's group meeting.'

Another buzz and the lock clicked, allowing Pink Puffa to push it open but before it swung closed behind her, she turned and smiled at the woman. 'Are you coming in or are you going to stand out here getting soaked?'

Pink Puffa waited and held the woman's gaze. Returning the smile she nodded and stepped inside.

'Don't be nervous, everyone is really nice and we're all here for the same reason. C'mon, you can sit next to me.' And with that, Pink Puffa gestured with her head that the woman should follow.

They made their way along the corridor, passing colourful stick-people paintings that merged with the information posters that outlined the services and activities available at the centre. Their wet shoes left footprints on the faded, tatty carpet and the woman could smell coffee and the unmistakeable aroma of burnt toast. They came to a halt at the open door of a small room that was already occupied by six or seven other women.

Pink Puffa turned. 'Here we are. Now, my name is Kelly, what's yours?'

'Er... Tina.'

'Right, Tina. Well, I'll introduce you and then I'm sure everyone else will do the same and remember, this is a place where we can relax and talk openly. If you just want to sit and listen that's okay too.' With that, Kelly took Tina's arm, strolled into the room and began introducing.

Seeing the welcoming smiles of women who looked ordinary, just like her, Tina began to relax a little, grateful that she'd bumped into such a nice person at the door. Tina had been about to bolt, just like she had the previous week when she'd turned up for the meeting but this time, Pink Puffa Kelly had given her the courage to go inside. In that brief moment, Tina had been grateful to be on the receiving end of kindness because it made a change from being on the receiving end of a fist.

Kelly wiped her eye with the cuff of her jacket and waited for the rest of the women to compose themselves after hearing Sharon's news.

They were seated on orange plastic chairs around tatty community centre tables. In the middle sat Bev, their support worker and opposite, her colleague Diane who was there to offer advice on housing, childcare, mental health and steps to freedom. Once everyone had helped themselves to a warm drink and biscuits or a few slices of burnt toast, they found a seat and began the meeting.

Most people would find it harrowing, listening to the stories that the women in the group offered up each week, snippets of their everyday life – if you could call it 'life' when every minute entailed walking on eggshells. Some women were survivors who came to offer support to others or share their memories, maybe to remind themselves never to go back, not to be fooled again. All their stories were different, and even the most minor incident was treated seriously and with suspicion because it served as a warning of a situation that might escalate. But there was a common theme and it bonded a group of strangers. Like an invisible current crackling from one to the other, around a circle of unlikely characters who, through no real fault of their own, had suffered and were still suffering at the hands of men.

Kelly saw Bev glance at the clock on the wall before she addressed the group. They only had an hour and afterwards the team were available for one-to-one chats, just in case something was too personal to share with a group. 'Okay, ladies, well that was a positive way to start the meeting and I'm sure you won't mind me congratulating Sharon. It's about time we had some good news to share and I'm sure this is going to be the new chapter she's been waiting for. We'll all be round for the flat-warming once she's moved in, won't we, ladies?' Bev winked at Sharon as a ripple of laughter lightened the mood.

'Now, would anyone else like to share with us?' Bev took a sip of her drink and let the question hang in the air, not focusing on anyone in particular.

A few women shuffled and the atmosphere shifted. Kelly could sense that those around her were thinking, maybe plucking up courage to speak while the clinking of cheap white crockery was the only sound that broke the silence. When Kelly raised her hand, her middle finger pointing in the air to attract Bev's attention, all eyes turned and focused in her direction. She was sure her gulp was audible, or maybe it was just the effect of being caught in the headlights that illuminated each of Kelly's actions.

Taking a deep breath, she spoke. 'Hearing Sharon's news has made me realise that there is light at the end of the tunnel but I feel stuck at the moment, in a dark hole I suppose, and over the past few weeks I've been trying to pluck up the courage to tell you why I'm here. I think today is the day, now or never, if you don't mind listening.'

Bev replied in a reassuring voice, speaking on behalf of the group. 'That's what we are here for, Kelly, so take your time and if you feel the need to stop for a moment that's fine. There's no rush.'

Kelly nodded and glanced at Tina who was seated beside her, eyes wide, perhaps in awe that she had the courage to speak out. This thought spurred Kelly on so she turned away, focused on the dust-clogged wall fan that sucked out toast fumes, then began.

'Last year I was raped by my boyfriend.' Kelly paused, just in case her words had shocked anyone, before realising they were all used to hearing horror stories. These ladies would save their comments and support until the end or for when it was needed. For now they were giving her time, space to share and the respect her bravery deserved.

'I met him at the gym. I went there twice a week, after work usually, or if I had a day off. I can't say training is my favourite thing, especially after a long day. I'm a dental assistant by the way, but I tried to stick to a routine and keep healthy. I don't belong to a gym anymore. Since it happened I've lost my confidence and I'm not good in crowded places and I can't stand loud noises. Not just that, there's no way I could be around so many men. The noise they make, you know when they are lifting weights and exerting themselves makes me shudder and my skin crawls. It's a horrible sound and reminds me of him, you know, doing what he did.'

Kelly paused and took a breath, keeping her eyes firmly on her hands that were clasped together and resting on her legs. 'We'd chatted lots of times, in between training as we swapped machines or passed each other on the way in or out of the gym. I could tell he liked me.'

Kelly looked up briefly and spoke to Tina first and then allowed her eyes to make momentary contact with the others. 'I'm not being big-headed, by the way, but you can just tell, can't you? I used to catch him staring at me and when I did, he'd give me a cheeky smile or a wink and a wave. He was really good-looking and always had a funny comment and once he brought me a bottle of water when I knocked mine over. I thought he was harmless.'

Kelly paused and took a sip of tea. 'Sorry, my mouth is bone dry I'm so nervous.' Her hand wobbled slightly as she lowered her cup and continued.

'Anyway, my car was in the garage so I'd taken the bus to work and walked to the gym after, but on the way home it was chucking it down, just like today. I was standing at the bus stop getting soaked when he offered me a lift and I was really relieved. There's a pub on the corner of my road and he asked if I fancied a quick drink. I said yes. We got on really well and ended up having dinner and staying till closing time. I did fancy him but I'm not into one-night stands or sleeping with someone on a first date but I could tell he was up for it. In the end we exchanged numbers and said goodbye. I hoped he would get in touch because I really liked him so when he texted the next day and asked me out, I was chuffed. I wish now I'd said no and never joined that gym because then I wouldn't be here.'

Kelly could feel her cheeks burning and she was too hot, so slid off her cardigan and folded it onto her lap. 'That's how it started. We were together for about seven months and at the beginning it was fine. He was very generous and took me to nice places but gradually he became pushy, demanding more of my time. I would stay at his house over the weekend but he soon wanted me there during the week too. I told him when we met that I liked to spend time with my parents. I'm an only child so I tend to gravitate towards them and I'm really close to my dad. I got the impression it irritated my boyfriend when I went to visit my parents and he turned down all my offers to meet them, saying he was too busy at work. It annoyed me slightly because he introduced me to his mum and brother and seemed pleased that we got along well, suggesting I went for lunch with her, that sort of thing.'

The plastic chair was making Kelly's bottom ache so she shifted position and chanced a glance at the other women, trying to gauge if she was boring them or not. None of them had nodded off so she took that as a sign to continue. 'That's another thing, he became more and more demanding, like wanting me to go to the plumbing business he owned and have lunch, you know, take him a sandwich and sit in his office or keep him company after work. It was the gym thing that really did my head in because instead of me going alone on the days I chose too, he suggested we trained together. I hated it because that's when he started making sly digs about my body and you'd have thought he was training Rocky the way he went on. I didn't notice it at first but soon he was commenting about my clothes and hair and he was moody too. He had a darker side and would take things out on me for no reason. He told me about his ex-girlfriend who'd left him but not in detail and I suspected she really hurt him because there were no photos or traces of her anywhere. It was weird.

'There were times when I couldn't do right for wrong. Like he asked me to go and watch him play rugby and then afterwards he left me standing in the cold for ages while he got changed. When he finally showed up he said he was going out with the lads and I should head home. I was so annoyed and felt stupid too. We had our first row that night when he rang me pissed up and wanted to know where I was. He expected me to go to his house but I went back to my flat and ignored his messages for a few days, you know, saying he was sorry and that he hoped we could start afresh. Stupidly, I gave him the benefit of the doubt.'

Kelly spotted some shuffling in the corner of her eye and one of the women was picking up her bag and folding her coat over her arm. 'Sorry, love, I just had a text. My Zöe isn't well and I've got to go and pick her up from school. Didn't mean to interrupt, love, I'll just sneak out.' With that she raised her hand and waved sheepishly to the others and then shot off.

Feeling a bit put off, Kelly looked over to Bev, worried that she might be taking too long but when the support worker nodded her head and smiled, Kelly took it as a sign to continue.

8

Once the door had closed and she had everyone's attention again, Kelly picked up where she left off in the story of her rape.

'Everything was okay for a while and then one night, for no reason at all, he went weird again. I know now that he was displaying narcissistic tendencies, something I'd never even heard of which is why I let him get away with too much. Anyway, we were going out for dinner and I was looking forward to getting all dressed up so made a special effort. We'd already had some wine and he was drinking beer when I came downstairs, expecting the taxi to arrive any minute. He took one glance at what I was wearing, smirked and said he wasn't going anywhere with me looking like that.

'Obviously we had a massive argument. He said awful things about my make-up and clothes so I told him I was sick of him and to piss off. I marched upstairs and started to get my stuff together because no way was I staying there. When he came in and saw me packing he went into a psycho rage, throwing my make-up everywhere and what totally freaked me out was that he wrote 'slag' all over the bathroom mirror and walls with my lipstick. I was petrified, especially when he got my new clothes and ripped them into shreds in front of my eyes. He told me I was going nowhere and to stay in the bedroom, then he stormed out and slammed the door. I think I was in shock to be honest and terrified of what might happen if I tried to leave so instead, I did as I was told. He didn't bother me again and must have drunk himself senseless and then fell asleep on the sofa. I was awake most of the night listening for him coming upstairs and at some point nodded off.

'When I woke up the next morning and went into the bathroom he'd cleaned it all up and the house was empty so I gathered my things and was about ready to leave when he came back with a shopping bag full of breakfast things. He was so apologetic and begged me to forgive him but apparently he'd just got over his ex walking out and seeing me packing my stuff brought it all back. He blamed the comments about my dress sense on jealousy and said he was paranoid. The thing was he'd really rattled me. I didn't want to be with someone who had issues and it seemed to me that he really wasn't over his ex. There was no way I was going to let him take her departure out on me so I let him go on and on but swore to myself I was going to end it.'

There was sweat on the top of Kelly's lip, it was making her feel uncomfortable so she brushed it away with her finger, wishing at the same time that someone would turn the radiators down because the small room was stifling. After a sip of almost-cold tea, she continued.

'I made an excuse up and managed to get away. But later that night, from the safety of my flat, I rang him and said I wanted a break. He was surprisingly cool about it and we agreed to a few days apart. I felt suffocated and had already decided to slowly cut down on the nights we were together, to give me some breathing space to work out how I felt about him.'

Kelly was momentarily distracted by the loud and annoying

reversing beeps of a vehicle outside but once they stopped, refocused.

'About three days later he rang and asked if I'd had time to think and if I fancied meeting up so we could talk things through. As it happened I was meeting some friends for a drink that night, not far from his yard and offices so I said I'd call in on my way home. He always worked late on a Wednesday. He said he liked to clear his paperwork up midweek so he could enjoy his weekends. I thought going to his work would be nice and neutral. I walked there from the wine bar – my friends were going on to the cinema.' Kelly looked down at her hands that she remembered being cold as she'd hurried through the yard towards Stan's office. Every detail of that night had been committed to memory.

'When I arrived he'd more or less finished and said he was starving so suggested we got something to eat and he'd drop me off at home. I didn't want to go to a restaurant so instead we went to the chippy and I thought it best if we ate it in the car. We still hadn't talked properly and no way did I want to end up back at mine. I needed to iron things out and set a few boundaries.

'Anyway, we parked up by Salford Quays and began to eat our food but it was only minutes before he asked me if I was going to dump him. When I tried to explain that he was suffocating me and I wanted to take things slowly he snapped. It was awful and I was terrified. He ripped my food off my knee and threw the carton and the contents at the windscreen then threw his kebab on me. That was it. I'd had enough so yanked on the handle and got out of the car. I told him where to go and I was so flaming angry, covered in stinky kebab meat and sauce that I kicked his car, really hard then stormed off. I knew then it was over and he was getting no more chances.'

Kelly uncrossed her legs because she was getting pins and needles and the bloody uncomfortable chair was making her back ache, too. Sighing, she focused on the wall and soldiered on.

'You know what the really ironic thing is, that everything I told you, he twisted and lied about. When I told the police all this, about his weird controlling behaviour, they questioned him and he tried to make out it was me who was the psycho. They caught me kicking the car on CCTV at the Quays and arriving at his yard. They have security cameras fitted there too, so the scumbag used that against me which is why I hate him even more. I just wanted them to believe me.'

Kelly heard the tuts and mutterings of 'typical' and 'pathetic' which she knew were aimed at Stan, not her. When she looked away from the extractor fan and caught the eyes of one or two of the women, their shaking heads and disgusted expressions spurred her on.

'I'd left quite a few personal belongings at his house so a week later I texted him to ask if I could collect them on the Friday after work. I was going away with my dad the next day. We like to play golf together and Mum hates it so now and then we head off to St Anne's. I wanted my stuff back and then I could forget all about *him*. He texted back and said it was fine and he'd have it ready so I left it at that. I was a bag of nerves all day and was hoping he'd pass me the stuff at the door but when I rang the bell he asked me to come inside, apologising that he'd not had time to pack it up.

'As soon as I stepped into the hall I had a bad feeling. He was on edge and smarmy too, then I smelt the food, Indian. He told me he'd bought us dinner as an apology for his behaviour, my favourite, chicken tikka, but I told him I wasn't hungry and I just wanted my things. I saw the look on his face and knew he was fuming but I brushed past him and made my way upstairs, determined to be as quick as I could. He followed me and I told him I could manage by myself but he kept cajoling me and begging, all the way to the bedroom. He was making my skin crawl to be honest, whining and pleading but I wasn't having any of it. Looking back I think that's what tipped him over the edge, seeing me taking my stuff because that's when he lost it... that's when it happened...' Kelly paused, and was on the verge of laying the most sordid of details bare when a piercing noise broke through the enrapt silence of the room.

Each of the women looked at one another and then to Bev for guidance, who quickly rallied and told them the obvious. 'I'm sorry, ladies but that's the fire alarm and we have to leave the building. Please leave your belongings where they are and follow Diane towards the exit.'

With that everyone did as they were told and headed towards the door. Kelly was in shock. After being immersed in her story, pacing each sentence so that it made sense, she was now plunged back into the real world and the moment was lost, and that bell was going through her. Its shrill warning made Kelly want to scream so she moved quickly, desperate to get outside.

Once they were in the car park she removed her hands from over her ears and then felt a gentle hand on her shoulder. It was Bev. 'I'm so sorry you couldn't finish your story, Kelly... we can continue next time if you feel up to it. I imagine the hardest part was about to come. Are you okay? I know you hate loud noises so that alarm must have rattled you.' Bev was rubbing Kelly's shoulder.

'It's okay, can't be helped and I'm fine, I promise... do you think there really is a fire or someone has burnt more toast?'

'Well, there are no teenagers in the building so I doubt they've set fire to the bins again. It's either a drill or a cooking accident, neither would surprise me. As long as you're okay, but if you need to talk privately, once they let us in I don't mind staying for a bit longer. It's no trouble.'

Kelly shook her head. 'No, it's fine, Bev. I've had enough of the past for one day. Maybe next time, if I feel up to it.'

Bev nodded and removed her hand, and focused on the arrival of the fire brigade.

While they waited for the building to be checked so they could go back inside to collect their coats and bags, Kelly joined the other women who were chatting in a group, some on their phones, some having a cigarette – they'd obviously thought on their feet and flouted the rules. Kelly was just glad it wasn't raining like earlier and the thought reminded her of shy Tina. Seeking her out in the crowd Kelly made her way over to check she was okay and maybe invite her to the secret Facebook group she'd set up for victims of domestic violence and rape. It was a great way of keeping in touch and supporting one another when they weren't in meetings.

When Tina looked up from her phone and saw Kelly she smiled, looked grateful. Maybe she needed some company. Kelly knew that feeling well. Being a victim changed your life in many ways. She hadn't expected that but gradually it began to dawn on her that people treated and looked at you differently.

Her parents avoided talking about it and overcompensated for the pain and suffering they imagined she'd endured. After all, the last thing they wanted was to hear the nitty-gritty and for this Kelly was glad. That's why she hadn't wanted them in court for the evidence. Why make them listen to that? Perhaps they felt guilt, too, about their inability to save their child from such an ordeal. It made them act weird and Kelly sometimes wished that she could turn back the clock and go back to how things were before. But what was done was done and she had to live with it.

It was a similar situation with friends because they also didn't know what to say to make things better. And men gave you a very wide berth, like you had the plague. Maybe they were ashamed to be male or were they afraid to approach a victim, someone damaged and fragile? Everyone seemed to walk on eggshells, were overly kind or they stared, and probably whispered behind her back. Kelly thought her life would go back to normal afterwards but it soon became very clear that normal was a thing of the past. What happened with Stan had changed everything. Gradually, she'd realised it was time to make new friends, some that understood, who would listen and not try to sweep things under the carpet.

If Tina had time, Kelly was going to invite her for a coffee, and include the other women too, if they wanted to join in. While they watched the comings and goings of the fire brigade, a seed planted itself in Kelly's brain and, as Tina chatted about where she lived and her kids, an idea blossomed.

By the time they got the all-clear to go back inside it had spread and Kelly's head was buzzing with bees that hovered over the garden of flowers in her mind. She was going to set up her own group for chatting about fun things, somewhere they could have a laugh and not necessarily discuss depressing stuff like drunken partners and how crap your life was. It would be a new start, a place to make friends, and right now, Kelly needed as many as she could get.

9

Billie couldn't wait to get inside the car, away from the rain and the stench of that prison. The place had stuck to her skin and hair and clothes so now she was desperate to get home where she could shower and change. But first things first, there was a call to make. Billie would keep it light, positive and informative. The rest she would save until they met. Billie tapped on Sue's name and waited. When she answered, Stan's mum didn't miss a beat. All she wanted to know was that he was okay.

'Billie, oh thank goodness! Have you seen him? How was he?'

'He's fine Sue, honest. He looked well. A bit thinner than last time I saw him but apart from that he was quite positive.'

'Good, that's good. I told him he was too skinny and needed to buy more snacks from the shop. He's got money in his prison account so there's no excuse, is there?'

'No, I suppose not.' Billie's heart went out to Sue who was still looking out for her boy, regardless of where he was.

Tears began forming again and she needed to pull herself together instead of behaving like an emotional wreck. Rubbing her eyes, Billie pressed on. 'Anyway, I need to set off for mum's and if I don't get my finger out I'll hit rush hour. She hates me driving over the Woodhead Pass when it's dark, and this rain never stops, does it?'

Sue laughed. 'No it bloody doesn't but you'll have to get used to it now you're home, and buy a brolly, too.'

'It's on my list, don't worry, but while I'm on, I was wondering could I come and see you, tomorrow?' Now Billie had asked the question she half-hoped Sue would say no and as soon as the thought entered her head, she felt guilty and chided herself for it. *Running away again, Billie? Always running away.*

'Oh, that would be lovely. Of course you can come! I'd love to see you. What time? I'll be in all day. You just say.'

'It'll be around midday. I'll be coming on the train and I need to check out the times but I'll text you for definite. Will Darren be around? I'd love to see him too.'

'Yes, he's on half-term. Wait till I tell him. He's upstairs on his PlayStation right now, like always.'

'That's lovely. I'm looking forward to it.' Billie's immediate thought was, *Liar.* Then she remembered the car and cringed because she didn't want Sue thinking that was the only reason she was going round there. She needed to set her straight. 'Oh and Sue, Stan wants me to use his car while I'm here, I hope you don't mind. I did try to resist but he insisted so I thought as I was coming anyway I could pick it up but if not, another time will do.' *Phew,* thought Billie, *that sounded okay.*

'Oh that's a good idea. It's standing here idle and, to be honest, it makes me feel sad. He loves that car and every time I look out the window it reminds me he can't drive it and where he is, not like I could ever forget...' Sue's voice trailed off, sounding sadder now, not as upbeat, like her brave mask was slipping.

'I'm sure it's been awful for you, Sue, so I'll do anything I can to help. All you have to do is ask.'

'That's very kind of you, Billie, but you need to get going

otherwise you'll have two mums worrying about you. I still think of you as part of the family, you know. I never stopped and I can't tell you how many times I wished you'd get back with our Stan because if you had, then none of this would've happened.'

And then it came, the crack in Sue's voice followed by silence. Billie knew she was crying.

'Come on now, Sue, I know it's hard but we all have to be strong. I'll be there tomorrow, as soon as I can and hopefully I will cheer you up a bit.' A million thoughts and scenarios whizzed through Billie's head as she listened to a few sniffs and imagined Sue, pulling herself together.

'Okay, love, and you're right. Getting upset isn't going to help our Stan, is it? I'll send Darren to the shops tomorrow for a few nice bits and I'll make us all some lunch. It'll be so good to have some company, it really will.'

'That would be great, Sue, but don't go to too much trouble.'

'It's no trouble, Billie, none at all. Now I'll see you tomorrow and take care. Will you text me so I know you got to your mum's safe and sound?'

'Course I will, Sue. See you soon.'

'See you soon, love.'

Billie heard the line go dead then sighed. She'd missed Sue so much. They had been a family, even though Stan had never actually got round to proposing. A ring hadn't mattered to Billie at the time: living as man and wife was as good. The rain had finally stopped so Billie wound down the window and let in some October fresh air, then sent it back up again when a bus drove past leaving a cloud of black smoke in its wake. After sending a brief text to her mum saying she was on her way home, Billie fastened her seatbelt, put the car in gear and set off, refusing to look at the jail to her left, knowing it would make it even harder to leave Stan behind her.

~

She'd tried to miss the rush hour but Billie had hit every red traffic light on the route out of the city and towards the pass. As she cleared Audenshaw, the small town where she grew up, Billie could just about see the slate-grey peaks of the moors up ahead. Resisting the urge to wander down memory lane and take a detour past her childhood home, and totally avoid the one she'd shared with Stan, Billie concentrated on the road up ahead. By the time she began the climb upwards, she admitted defeat and prepared herself for her journey across the tops in darkness, with only tail lights of the car in front to show the way.

Her parents had lived in the shadow of the sullen Pennines all their lives and spent many weekends rambling across the moors, vowing to settle in the area when they retired. It was a mystery to Billie why anyone would want to trudge along footpaths in all weathers or what possessed her dad to spend hours and hours alone with a map-bearing control freak, when he could've been at home enjoying some peace and quiet. Still, Billie had always encouraged their dreams, and at the time, imagined the distance that the winding A628 put between her and her mum could only be a good thing. But on hideous winter nights like this, their country village idyll was a pain in the arse to get to.

At least the slow crawl had given her time to think and get her head straight because she had a lot of decisions to make, speeches to rehearse and, no doubt, a huge battle with her mum. But then that was nothing fresh.

Claudia and Billie had been fighting for as long as she could remember and had rowed about almost everything. Dull-black Clarks school shoes or the patent red ones in the window, eating green veg, not eating meat, playing loud music, GCSE options, low-cut tops, crop tops, make-up, rubbish jobs that were beneath her, and – right at the top of the list – boys and, inevitably, Stan. Claudia had sucked the life and joy out of Billie's teenage years. When Billie finished her A-levels and insisted on a year out to do what the bloody hell she liked, it hadn't gone down well.

Billie dug in and found a job at a pet store which she loved until it went bump and everyone lost their jobs – hardly her fault. So she tried her hand at waitressing at Nando's which she enjoyed, apart from serving dead chickens, and the late shifts weren't conducive to partying. Next she worked in B&Q but that almost sent her mad so she went self-employed and delivered parcels, which was fun, being master of her own round. She got to know the regulars in between bopping along to the radio and whizzing around town. Then, when her little Corsa broke down and cost a bomb to fix, right before Christmas, Billie decided that a regular income might come in handy and anyway, she was knackered. The sheer amount of stuff people ordered was staggering and her nice little earner became an unrelenting routine of dull brown boxes and a race against the clock.

It was a chat with a friend of a friend, on New Year's Eve that sent Billie in an unexpected direction and after listening to the rather exciting tale as told by a fresh and eager new police officer, her mind was set on joining the force. For once Claudia had been impressed and threw her full support behind Billie, whose reaction to her mum's involvement could have gone either way. However, this time the daughter indulged the mother and gave the father a break.

She also turned a blind eye to Claudia's bragging and interfering. You see, Billie had a plan and knew the moment she'd qualified and had a few months' wages in the bank, she would be moving out and into somewhere of her own. Anywhere would do.

Becoming a fully-fledged police officer coincided with Billie's twenty-first birthday and it was here, in a hired room at the town hall, that she gathered all of her family and friends. Some of the latter she'd known for a few weeks or months via training, others had been around for years but six or seven special party-goers had been in Billie's life since secondary school and one of them, fresh home from two weeks in Ibiza, was Stan. Despite feeling borderline invisible for years, Billie found herself on Stan's radar, without needing help from the strobe light or even having to stand under the glitter ball. On that special night, when she least expected it, Cinderella bagged her prince.

In the end there had been no need to rent a room in a shared house or fill in dreary mortgage forms and fall on the mercy of the bank manager because within four months, they progressed swiftly from dating to exclusivity and then referring to each other as 'my partner' when Billie moved into Stan's house. There was no doubt about it, they were in love, loving life, their careers and neither could fathom how it hadn't happened sooner. And nor did they spot the storm cloud that was hovering, like a portent of doom gliding their way.

Bright lights coming in the opposite direction, some arsehole using full beam, caused Billie to squint and hold up her hand to shield her eyes from the glare.

'Bloody idiot,' she muttered under her breath while at the same time feeling relieved to be released from reminiscences. The past was still as painful as the injuries she'd sustained that awful night. In some ways, they had marked the beginning of the end for her and Stan.

Seeing the sign for Thurlstone, Billie indicated and began the short drive towards the village, eager now to get out of the rain and home, well her parents' cottage at least. Despite the gloom that had settled on her the moment she set off for Manchester earlier that day, and knowing full well that she was walking straight into a battle with her mum, when she spotted the yellow glow from the leaded windows, her heart lifted and all she wanted to do was get inside.

After pulling onto the driveway, Billie heaved herself out of the car and stretched creaky bones, inhaling deeply the Pennine air before locking the car and almost running up the path and worn stone steps that led to the front door. There was no need to use her key because her mum had obviously been keeping look-out. Through the frosted glass, Billie could see Claudia coming along the hallway, a misty form, and then the sound of her voice, chattering away. As the door swung open, Billie heard the word that always made her heart sing and then, a second after she saw her mother, the face that set her world alight.

Claudia's sing-song voice couldn't even break the spell. 'Here she is at last, look who it is, here's Mummy, there you go, told you she wouldn't be long.'

Stretching out her arms, Billie reached out and took her precious baby in her arms, beautiful Iris, her daughter, and Stan's.

10

Stan was sitting on his bed, head in hands, sucking in air and willing the migraine that was building in his temples to desist. The last thing he needed was a full-on attack or, for that matter, to endure the rigmarole of the medical centre. He preferred, for many reasons, to stay exactly where he was and tough it out.

'Don't be sick, don't be sick,' Stan muttered under his breath, shutting his eyes to block out the light, until his mantra was interrupted by the sound of something hitting the bed opposite, breaking his concentration and forcing him to open his eyes. Better safe than sorry.

Looking up, Stan was first aware that the doorway was partially blocked by a substantial form. Folded arms were embellished with tattoos that matched the one snaking up a thickset neck the size of Stan's thigh towards a domed and well-polished scalp, Then, as his eyes focused, Stan was caught in the glare of piercing blue eyes. He waited for the inevitable, knowing the sneering mouth would have plenty to say.

'Hope you're not having a cry, soft lad? What's up? Did Pinky give you the elbow?'

'Fuck off, Doog. I'm not in the mood and no, she was okay. It went better than I expected.'

'So why you sittin' there looking like a mard twat?' Doog pushed himself away from the door then launched himself onto his bed, landing on his back before folding his arms behind his head and waiting for his cellmate to reply.

'Cos I'm getting a fucking migraine, okay? Now shut it and let me rest. I need to keep my eyes closed then it might ease off. Don't suppose you could get me a mug of water, I need to sip it, cold as possible.'

'Who do you think I am, your bleedin' slave?' Regardless, Doog heaved himself off the bed and grabbed Stan's mug then filled it with water. 'Here, don't say I don't do owt for you.'

Stan took the mug and raised his head, sipping at the luke-warm water then flopped down on his mattress, taking once more to prayer but this time asking for divine medical intervention.

'She's a bit of all right your bird, sort of weird lookin' but I wouldn't say no.'

'Fuck off, Doog.'

'Ah, don't be like that, mate. I'm only messin' with you. Did you give her the line about it being hell in here and havin' to watch your back, like I told you?'

'Yes, I did and it really shit her up, if she wasn't freaked enough already. I felt really bad especially when she filled up.'

'Stop being wet. You gotta make her see how bad it is in here for the likes of you.'

'Oi, I'm not one of them and you know it.' Stan indicated to the cell next door with his thumb.

Doog chuckled. 'Yeah, I know, mate, you and me both, but you might as well tell it to that wall for all the good it'll do. This place is full of innocent bastards like me and you, so get used to it.'

'I'll never get used to it. And stop acting like you're a fucking big-time lifer who knows it all. You'll be out soon and I'm going to rot in here if I don't do something fast. I'm banking on Billie giving that private dick a kick up the arse; or asking some of her old copper mates for help. Anything is better than wasting away in this shithole. And what are you talking about... innocent? You told me you sent those photos to all your mates, so I reckon they got you bang to rights.'

Doog sniggered. 'Yeah, yeah, I s'pose, but I was provoked and they didn't take her being a slapper and a cheat into consideration.'

When Doog smirked at Stan he merely tutted. Rolling his eyes was too painful.

'Well just so you know, I did my bit and gave Pinky the evils when I passed earlier. I caught her eye when she arrived, then at the end of visiting. I swear she looked like she was going to shit herself when I eyeballed her. Job done.'

Stan groaned and it was nothing to do with his migraine. 'Poor Billie, she doesn't deserve all this.'

'And neither do you, mate – apparently – so stop acting like a tart. Do you wanna get out of here?'

Stan snorted his derision. 'Stupid question of the year.'

'Well then. Let's see if she goes and sees the dick, then you'll know if she's serious about helping you and if not, we go to plan B.'

'Er, what's plan B?'

'I'll give you a quick slap and make it look like you've had a good hiding... that'll give her a nudge in the right direction, I bet you.'

'Fucking great. That's all I need, you giving me a kicking. This is the cell that just keeps on giving.'

Doog laughed, 'Ha, so you'd rather be in with the kiddy-fiddler next door and get bummed in your sleep. Whatever, mate. You stick with your Uncle Doog and you'll be right. I won't let owt happen, don't you worry about that.'

Stan was too depressed and in pain to respond so instead, wiggled onto his side and pulled the thin duvet over his head to block out the light and the misery, and Doog's voice. There was nothing he could do about the pain, though. The migraine had taken grip so he'd have to ride it out, like his sentence unless someone or something could save him. What the hell that could be, he had no idea. Maybe he had to face facts and get used to the possibility he might be in there for years, six of them to be precise, three if he behaved himself.

The thing that tortured him even more was that now, after seeing her again, was the fear of losing Billie forever. If he didn't get an appeal, and win, how could he expect her to wait for three years, never mind six? He'd have to set her free. Now there was a word he really struggled with for so many reasons.

If he did the decent thing, she'd probably go back to Greece, meet some beach dude, or even the imaginary millionaire with a yacht he'd obsessed over, and he'd never see her again. When the fog of despair settled like this, Stan quickly spiralled into a pit of misery and had found it hard to climb out – and why bother? Even when he was released he'd be an outcast, shunned by his mates, a burden to his family, their dirty stain. How could he carry on, go back to his life before, or ever forget all this? Stan could feel the bitterness that was now a part of him swirling like poisonous bile in his gut.

While the pain thudded in his temples, Stan began another battle with his mind, one that told him not to get up and put his foot through the telly that was now blaring out the tune for *Homes in the Sun*.

Sleep, try to sleep. Stan repeated it over and over again and willed his pulsating swollen brain to comply. All he wanted was a few hours off. He'd settle for a few minutes of oblivion, respite from the world he now inhabited and the uninvited guest named torment that had taken up residency in his head.

~

It was 4am before the pain started to recede and even though he'd not had a wink of sleep, Stan felt like he'd got off lightly because sometimes, a migraine attack could last for days. Perhaps his prayers were starting to work. After all, Billie had come home and he'd not heard from his solicitor to say the appeal was a non-starter.

Turning on his side, Stan looked over at Doog who was snoring and whistling at the same time, a weird hoot with his inward breath, a phlegmy snort on the way out. Stan thought Doog looked like a beached walrus, lying there in his underpants, his mammoth frame sloping downwards, giant tattooed thighs, then hairy footballer's calves that led to size thirteen flippers. There were different types of cell in the prison and where you ended up depended on your crime, sentence length and how full they were. Stan had prayed for a single cell and definitely not the lower mattress of a rickety bunk bed that rattled for a few minutes every night. The day Stan was shown to his cell he nearly died of fear when he saw Doog, thinking that all those stories of hideous beatings and sexual assaults were about to become reality. At least one prayer was answered, they had separate beds.

Twenty-four hours passed before Stan felt safe. He really did thank God that he'd been spared sharing a cell with a nutjob perv. Over the following days, he also began to realise that in his sarky, sometimes mildly amusing cellmate, he'd found sanctuary.

Doog was a jack of all trades – well, not actually any trade he'd trained for, or one of any practical use. He was more the kind of bloke who followed the money and could turn his hand to this and that, nearly all of it dodgy. He ran his own team of bouncers and according to his own legends had some very useful contacts (Doog would tap the side of his nose every time he mentioned this). So he was known and accepted amongst the other prisoners and given a modicum of respect. Even his crime wasn't regarded as heinous. He'd heard Doog joking about it now and then. It was like he had kudos. Maybe the way he looked helped. And he wasn't a threat to any of the blokes who ran the wings, but at the same time he knew the score and had picked up the ropes quickly. Most important of all, was that Doog could handle himself and once outside the cell doors, a look from him could curdle milk and most inmates gave him a wide berth and by association, up to now, Stan too.

They got on all right considering they were stuck in the cell all day but then again Stan was in no position to dictate what game show they watched or who should take a morning dump first. The weird thing was that after spending all his life playing by the book and keeping out of trouble, Stan was beginning to mellow towards Doog and his casual attitude to lawlessness. The notion of a life of petty crime didn't seem quite so appalling. How bizarre was that? After all, the stuff that Doog purported to be involved with hadn't landed him in jail. That was the result of being a hothead and losing control of your mind and mobile while pissed. Not only that, going by the photos of Doog's house, and the three cars on his drive, crime did actually pay. Maybe Stan was becoming institutionalised and criminalised after four weeks, two days and four hours.

Stan did constantly remind himself that this wasn't some TV soap opera where he was befriended by a lovable rogue. This was real life and from what he said, Doog could be very unlovable if he set his mind to it. Regardless, in the quiet moments, like now, when you tried to banish images of home, there was sod all to think about other than what was going on inside the cells all over the prison, and, occasionally, under Doog's duvet. Surprisingly, Stan had wondered if he might fancy a bit of that. Not going under Doog's duvet, a chance to make some easy money once he was on the outside.

Stan had done really well, carrying on with his dad's plumbing firm and expanding it, then adding to his own property portfolio of rented houses and the three self-store facilities, but that was hard slog. Being legitimately self-employed wasn't always a barrel of laughs and once everyone was paid and the tax man got his share, Stan had ploughed the rest back in, for the future, whatever that meant now.

Maybe he was jaded. He was definitely resentful and disillusioned. It seemed a fair assumption to make because clearly, being a decent bloke meant sod all in the eyes of the law. You make one stupid mistake and bam; they treat you like every other scumbag they've shoved inside the back of a van. Nobody listened to him; even character witnesses were ignored and ridiculed in the dock, their words twisted out of shape, but not where that bitch was concerned. All she had to do was give evidence from behind a screen, snivelling and telling lies, making him out to be a psycho control freak.

It was the looks he couldn't get out of his head. The coppers, the courtroom staff, even when he had meetings with his solicitor and barrister, he could've sworn there was an attitude – 'we all know he did it but let's take his money anyway so we can buy some lovely new rope'. He also didn't imagine that subtle something in the tone of their over made-up, stuck-up secretary who asked if he'd like tea or coffee, and probably a dollop of spit when nobody was looking.

Paranoia came next. That was par for the course. He trusted

no one, not anymore, apart from his mum and Darren, and Billie of course. Even that private detective was probably ripping him off. And God help anyone found with their fingers in the till, now he was out of the way they could all be lining their pockets at any of his businesses. In that instance Doog and his cohorts would come in very, very handy, Stan's soft touch days were over.

That rage was swelling up inside him again and he had to keep it under control otherwise it might trigger another attack, migraine or anxiety.

'Fuck my life,' Stan whispered under his breath, just as Doog broke wind followed by an epic snort, as if to prove the point that he'd reached rock bottom.

What was it his dad used to say? Something about when you've reached the bottom the only way to go is up. Well that was all he had to cling onto for now, and Billie and, in some ways, Doog.

Stan wasn't naive enough to believe that Doog was looking out for him from the goodness of his heart, although he did like to think that there was a fledgling bond between them. In reality, it was more than likely that during their chats, divulging facts not fantasy, Doog had realised that in the future, on the outside, Stan could come in very handy, his storage facilities in particular. In return, the simmering bitterness that festered inside Stan along with the sheer desperation of his situation, made him more than open to suggestions of a mutually beneficial collaboration. Freedom and a bit of tax-free cash on top weren't to be sniffed at and a vague understanding had been reached.

Stan had told Doog the truth about the night with Kelly. Doog had told Stan he didn't give a fuck. He thought Stan was okay, wet but harmless. It made no odds to him if Stan was guilty or innocent and for the time they were banged up together he'd do his best to keep him sane and safe. No firm plans or deals were made, apart from who took a dump first and got control of the remote. Doog said it was down to con's honour, which Stan said sounded cringey and probably wasn't actually even a thing. They didn't even shake on it which made Stan worry in his paranoid moments. He thought that maybe Doog didn't expect a rapist to make it out. But now and then maybe you had to have trust, despite your circumstances and experiences to the contrary. Thus far, Doog hadn't let Stan down so for the moment, he would keep on praying, and have faith in the few.

Taking deep breaths, Stan focused on the two things that might just save him from himself: the face of a mermaid, and, once that faded, the face of a witch. Sometimes it was the only way to cheer himself up: making step-by-step plans. One day, no matter how long it took, he was going to take his revenge on that evil fucking slag, Kelly.

11

Billie was doing her best to remember all the baby paraphernalia she needed for the day while trying to drown out her mum's voice which was seriously grating on her. The only thing that prevented Billie from snapping and telling Claudia to 'shut the fuck up' were the big brown eyes of her daughter, who was watching every move from her bouncy chair. As she stuffed a few extra nappies into her baby-bag and checked it over one last time, Billie sucked in air then exhaled, giving Iris a cheeky wink which always made her smile.

'I just wish you'd reconsider... take a couple more days to think it through, that's all I'm asking.'

'I have thought it through, in fact I'm going mad from the sheer mind-boggling enormity of the whole situation so, please Mum, give me a break, that's all *I'm* asking.' Billie bent down and unfastened Iris from her chair and hoisted her upwards. 'Right, I'm off. Dad, are you ready? I need to get going.' Billie raised her voice and heard a hint of temper, maybe panic, so swallowed it down as she listened to her mum give it one last shot.

'You do realise that once you've done this there is no going back and God only knows what trouble it could cause. You'll be tied to Stan and his family forever and there'll be no more running away. You can kiss your idyllic island goodbye, too, because he'll probably take you to court and get a restraining order or something, you know, to stop you from travelling abroad.' Claudia blocked the doorway and locked eyes with her daughter.

'Surely you'd be glad of that. It'll suit you down to the ground to have your granddaughter close by, another child to boss about and drive half mad with your never-ending bloody rules and regulations. Now move out of my way! I mean it, Mum.' Billie glared at Claudia, furious with herself for losing her temper and swearing in front of Iris.

She could see that her mum was fighting her own inner battle. It was a scene they'd played out hundreds of times over the years but the timely arrival of her dad broke the impasse and Claudia stepped to one side.

'When will you be back?' Claudia sounded sullen.

'No idea, I'll text you later.' Billie sounded impatient.

'Let me know you've arrived at Sue's, though.'

Billie puffed out her annoyance especially at her mum's mardy tone. She never changed. In a very exasperated way that she hoped would indicate how bored she was of the whole conversation, Billie replied, 'Yes, I'll text you. Come on, Dad, I'm going to miss the train if we don't get a move on.' And with that she allowed Claudia to kiss Iris goodbye, before marching down the hall.

Once they were all strapped into the car and off the drive, Billie began to relax slightly. There was still her dad to deal with, but he was a pussycat compared to the velociraptor who was now staring out of the window, arms folded across her chest. Billie knew exactly what her dad was going to say so before he opened his tight lips, she nipped his peace-making speech in the bud.

'Don't say it, Dad... that she means well and has my best interest at heart because I've heard it all before and it won't wash. Mum only ever thinks of number one and manipulates everyone and everything to suit herself. And you know it's true, otherwise you'd be living in sunny Portugal by a golf course, not in a remote village on the edge of the moors of death and doom. Can you see the ninth hole from here? No, thought not. I rest my case.' Billie's voice was laced with sarcasm and thinly-veiled fury as she raged on.

'Why can't she support me, just this once, over a *huge* and blood– *blooming* important thing like this? I ask you, is it so difficult to see that I have to think of Iris, and Sue and Darren too? It's not always about her. Aargh, she makes me so flipping mad.' Sometimes it almost killed Billie not to swear in front of Iris even though it was unlikely she'd repeat it. She hadn't even said 'Mum' yet, but then again, knowing her luck, her daughter's first word would be an expletive. Claudia the controller would love that.

Billie could feel a sulk settling on her until she felt her dad pat her on the knee. Out of earshot of the velociraptor, he took his daughter's side. 'Well, if you must know, I was going to say that I think you're doing the right thing and I will support you all the way. Why do you think your mum is so wound up?' Mike looked at Billie who shrugged and stared straight ahead, channelling her teenage years.

'Because I told her last night that I agree with you and she needs to back off. It didn't go down well so now she's doing her "one woman against the world" routine.' Mike slowed the car and pulled into the station behind a queue of cars in the drop-off zone.

At her dad's words Billie was overcome by a rush of gratitude and no small measure of admiration. Smiling at last, she nudged his arm. 'Thanks, Dad, that means a lot, in many ways.'

'Look, I can't say I'm happy with Stan for the obvious reasons but before... you know... what happened, I always liked the lad. So if there's any way you can help him prove his innocence or help him through his sentence, then I'm behind you one hundred per cent. Okay?'

'Okay.' Billie leant over and planted a kiss on her dad's cheek. 'Look, there's a space. Pull in quick and I'll get the pram out.' And with that, Billie's mind focused on unloading the car and not missing her train.

At least her dad was on her side and his words had settled her nerves because Claudia had been just the first hurdle of the day. The next would be explaining to Sue and Darren all about Iris and why it had taken her almost a year to tell them – and then Stan – that they had a new family member.

12

Iris was fast asleep in her pushchair when the train pulled into the small suburban station and for a moment Billie wished she was awake so she could tell her daughter all about Fairfield and where she'd gone to school, and the places she'd hung out when she should have been in lessons. It was a fifteen-minute walk to Sue's house and Billie used the time wisely to go over what she was going to say when she arrived. That would just be the start of it, though, because once she'd told Sue, she would have to find a way to tell Stan and – to be honest – that was her main concern. How can you tell someone something as momentous as this when they are surrounded by other prisoners and their families? Should she write to him first, send him some photos and a letter, explaining things step by step, or take Iris in, on the next visiting day and say, 'Ta-dah, surprise'?

This is what her mother didn't give Billie any credit for. Actually, her mum hadn't the humility or headspace to even consider what Billie was going through, let alone the hours and hours she'd agonised over the Stan situation.

Turning the corner into the quiet cul-de-sac, Billie made her way to number nine and hoped she'd make it up the driveway before Sue spotted her. Iris was stirring now and would soon be wide awake which was perfect. Billie had planned the scene carefully but it was the black Range Rover parked on the drive that immediately threw her into disarray. Her brain was befuddled by snapshots from the past and for a split second she had the stomach-churning notion that Stan might be inside. Billie understood how Sue must feel every time she looked out of the window and saw her son's precious car. Swallowing down her nerves and sucking in air, Billie shook off the image of them in the showroom, the day they collected Stan's shiny, spanking new car. Instead, she manoeuvred Iris alongside then parked the pushchair where it was hidden from view by the porch.

Watched intently by Iris, whose dummy was bobbing up and down, Billie rang the bell and opened the porch door, stepping inside onto the mat. As she expected, Sue appeared through the glass almost instantly, obviously on pins and waiting for her arrival. When the door swung open Billie masked her shock at Sue's appearance with cries of 'Hello' and 'I've missed you', and during their embrace held in tears as she hugged the skeletal frame. Darren hovered behind, taller and ganglier than she remembered, still shy but he reciprocated when Billie rushed forward and squeezed him tight, too.

'Come in, come in, it's chilly out and I bet you need a brew. Darren, go and flick the kettle on while I get Billie inside.' Sue was clinging on tightly to Billie's hand.

'I'd love a brew but before you dash off, Darren, stay there because I've brought you a little surprise from Greece... two ticks, don't move.' Billie stepped backwards; her palms held up to signal they should wait then quickly bent down and unfastened Iris who was hugging her teddy, totally oblivious to her upcoming starring role.

Carrying Iris into the porch, they were met by two understandably surprised faces who looked at each other in bemusement, then back to Billie who blurted it out. 'There's no other way to tell you this, so here goes. Say hello to Iris... your granddaughter and niece, Stan's little girl. Iris, say hello to your granny Sue and Uncle Darren.' Billie took Iris's chubby hand and waved it, causing her daughter to chortle, as Sue's face crumpled, her hand shaking as it covered her mouth, holding in a sob.

It was Darren who recovered first and broke the spell. 'No way! No way! That's ace. Hi, Iris.' He stepped forward and jiggled her hand, blushing slightly but smiling like his face would split.

Sue had regained some composure and although her voice sounded wobbly and her eyes spilt tears, she reached forward, looking to Billie for permission then took her granddaughter in her arms. 'Oh Iris, you are so beautiful and such a wonderful surprise. I'm so happy to see you, my darling, just so happy.' As Sue hugged Iris, Darren placed his arm around her shoulders and guided her towards the lounge, winking at Billie who then signalled she was getting her things.

After grabbing her baby-bag and folding down the pushchair which she dragged inside the porch, Billie closed the front door and followed the sounds of a cooing granny. That was the fun, special part done with. Now all she had to do was explain why it had taken all this time to get here.

When Billie arrived on Alonissos she swore off men for the foreseeable future, so chucked her contraceptives in the bin and avowed herself to detoxing mind, body and soul. She then focused on having fun, forgetting Stan and most important of all, fixing her mind that, after all, was still fragile and the root cause of their split. Her PTSD was more or less under control, though she was prone to triggers. She thought that surely in the fishing village of Votsi, she could avoid anything that might bring on a flashback and the ensuing crippling attack.

It was Marissa that jokingly mentioned the P-word, when she found Billie with her head down the loo when she collected her for work one morning, commenting that her friend's normally ironing-board-flat stomach looked a bit on the round side. Billie laughed it off but then, while they walked to work, did the maths. She'd missed two periods, surely not... but that would be just stress. It had happened before when she lost weight, and after she was stabbed, when her and Stan broke up. Still, Marissa insisted they went to the chemist at lunchtime.

Dr Apostolu seemed most pleased when later that week he confirmed that Billie was thirteen weeks pregnant, while she was almost catatonic with shock. Her mind literally froze, unable to compute the information, accept there was a baby growing inside her, Stan's baby.

As they sat on the rocks overlooking the village watching waves crash and foam below them, Marissa put it all into perspective. 'Billie, don't overcomplicate things. Focus on growing that little life inside you. We need to keep you well too, so save any big decisions for when you are ready. You have everything you need for now and we will take care of you, I promise.'

'But what about Stan? I should tell him but it was all such a mess when I left. He let me down when I needed him the most and I feel so bitter about that.'

'You still love him, don't you?'

'Aargh... yes I do! That bloody man broke my heart and I still can't be rid of him... And now this.' Billie placed her hand over her stomach. 'But you're right, as usual. Now's not the time for grand gestures. I need to get used to the idea I'm going to be a mum so Stan can sodding well wait till I'm good and ready to tell him, and then I'll decide if I'm going back or staying here.'

'Sounds like a plan.' Marissa smiled and nudged Billie who grinned.

'Yep, sounds like a plan.'

A corny saying came to mind on the night Billie's heart finally won the battle with her head and prompted her to send Stan a text. 'Life is what happens to us while we are making plans'. She'd read it on a tea towel in the tourist shop. The bump was growing and she stroked the smooth dome while she waited for a reply. She'd started casually, checking in to say hi. By the end of the week she had told him she was coming home. He was single, doing okay and seemed chuffed to hear from her and from what she could tell, was looking forward to meeting up. He could still make her smile even via text and there had been no talk of anything serious, no hints about reconciliation or mushy missives, just Stan's jokey, friendly self.

Her flight was booked for two days after Marissa's big birthday shebang. Three days before the candles on the cake were lit, she received a text from her cousin Debbie saying she'd heard via Facebook gossip that Stan had been arrested for rape.

She'd tried to get hold of Stan the minute she received the message but his phone was off. Instead she rang Sue: it was the sensible option. His mum would set her mind at rest, tell her it was all a misunderstanding and Stan was fine. Instead, Billie's world came crashing down. By the time she ended the call, Sue had told her all about Kelly, his girlfriend of seven months, who seemed lovely, yet had accused Stan of rape. Billie said she would be in touch, mumbled something about hoping Stan was okay and it would all be sorted out, then disconnected. He'd lied again.

One day later, Billie spotted the blood in the toilet.

It's funny how the past comes back to haunt you when you really, really don't need it but in Billie's case it trolled her merci-lessly. Not only had Stan wounded her again when she was about to chuck him a very tenuous lifeline, but those triggers that she'd avoided so well were now all around her.

Hospital. She hated it. The smells, the sounds, the bright lights, the needle prick, the cherry-liqueur blood, the tinge of fear that was building with every moment she waited for the nurse to do the scan, and the doctor to tell her the worst. She had been lucky. The drugs they dripped into her slowed things down and Billie swerved early labour. Her blood pressure was high and would have to be kept under control which also meant bed rest, keeping calm and avoiding stress.

Marissa took Billie home and insisted she stayed with her and Nikos, so that she could keep an eye on her. There was no need for vigilance, though, because in those terrifying hours, waiting, being prodded and infused, Billie had already decided that from that moment on, she and her baby came first. Whatever it took and if that meant wiping Stan from her mind, so be it. But it was hard, not wondering what was happening thousands of miles away, trying not to imagine Stan doing what this Kelly had said he'd done, hoping that it was all a stupid mistake.

Billie had intended telling her parents about the baby when she went home, two birds with one stone and all that. Marissa thought they deserved to know but Billie wanted to hold off, mainly because her brain just couldn't take any more hassle. It could have been the message from Debbie, the veritable harbinger of doom, saying that Stan had been charged with rape, or nature taking its course, a coincidence or a multitude of combined factors that brought on Billie's labour pains.

Once again, the triggers were switched on full when at thirty-two weeks, the dull backache started, then the cramps that felt like her insides were being ripped apart, and Billie was transferred by emergency helicopter to Skiathos. Ambulance sirens wailing as she was whisked from the airport to the hospital, the bright ceiling lights seen from a stretcher as it raced through corridors, voices shouting orders, pinpricks on skin, bags of cherry blood, then sleep, blissful black nothingness.

When she awoke to find her parents by her bedside, they told her she had a little girl, who was perfect and tiny but a fighter. Marissa had done all the hard work on Billie's behalf so there were no recriminations. Claudia and Mike understood the situation: they were there for her now and that's all that mattered.

'So, what's our granddaughter called? Have you thought of names?' Mike held Billie's hand gently, giving it a slight squeeze.

'Iris, she's called Iris. It means colours of the rainbow. That's what Votsi reminds me of.' Billie smiled, she was sleepy and sore, yet calm and happy. 'When can I see her? I need to see Iris.'

'Just sleep now, love, you had a caesarean so you'll be sore but as soon as the doctors say you can get up we'll take you to see her but look at this, dad took a photo.' Claudia grabbed her phone and held the screen to Billie's face that was awash with tears.

It was seventy-two hours later, as Billie sat in ICU, watching her daughter's chest rise and fall that she noticed something was wrong. While she kept vigil beside Iris, Billie's body had been slowly failing. Postpartum eclampsia had crept unnoticed and was about to strike. The headache she'd woken up with was now pounding, she felt nauseous and couldn't see clearly, like everything was blurred. Rubbing her eyes, Billie tried to focus while ignoring a jabbing pain under her ribs. When she spotted the nurse, her intention had been to stand and shuffle her way over, perhaps ask for some paracetamol but she didn't get that that far.

Weeks later, when Billie and Iris were finally allowed to leave hospital, they took the two-hour ferry ride back to Alonissos accompanied by Claudia and Mike. Billie had no intention of going back home to England. Those hours of fear, being separated from Iris who had to fight an infection alone, while Billie fought her own battle of mind and body, praying the medications she had been given would prevent seizures and tame her blood pressure, had made her bitter. There was only one person to blame for all of it, for them being in that situation, and that was Stan.

Everything led back to him. Had he not been selfish, a liar, a dickhead, Billie would have been at home in the UK. She and Stan would have been together, no dramas. No packing bags and jetting off, no stress, no rape charges. Blaming him focused Billie's mind, it made sense of things, it helped her deflect everything onto him. It was easier that way.

It also proved that miracles do sometimes happen because for once in their lives, Claudia and Billie actually agreed on something.

'I think you've made the right choice, by staying here. You need to get properly better and I don't think you're strong enough to cope with all this Stan business, not right now.' Claudia was feeding Iris while Billie gazed out of the window, across the tops of the buildings to a strip of the Aegean Sea. She remained silent as her mum forged ahead.

'Me and Dad have been talking and we want to stay on, if you want us to. I've told everyone we are spending some quality time with you after the holiday season and they all think we shot over here because you were poorly. We can tell the rest of the family about Iris when you are ready. They'll understand.'

'Don't you have things to do? And Christmas is coming up. You'll need to go home, won't you?'

'We are retired and can do whatever we want. It's not like we can't afford to stay, is it? I can send Dad back to check on the house and maybe get some bits and bobs. He's a big boy and I'm sure he'll manage by himself. I'd like to stay, Billie. I want to look after you and Iris.'

'Is that code for keeping an eye on me and taking control?'

'No Billie, it's code for I love you. Look, I know we have our differences but just this once let's try to get on. Let's agree that you won't push me away and I won't boss you about. How's that for a deal?'

Billie turned to face her mum who was smiling, a hopeful look on her face, which Billie managed to return. Just. 'Okay, it's a deal. It'll be nice to have you here for Christmas... not that I have any idea how they celebrate, but let's give it a go. But you need to remind Dad, or I will, that he has to keep quiet about Iris. I mean it, Mum, nobody is to know. Otherwise our Debbie will spread it all over Facebook and then Stan is bound to find out. I can't deal with him being on my case. Or Sue. I know it's wrong but right now I don't care. I really don't care.'

'It's okay, love. I understand, I really do. Right, I think this one is ready for a sleep so I'll put her down then go and find that husband of mine. Will you be okay for an hour or so?'

Billie nodded and turned back to the window, listening to the rain pattering against the glass and her mum muttering nonsense to Iris. As she took in the scene, Billie saw it in hues of blue. Not the true-to-life white buildings and rooftops, or a November grey sky dotted with moody black clouds and a strip of rain-blackened beach to the right, touching the dull green sea that stretched to the horizon. It was turning blue, like the mood that was enveloping her, numbing her senses, smothering her emotions. Even when she looked at her beautiful baby swaddled in a pink, flowery blanket, the colours were fading which was the real reason she'd accepted her mum's help and also, why she'd called Marissa that morning. Billie knew she was in trouble and needed more than assistance with nappy changing and bottle feeds. And it was all because of him. Stan.

Thanks to the prescription from nice Doctor Apostolu, and counselling sessions with one of Nicos's cousins twice removed, along with an incredible amount of patience and understanding on everyone's part, Billie began to make progress. By early January Claudia and Mike recognised that it was time to go and went home, safe in the knowledge that Marissa was on hand.

Month by month Billie improved. Iris got stronger and the fear of everything, infection, relapse, triggers, began to loosen its grip. And as Billie healed and started to feel again, her perspective gradually changed. She mellowed and could work things through in her mind.

What had happened wasn't all Stan's fault. Some of it maybe, the actual break-up for sure. But getting pregnant was down to her. She'd taken responsibility for contraception, not Stan. And after a talking to the midwife, she understood that it was her body, nature perhaps, that was to blame for what happened with Iris, not a man thousands of miles away, a man who had a child, a father.

Ironically, Billie was slowly coming around to the inevitable when her mum rang to tell her in the gentlest way possible, especially for Claudia, that Stan had been found guilty and sentenced to six years in prison. This time, instead of falling apart, Billie coped.

She knew that one day – but at a time of her choosing – she would have to tell Stan, Sue and the world about Iris. Until she was ready and had decided how and when, she was staying put. Billie also didn't allow her brain time to worry about how you would tell a child her daddy was in prison, that her daddy was a rapist. This too would be solved in her own time.

Billie continued to heal, Iris grew stronger too. She genuinely thought that Stan had forgotten all about her, that her silence and lack of support and contact had sealed the deal. This notion suited her down to the ground.

It was the arrival of a brown bubble envelope bearing her dad's handwriting and containing a huge bar of Dairy Milk and a letter that flipped Billie's world and stomach in the space of minutes. She read Stan's letter seven, eight, maybe nine times and everything she'd thought and believed, her resolutions and resolve, immediately dissolved like a sandcastle washed away by the sea.

It was time to go home and face the music. Stan had reached out, explained, begged almost. He needed Billie and even if she couldn't help him in a practical way, she could at least give him a chance and some moral support. Most of all she could give him the truth, his daughter, and something to carry on for. It wouldn't be easy but compared to being in prison, what Billie had to face was negligible.

Claudia had a fit when she told her she was coming home and why. Marissa cried but said she understood. Iris slept through the entire flight unlike Billie who spent every minute preparing to face her mother, rehearsing her lines over and over, but most of all, thinking about Stan.

13

Sue and Darren had listened in silence to Billie's explanation and now Iris was beginning to nod off, she feared that they were waiting, not wanting little ears to be privy to recriminations. She was wrong.

'Look, I understand if you are annoyed with me, I expect it, to be honest, but all I can do is tell you the truth. It's not an excuse. It's just fact and as I've said, if I could turn the clock back I would and I am sorry that it's taken till now to face up to things. But I was so ill, and Iris too, so I hope you can forgive me.' Billie stroked her daughter's forehead and focused on her mouth which was open slightly, her dummy about to tumble out.

Sue spoke first. 'Billie, love, there is nothing to apologise for, really there isn't. Dear me, it sounds like you've been through the mill and what, with being so far away from home and knowing what a mess things were here, no wonder you went to pieces.'

Billie relaxed slightly. 'You don't know how much that means to me, Sue. I want Iris to be part of your lives and for you to spend as much time as you can spare with her. Here, do you want another cuddle while she's asleep?'

Billie stood and took a few steps towards Sue, passing sleeping Iris into her arms. Once she was seated, Darren spoke up. 'But what about Stan? I get all the reasons you stayed away but he needs to know about Iris. You have to tell him as soon as possible.'

There was an edge to Darren's voice and Billie sensed he was still slightly mistrustful and felt he should speak on behalf of his brother.

'I agree, Darren, and I plan to tell him straight away, I'm just not sure how to go about it so I thought I'd ask you and Sue. How do I do it? What's the best and kindest way? Because he's going to be as shocked as you were earlier.' Billie hoped she'd defused what sounded like mild anger, a hint of accusation in Darren's voice by throwing the problem back to him, see if he had any bright ideas.

'Can't you tell him when you go in to visit him?'

'I thought of that but since actually seeing what it's like, I don't think that a hall full of prisoners is the right place to give him such massive news, and a phone call is just as bad. I don't know, it's seems cowardly and feels wrong. Imagine being stood by a phone box with a queue behind you and hearing that you have a daughter.'

Sue spoke next. 'You should write him a letter and put photos inside. He can read it in his room and have time to process all the information, and you can explain it all like you have to us. It will be a shock but a lovely one and it will give him something positive to focus on.'

'That's what I was thinking, about a letter, but as for being positive, it's worried me for ages that it will make everything worse, you know, missing out on Iris growing up. I'm scared it might drive him mad.'

Darren sounded equally as cautious. 'Billie's right, Mum. Knowing he's got a baby will freak him out because he can't see her and by the time he's out she will be three, that's if he does only serve half his sentence.'

'Well there's no way we can lie, I know I couldn't. How can we keep this from him? I can't sit opposite him in that place and lie, and you wouldn't either, Darren. Whether it makes things worse or not, he has to be told.'

Billie felt slightly awkward because they all knew she had done just that, looked Stan in the eye and kept a huge secret. 'Your mum's right, Darren. And it was awful yesterday, for so many reasons. Throughout the visit I could see that Stan was holding onto his emotions. We both were.'

'I know, love, I'm the same and I always end up in tears, no matter how hard I try not to. It's not easy for anyone.'

'I stupidly convinced myself I'd have the guts to tell him but once we were face to face, there was never a right moment. We had other stuff to discuss and everyone seemed so near. I could hear some of their conversations and what I wanted to say was really private, epic really.'

Darren let out a dramatic breath, not quite sarcastic, more emphasising that Billie was stating the obvious.

Billie ignored him and carried on. 'And I was terrified that if I just blurted it out he might break down in front of all those people, or lose his temper... and I didn't have a photo of Iris. I wasn't allowed to take anything in, and that would've been the next thing he'd want to see, so I just knew it wasn't the right time.'

Sue was firm. 'Billie, you did the right thing so stop fretting. The most sensible thing to do is write it all down and get it to Stan as soon as possible. If you write it today and get it in the four o'clock post, it might even be there by tomorrow. I don't know how long it takes for them to process the mail in there but the sooner you get it over with, the better. We're going to feel so awkward if he rings. He won't like the thought of us keeping secrets from him.'

'Okay, that sounds like a plan, and I've got lots of photos with me: I brought a whole set for you, right from the minute she was born. I'll put some in with my letter.' Billie felt a huge burden had been lifted and even Darren looked less tense.

'Now that's all sorted, why don't we settle our little princess on the settee and I'll make us something to eat, and then we can look at these photos. How does that sound?' Sue smiled encouragingly at Billie.

'Sounds fab, and I'm starving. Let's have a look at the photos, Bill, while Mum makes dinner.'

Just hearing Darren refer to her like he used to caused Billie's heart to flip and tears sting her eyes. He'd forgiven her, she knew that now. Looking quickly at Sue who gave her a conspiratorial wink, Billie stood and made her way over to Iris before settling her on the settee, wedging her in with a row of cushions.

'I'll get them now... there's two sets, one for you and one for Stan.' It was just as she covered Iris with the blanket that her resolve broke and she burst into tears. Relief and a year's worth of emotional turmoil bubbled over. Billie felt stupid and overwhelmed until she became enveloped in a hug from Sue who shushed and cajoled her.

'Now, now, there's no need for tears, love. Everything's going to be just fine. We're family and we will get through this, I know we will.' Turning to Darren, Sue gave him his orders. 'Don't just stand there, go flick the kettle on and then bring us some kitchen roll.'

Darren shot off while Billie attempted to compose herself. He was back in a flash bearing the kitchen roll, still on the wooden stand which he passed to his mum. Rolling her eyes at her son, Sue tutted and pulled off a length before passing it to Billie who, seeing Darren's bemused face managed a smile.

'Thanks Darren, thanks Sue. I'm so glad to be here you know, back in this house with you. It reminds me so much of Stan... and everything. But you're right, we are family and no matter what, that's how it will stay, I promise.' As Billie wiped her eyes she felt Sue plant a kiss on her forehead.

'Right, food. Our little rainbow will be waking up soon so let's get something to eat, and I'll find you some writing paper then you can get cracking on that letter.' With that, Sue hurried off towards the kitchen.

Billie wiped her nose then turned to Darren. 'So we're okay? I missed you, little brother.'

Darren flushed then gave her a shy smile. 'Yeah, course we're okay and I missed you too, big sis. Now, let's have a look at the photos. I think Iris looks like our Stan, don't you?'

'Yes. She's the image of him, she really is.' Rummaging in her baby-bag, Billie pulled out the wallets containing the photos and passed one set to Darren before plonking herself by his side on the arm of the chair.

As he studied each one carefully, Billie talked him through the image and as she did, thought of Stan doing the same thing. Sue was right, he had to know and as soon as possible. It would knock him for six but after he'd got over the shock it would give him a focus, another reason to survive his sentence. In the meantime, if she could do anything at all to help, she would. Not just for Stan, but for Iris, and for all of them.

14

Stan was perplexed as he settled himself on the bed and pulled Billie's letter from the envelope. It irked him that it had already been opened, as had the smaller one that said 'OPEN LAST' in red biro, and that her words would have already been read by some faceless officer. That was the rule though and, as with all the others, Stan just had to deal with it.

He'd been waiting for this letter and hadn't stopped wondering about its contents since his phone call with Billie. He'd rang her two nights previously, wanting to know how her visit with his mum had gone and whether she'd taken his car. After Billie had assured him that his mum and Darren were fine and they'd had a lovely time together and yes, she'd collected his car, filled it with diesel and felt very safe driving back to her mum's in it, she went all mysterious on him. He'd gone over and over her words ever since, trying to guess what she meant.

'So when are you going to see Aiden? Do you know where his offices are? I told him to go through everything with you.' Stan was eager for Billie to visit the private detective. Even though he knew he was grasping at straws, just maybe she'd think of another angle, some way to discredit Kelly or pour cold water on her testimony. If not, his appeal would have to be withdrawn.

'I'm going on Friday. He said he was working away on a case and that's the earliest he could fit me in. He sounded nice enough though.'

'Yeah, he's okay, old-school ex-copper but he employs a tech guy to do all the online digging.' Stan lowered his voice so nobody in the queue could hear. 'It's probably dodgy as fuck but who cares as long as he finds something and it's worth the money I'm shelling out.'

'Well I'll let you know what he says once I've seen him but, Stan, there's something else I need to talk about and it's important so listen. Okay?'

Stan's stomach lurched, always fearful of bad news from home or a knock-back from Billie. 'Okay, what's up? Is something wrong with Mum?' He'd already convinced himself that's what it was before Billie got a chance to reply.

'Stan, I swear she's fine, honest. When I left her yesterday she was in really good spirits so stop stressing and listen because I'll be pissed off with you if your phonecard runs out. So shut it.'

Relief swam through Stan's veins as he laughed. He liked it when Billie was bossy. 'Okay, but don't worry, I've got plenty of credit so go on, I'm all ears.'

'At last. Right, I've written you a letter and posted it earlier, first class so it should get to the prison tomorrow. I don't know how long it takes to process them so you might not get it till the day after. When you do, save the smaller envelope till last. It's got some photos in it but I'd like you to read the letter first, so do you promise to do as you're told for once?'

Stan thought Billie sounded anxious.

'Yeah, of course, I promise. But why the big mystery, and

what are the photos of?' Stan knew better than to suggest they were naked ones of Billie: that wasn't her thing at all.

'Just wait and see. I took them when I was in Greece and once you've read the letter you'll understand.'

'You're not giving me the push again are you? Not that we are, you know, together or anything but you've only just got back and made friends so it sounds like a Dear John letter is heading my way with some "remember me" photos inside.'

When Billie spoke Stan could tell by her tone she was serious and most of all, sincere.

'I promise you it's not a Dear John letter. I just want to explain a few things about how I was feeling when I left and stuff that went on when I was in Votsi. It'll save time at visiting, you know, going through the ins and outs of my life while the people on the next table earwig, so I put everything I needed to tell you on paper. Just like you did when you wrote to me. The photos are to help make sense of the things I describe... so just behave and keep your promise, and then ring me once you've read it. I'll be waiting.'

Stan let out a silent sigh. Billie's comments had set him at ease although he was still curious. 'Okay, as long as you don't tell me you had it off with some Greek millionaire with a yacht.'

He heard Billie tut loudly. 'What on earth are you going on about? I don't know any millionaires with a yacht. Not even a rowing boat, so quit the questions and be patient.'

'Yes, boss, I will, boss. Whatever you say, boss.' Stan was smiling and he imagined she was too.

Billie sighed. 'Right, I'd better go. Mothership is waiting to serve tea and she's had a right face on her since I got in. Don't forget to ring me – and send me a visiting order for early next week if you can.'

'Will do and, Billie, thanks for everything, you know, going to see Mum. I feel better knowing you've been and she's cheered up. Say hello to your mum and dad for me, or not. Don't want our Claud projectile vomiting all over her tea.' Stan always used to joke that when she was annoyed, he expected Claudia's head to spin round like in *The Exorcist* and he knew from Billie's reaction she remembered.

'It's okay, I've got my crucifix ready, just in case. See ya, Stan, please take care and I'll speak to you soon. Bye for now.'

'Bye Billie, see you soon.' Feeling that choking sensation in his throat and the threat of tears, Stan was almost relived that the call was over and that unmistakeable disconnect sound was ringing in his ears.

Billie had been right about the delay and two days later, Stan finally had mail. Glad to have the cell to himself while Doog mopped the corridors, Stan lay back on the pillow, unfolded the sheets and began to read.

Dear Stan,

I have thought about what I'm going to tell you in this letter a thousand times, maybe more, and now the time has come to actually write the words, it seems the only way to explain what happened is to come right out and say it, so here goes.

When I left Manchester and you, I had no idea that I was pregnant and eight months later, a lot earlier than expected, I had a baby girl: our daughter. I named her Iris and she was born on the 20th of November, the most beautiful, adorable little girl in the world. Her name means colours of the rainbow and that's what the tattoo means on my arm. I know you will be in complete and utter shock right now so take deep breaths and read the rest of my letter. I hope it will explain everything. By the way, I am writing this in the dining room at your mum's. I brought Iris to meet her gran and uncle today and they are both so happy and love her already. I've been through the

*whole sequence of events with them and they understand, so now all I
have to do is tell you and hope that by the end you feel the same.*

*You can open the other envelope now and look at our perfect baby
girl.*

Stan's right hand was covering his mouth, holding in his
utter shock and disbelief while his eyes were pumping out tears
that prevented him reading any more of Billie's letter. Pushing
himself upright, he wiped his face and with trembling hands,
slid the photos out of the smaller envelope. When he saw the
face of his daughter, Stan gasped and touched the photo of Iris,
imagining the feel of wispy blonde hair that just about reached
her ears. She had soulful brown eyes, not as dark as his own.
Maybe somewhere in between mine and Billie's, he decided. She was
grinning into the camera, two tiny bottom teeth popping
through her gums.

Sucking in air, Stan moved on to the photo underneath and
here she looked slightly younger. She had less hair, and was
wearing an all-in-one, pale lemon with rabbits. Quickly, Stan
flicked through each one and he was right, they were going
backwards in time and the final one was of an incubator and
inside, a tiny scrap of pink in a nappy that looked far too big.
There were wires and tubes everywhere, linking Iris up to a
machine that, from the looks of things, kept her alive.

The next set was wrapped in a sheet of paper and on the
front it said, 'Me and the Bump'. There were five images
showing different stages of Billie's pregnancy and the final one
of mother and daughter, presumably the first time they were
properly united. Billie looked so frail and tired, thinner than
he'd ever seen her and Iris was swaddled in a blanket, only her
face on show. What had happened? Why had Iris come early?
The last one was of them recently, on the beach, possibly before
they left Votsi. It was as Stan reorganised the photos he noticed
that Billie had written on the back of each, a short note giving

the date and stage of Iris's life. He decided to read them later because now he was more concerned about the contents of the letter and the series of events that had led to his daughter's birth, and her being so poorly.

Picking it up, Stan continued where he'd left off, hoping that Doog would stay away for a while longer, just until he'd got his head round everything. Finding his place, Stan read on and as he did the pieces fell into place and it slowly dawned on him how his life in England, the one that involved that slag Kelly and ran parallel to Billie's, could have had a profound effect on the outcome. Swallowing down an impending sense of fear, Stan pre-empted guilt and by the time Doog came bounding into the cell, he was awash with it. Billie had gone through hell and reading between the lines, he was more than likely the cause of her descent into the abyss. Once again he had let her down.

'What's up with you? Ah, the mystery letter. Did she give you the elbow then?' Doog was relaxing in his bed, unwrapping a Mars Bar and didn't wait for Stan to answer before taking a huge bite.

Looking up from the letter, Stan was in no mood for Doog's piss-taking so decided to nip it in the bud, glad that his cell-mate's mouth was full of food.

'No, she told me that I'm a dad and she had my kid while she was in Greece.'

'No shit. So how do you know it's yours then?'

Doog always talked with his mouth full and it really got on Stan's tits at the best of times but the comment touched a nerve. 'Because I know she fucking is, so watch your mouth.' Stan was trembling but regretted his outburst so softened his tone. 'Leave the jokes out, Doog, okay, just this once.'

Doog raised his hands in mock surrender, a stump of Mars Bar held between his finger and thumb. 'Hey... chill out, mate, fuck me I was only messin'. Congratulations by the way. Seriously, I'm chuffed for you, I really am.' Doog sat up and swung his legs onto the floor.

Stan was riled and his head was on fire with questions and recriminations, and so much hate. He could feel it running through his body like molten lava.

'Come on then, let's have a gander.' Doog's tone was more serious now and as he caught Stan's eye, he gave him a smile.

'Here, and don't get chocolate on them... look, that's her. I can't believe it. I'm a dad.' Stan brushed his hands over his face, still reeling from the shock.

Doog studied each of them before handing them back, chocolate-free. 'So what's the story then? How come she's just told you now?'

Stan could see that Doog was suspicious. It was just his nature but he wouldn't have Billie tarnished, so decided to explain, thinking it might also help to go through it all again. 'Do you really want to hear or would you rather watch *Only Fools and Horses*, again?'

'Nah, can't be arsed. You look like you could do with some words of wisdom from Uncle Doog so fire away... I'm all ears and, as they say in Asda, happy to help.' With that he lay back down and folded his arms behind his head and waited.

Stan glanced at the small clock on the side. He needed to ring Billie and his mum too, but he wasn't allowed out yet and had hours to wait. There was a very good chance he'd go mad in the meantime, but at least now he had Iris to think about, her gorgeous face to focus on which was a good thing really. Because once he'd spoken to his family and asked Billie to bring their daughter in, like she promised in her letter, the next item on the agenda was getting out of there.

The other matter he forced from his mind. *Her* face, her name, the stain she had left on him and his family. She was not going to ruin today, not like she'd ruined his life. And God help him, no matter how long he waited, one day she would suffer. He would destroy her. That was exactly what she threatened him with, and boy, had he suffered. But when it was her turn, once he was out, he'd make damn sure the evil slag knew the true meaning of the word. One way or another, Kelly would pay.

15

Billie was waiting to see Aiden, the private detective, who was on an important call and had been for the past fifteen minutes; long enough for Karen, his secretary, who had apologised twice for the delay and appeared rather annoyed with her boss, to offer Billie another cup of coffee. She'd accepted, grateful for a double hit of caffeine because she was mentally and physically exhausted.

The strain of the past two days was taking its toll and Billie could really have done without Iris keeping her up all night teething. Poor little thing was really struggling with her achy gums and hot, rosy-red cheeks. She'd finally settled in the early hours of the morning and allowed Billie a couple of hours of blissful unbroken sleep. It hadn't been anywhere near enough, not to replenish her reserves let alone recharge her battery.

Whoever said confession was good for the soul was deluded because after going over the past, dredging up parts of her life that had caused such anguish, all she was left with, lingering in the background were the faint murmurings of fear. Billie was scared – that she would let Stan down, that she wouldn't have the strength to support him through years of a prison sentence, or explain to Iris where her daddy was. All of this had swirled inside her head as she paced the floor during a very long night, trying to soothe Iris.

But there was one good thing to come out of it. Stan had forgiven her. He was adamant there was nothing *to* forgive, just like Sue and Darren. Billie had cried through most of their phone conversation, an outpouring of everything held in for so long. Thankfully, by the end, Stan had made her smile and somehow, convinced her that the scales were equally balanced, well, almost. He insisted on taking the blame for their break-up.

'Billie, I get it, I really do and if anyone is to blame it's me for messing up and causing you to run away. I've read your letter over and over and the only bit that's missing is my part in it all, before and after you left. So can we just move on now?'

Billie hiccupped and then blew her nose, trying hard to get a grip and stem the tears and snorty sobbing noises. 'Okay, okay... let's just start again, we have Iris and that's what matters.'

'Good, that's my girl, well my big one anyway and I can't wait to meet my little one but Doog says I'll have to be assessed first, and so will you, by social services. How fucking ridiculous is that? They need to make sure I'm not a threat to my own child! It makes me sick.'

Billie's stomach lurched because she was going to explain what the prison had told her when she rang to enquire about visiting, but he already knew, thanks to his cellmate. 'I know, it's ridiculous and I couldn't believe it at first but I've already rang up and started the ball rolling, and I explained that you hadn't seen Iris yet so fingers crossed everything should be in place by next visiting. Just hang in there, okay?' Billie was so disappointed and couldn't hold it in anymore, and set off crying.

'Hey, stop that, please, Bill, don't cry...'

'Sorry, sorry, I don't know what's wrong with me. I think it's just relief and anger and disappointment all mixed together, that's all. I just wanted you to see her.'

'Look, I'm disappointed too, and I'm pissed off that you have to be assessed, you've done sod all wrong but we'll get through it. Now come on, let me hear you smile.'

Billie sniffed. 'How can you be so brave and sensible while I'm being a complete mard-arse?'

'You're not mard at all... and I'm not brave but for the first time in ages I do feel what I can only describe as a bit of happiness, knowing I've got a baby daughter, and you on my side. It seems a weird thing to say when I'm stuck in here but this is like a fresh start and I swear, once I'm out I will do whatever it takes to make things right and look after you and Iris. That's if you want me to.'

Billie could feel Stan's loaded question radiating down the line, a bright white beam of hope travelling through space, hitting a lonely satellite before pinging back to earth then zapping her phone, bringing his words to her ears. In that moment she knew the answer. She'd known it all along, even on the day she boarded a flight for Greece and then one home again. She did want Stan, more than anything.

'Of course I do. We both do.' Billie wiped away more tears and listened. Silence, and she knew Stan was fighting his own battle at the other end of the line.

When he managed to speak, just after a throat-clearing cough, his words made her smile. 'Right, well that's a plan then, the three of us against the world. And I'll be counting sleeps till I see you all again. I've missed you so much, Billie.'

'I've missed you too, Stan. Now bugger off before you make me cry again. Ring me tomorrow night if you can.'

'Will do, Billie...' There was a pause, then Stan said softly, 'I love you, Billie.'

Billie smiled. 'I love you too, now go!'

When the detective's receptionist-cum-secretary returned from the office kitchen carrying another cup of coffee for Billie, it broke the spell and forced her back to the here and now. She managed to say thank you and take a sip before the wooden office door swung open and out stepped Aiden. Billie hadn't given much time to thoughts of what he would look like, but somewhere in the recesses of her mind she had stored the image of a short and portly chap, balding obviously, in his early sixties, wearing a weary expression and a badly-fitting suit to compliment his irritable and shambolic air. The private detective who stood before her, smiling kindly as he offered his hand and apologised for such a delay, was nothing of the kind.

Aiden Walsh was, from Billie's estimations, six foot four, because she had to look upwards to meet his gaze. His suit, gunmetal grey and well cut, covered a crisp white shirt that was open at the collar, no stuffy tie. Aiden's handshake was firm. His clean white nails contrasted skin that held the olive tinge of a recent summer holiday. He was handsome, slightly rugged, firm of jaw that hadn't yet started its journey south, while gentle wrinkles rested under grey eyes which were alert and bag-free. The salt and pepper, well-groomed hair was parted precisely and swept back from his face and was the only thing that suggested his age, perhaps just sneaking into his sixties.

Gathering her wits and pushing Detective Columbo and DI Frost from her mind, Billie followed the direction of Aiden's outswept arm, entered his office and took a seat. They exchanged pleasantries about the genial location of his offices in a newly-converted mill, and about the turn in the weather, before Aiden got down to business.

Settling into his chair that rocked slightly with each move-ment, he rested his arms on the side and with his hands clasped together, looked relaxed and in control as he spoke. 'Right, Billie, it's okay if I call you Billie, isn't it?'

Billie nodded, all of a sudden nervous. This was getting a bit real, serious.

Aiden began. 'Stan has given me permission to speak frankly and instructed me to make any information I've gathered avail-able. He clearly trusts you and is convinced that between us we can unearth some new evidence to exonerate him.'

Billie sighed, the weight of the task and the huge responsi-bility already daunting. 'I know, but I've already explained to him that I haven't really got any contacts in the force, not that that will be of any help. I was only with them for eleven months before my... before I was attacked. I honestly don't think I can help him.'

'Yes, Stan explained briefly what happened. Are you fully recovered? He said you struggled afterwards and it caused prob-lems between you.'

Billie nodded, bristling slightly that such a catastrophic event, not just for her, had been described as a mere struggle. One she had no intention of discussing with a stranger. 'I'm not sure I'll ever be fully recovered from it. The wound has healed and left a scar, not just on my skin but here too.' Billie tapped her head then continued. 'But I'm doing okay and need to focus on Stan, so tell me, have you found something we can use?'

Billie saw a flicker of understanding in Aiden's eyes then he nodded, and without further comment picked up an A4 manila folder and slid it across the table to Billie.

Rather than open it, Billie preferred to hear whatever news it contained from Aiden, suspecting also there would be photographs of Kelly that for many reasons she had no desire to see, so instead she held Aiden's gaze and waited for him to speak.

'To be honest, Billie, we've drawn a blank. Tom, my tech guy has dug around and taken her life apart but as far as hard evidence goes we have nothing. The police took her phone and devices as soon as Stan was arrested. It's protocol now but there was nothing on them that implied she was lying. Every piece of her testimony stacked up, even if it was her word against his. I was hoping that they'd missed something, a text, an email, even a photo to suggest she was a liar. Even her bank accounts show nothing untoward.'

'But we have to find something, anything to give him hope. He's getting desperate in there and recent developments between the two of us have probably made the situation a whole lot worse.' Billie could feel herself blushing and shuffled in her chair, uncomfortable under the detective's scrutiny and wishing she'd kept her gob shut.

'Oh, he didn't mention anything when he rang. Has something happened that I should be aware of?'

Billie sighed. 'When he rang you he didn't know, I've only just told him. You might as well know it all and I suppose you need to understand where his head's at.' Glancing upwards she was relieved to see that Aiden wasn't eyeing her suspiciously, he merely waited.

It dawned on her that in his line of work nothing would surprise him so the news of a secret baby wouldn't cause him to flinch, or make the front page of *The Private Detective's Weekly*. After taking a sip of her coffee, Billie adopted Aiden's pose, attempted to relax and told him all about why she left the force, their break-up, and Iris.

If Billie had had to describe how she felt in one word, it would be 'drained', like her energy was being sucked into a swirling vortex then dragged down a black tunnel before ebbing away, probably on some shitty beach full of brown frothy slime and plastic waste.

Aiden had listened patiently and certainly hadn't judged. Instead he'd told her he'd seen PTSD countless times during his years on the force. He understood and for that and his patience, Billie was grateful. When he looked at his watch then broke the silence, cutting though the serious atmosphere in the room, Aiden's tone was friendlier, more pally than professional.

'Listen, it's almost lunchtime and you look wiped out so why don't we get out of here and grab something to eat. We can continue this in a more relaxing environment and anyway I'm starved. What do you think? And I promise I won't put it on Stan's expenses.' Aiden grinned, his grey eyes held a hint of mischief.

Billie wasn't expecting that or the big flappy butterfly that was going crazy inside her chest and to make matters worse, she knew she was blushing, which annoyed her. She was acting like a silly teenager for God's sake.

'I'm quite okay here, honestly, there's no need to go to any trouble. Anyway, we haven't gone through the file and there could be something important. What if you've missed something?'

'I promise you, I've been through it, and so has Tom. There isn't anything in black and white that will help Stan, but there are some interesting anomalies that I'd like to discuss, more a hunch than anything. We dug about on social media and delved into Kelly's private life and that turned out to be far more interesting than her credit history. Now, do you want some lunch or not?' Aiden tilted his head to one side and raised his eyebrows slightly.

'Okay, I'm intrigued and I'm starving too, so let's go. What've we got to lose?' As Billie said the words her heart contracted slightly.

This was no time for being flippant, not while Stan was locked up just down the road, probably eating crap food and imagining what was going on inside this office, hoping and praying it would be good news. For a second Billie hesitated and regretted agreeing to lunch with a handsome, rather cocksure man who was already in reception leaving instructions with Karen.

'And if Jed rings, will you tell him where I am. He's supposed to be in court all day but said he might pop in if he finishes earlier than expected.' Aiden signed whatever document Karen had passed to him and once he'd returned her pen, opened the door with a flourish, allowed Billie to pass then pointed the way in a chivalrous manner.

Billie was becoming more flustered by the minute, nonplussed by the ever-changing persona of Aiden Walsh, private investigator. Memories of jack-the-lad detectives and rumours of affairs between married officers flooded back and now, she was off to lunch with an ex-copper who definitely had a glint in his eye. As they made their way down the worn mill steps, Billie attempted polite conversation.

'So who's Jed? Is he one of your employees? Has he been working on Stan's case too?' Billie waited as the modern glass doors swooshed open. As they stepped onto the pavement the glare of winter sun caused her to shield her eyes.

'Oh no, Jed's a barrister and, for better and worse, my husband. He deals with the dreary side of the law, financial dastardly dealings, I'm more cut-throat, you know, cheating husbands, bitter wives, missing persons, even the odd dog-napper.' Aiden was marching along with Billie at his side and as they stopped at the pelican crossing he turned and gave her a wink and an amused smile. 'So there's no need to worry, you'll be quite safe. I really do just want some lunch and a chat, okay?'

Billie threw back her head and laughed, just as the green man started flashing and beeping. As they crossed the road then headed into Wetherspoons, she allowed herself a moment to embrace the glimmer of hope that Aiden's hunch, whatever it was, would somehow set Stan free.

16

The pub was filling up as Billie said goodbye to Sue and disconnected the call, safe in the knowledge that Iris was fine and was watching CBeebies with Darren. The difference in Sue was remarkable and although nothing was going to replace the two stones in weight she'd lost, not overnight anyway, Iris had definitely put a spring in her step. Billie could also do something about the frizzy streaks of grey in Sue's usually shiny, bobbed hair, and be the company she so clearly lacked since her fair-weather friends had turned their backs.

No matter how much her mum hated it, Billie was also adamant that Claudia was going to share Iris with Sue. And if she carried on making the atmosphere difficult every time she left the house, questioning and haranguing, then Billie had told her mum straight that she would find alternative accommodation. Claudia knew that Stan's room remained vacant and this was possibly the only reason why she had kept her mouth firmly shut earlier that morning. Billie had chuckled, knowing that it would be bloody killing her.

Iris was a very genial baby and loved cuddles and attention so had taken to Sue and Darren immediately. Stan had told his mum to buy whatever baby stuff she needed for the house and to make sure Billie and Iris wanted for nothing until he could sort out some proper maintenance for them. Sue had taken Stan at his word and according to Darren there was nothing he didn't know about Mothercare products and was dreading the delivery van arriving later that day. He would soon have plenty of flat-pack furniture to keep him occupied in between CBeebies and college work.

Billie needed to make another call but that could wait. While she was in Manchester there was a special person she wanted to visit. It was someone who she'd come across during her short time in the police and had left a lasting impression. Carol was a victim, a young woman Billie had tried to help, and another player in the events that led to the split with Stan. They had become friends and emailed back and forth, forging a long-distance friendship. Billie wanted to check in on her, to see Carol in a happy situation now she was free of her abuser and had begun a new life.

Dragging her thoughts from the past, Billie concentrated on watching Aiden as he ordered and paid for their food. After joking with the barman who he was on first-name terms with, he strolled back to their table with drinks, attracting admiring glances from the two women seated opposite. Billie thought there was an energy about him, determined and in control, like he knew exactly what he was going to do or say in advance, especially in conversation. It was as though he was weighing you up, his brain ticking, evaluating you and whatever you said. No doubt his twenty-five years on the force was ingrained in him but he had an edge. Aiden wasn't like anyone she'd met before and she felt drawn to that aspect of his personality. Billie had always liked 'different'. Aiden took a sip of his pint and then settled into the booth to continue his tale.

'Right, where was I? Like I said, we went through her

evidence and personal data with a fine-tooth comb and it revealed zilch – but that's what I expected to be honest. We have to face facts because the CPS had a cast-iron case against Stan. The external injuries Kelly sustained that night along with the DNA evidence, plus the testimonies of the neighbours who she ran to for help, not to mention the CCTV footage of the incident at the Quays, all went against him.'

'I know, he's explained all this. So why aren't you giving up on him if it's all so cut and dried? Is it this hunch of yours or is it because Stan's not short of a bob or two and he's desperate? You keep digging, he keeps paying.' Although Billie said it in a jokey way so not to cause too much offence, she meant it and wanted to let Aiden know she wasn't a mug. Neither was Stan for that matter.

Aiden raised both palms in surrender but seemed amused by Billie's direct approach. 'Hey, don't get me wrong, Stan's bill won't be cheap but I'm not a con man. If I thought for one minute we were banging our heads then I'd throw in the towel. I've got plenty of work on but I'm on the level here... there's just something about Stan's case that makes me want to have one last try.'

'Well, that's very noble of you and I appreciate it, and your honesty, like I hope you appreciate mine.' Billie took a sip of her fizzy water, relieved he'd not taken the huff.

'I do, and there was no offence taken, I promise. Just remember, if this was official police business we wouldn't even be having this conversation. There aren't resources available to go off on hunches and spend hours trawling through someone's chat history, especially when Stan's case is more or less bang to rights. The difference is that I *do* have the resources but they cost. It's as simple as that. And those resources, plus old-fashioned coppering instinct, led me to my hunch.'

'Fair dos, so come on, let's hear it.'

Aiden changed position and leant forward, his arms on the table, hands clasped and lowered his voice slightly. 'It was Tom who suggested we dug further into her personal life. I think that's because he hasn't got one and is in love with his laptops.'

'How many has he got?'

'In the office, three, at home he has a wall full of tech stuff. It looks like the bridge of the Starship Enterprise in there. Anyway, after he'd spent hours going through her Twitter, Instagram and Facebook profile he noticed it.'

'Noticed what?'

'To put it bluntly, Kelly has no friends... well not close ones or any that seem to want to engage with her. When he checked, right back to the time of the attack then beyond – she's deleted anything relating to Stan by the way – you get the impression that she's a bit of a loner.'

'But how does that help Stan? And by the way I don't use Facebook and neither did he, unless he started after we split.'

'No, he didn't, we checked.'

'Well I despise it, the trouble it causes, but I will admit to checking her out online. All I could see was her profile photo and I only looked at that out of curiosity and so I had a face to focus my hate on.' Billie didn't care if she sounded bitchy or childish. She fucking despised Kelly and was happy to tell anyone who'd listen.

'Ah, I see, well I might need to explain then. When friends post, a picture or some news, you often see comments and reactions as well as likes. You can gauge someone's popularity by how much interaction they get, but it's not an exact science by any means. In Kelly's case, she's lucky if anyone bothers to give her a blue thumbs-up, let alone chat with her. Even before and during her relationship with Stan, Tom gleaned that while Kelly tried hard to connect with her limited number of friends, it wasn't reciprocated. After the rape, none of them deleted her, but it's not as though they went out of their way to publicly support her despite her relentless posting of memes and links to newspaper articles relating to domestic violence and rape. She favours anything that's pro-women and definitely anti-men. She's even been on the radio, some phone-in, then told everyone on Facebook but she had a very muted response.'

'Do you think that's because they don't like her or don't believe her?'

'I'm not sure. Maybe it's because she comes over as attention-seeking, but in a sisterhood way. They can't openly say she's annoying or totally ignore her because it would come across as unsupportive after what she went through. You'll find that Facebook users hide behind their profile and can be as fake or genuine as they like. From an outsider's perspective, Tom and I get the feeling they wish she'd go away. Do you get what I mean?'

'Yes, I think so: she doesn't sound very popular.'

'Mmm, I agree, which is why we made enquiries into her background and came up with a few surprising facts that weren't disclosed in court.'

'Like what?'

'Like she lied her arse off to Stan about the relationship with her dad; that she's had an affair with a married man and is prone to a bit of blackmailing and theft and, although they weren't reported to the police and were dealt with internally, Kelly has made three separate complaints of harassment in the past, two sexual, one in the workplace.'

'Oh my God... seriously?'

'Seriously?' Aiden raised his eyebrows in a knowing way.

Billie was completely gobsmacked. 'How did you find out... Who told you all this?'

'We have our ways and sources and you'd be surprised what people tell you when they've had a few to drink and especially if they aren't fond of the person we're enquiring about. I also find that hefty tips loosen lips.' Aiden paused for a second. 'Actually that's catchy, we could use it as a slogan... or perhaps not.'

Billie's head was spinning more so with the technical aspect of Aiden's work, and the dubious nature of this Tom's activities. 'Can I ask you something? Is what you do illegal, you know, the methods you use?'

'I couldn't possibly say, apart from it's a damn sight easier than plodding down the legal route we used in the force, but the less you know about that the better. Just leave all that to me and my team, especially Tom.'

Billie had a feeling he was going to say that and to be truthful she'd gone past caring. If it helped Stan, sod it, and the law. 'Okay, enough said. So go on, tell me everything about Kelly the cow and her sad life.'

Aiden smiled then was distracted by the arrival of the waiter. 'Oh good, here's our food.' After he'd introduced Billie and thanked Luke, Aiden rubbed his hands together at the sight of his lunch. 'Come on, tuck in. Let me eat my pie and half my chips then I'll begin, I'm absolutely starving.'

Billie gave Aiden an exasperated look then relented. She was hungry too so picked up her cutlery and began to cut into her pizza. 'Just half the chips, then you tell me, and I'm counting.' Giving him a nod in the direction of his plate, Billie saw Aiden smile and then sprinkle salt and vinegar on his huge pile of chips. As he did, she swallowed down the swell of anticipation caused by his vague but faintly promising revelations.

Please let this be good, thought Billie, *please give me something to take back to Stan.*

17

Going by the information Aiden had gathered at the golf club where Kelly's dad was a long-standing member, it appeared he had an excellent relationship with his daughter who also enjoyed the odd round of golf. She'd had her eighteenth and twenty-first birthday celebrations there, not huge affairs, more small family gatherings in the restaurant. But it was clear she was the apple of her father's eye and vice versa. More digging uncovered that after her ordeal, Mr Langton and his wife had treated their daughter to a holiday in Tenerife, all three of them jetting off for some family time and then after the court case, father and daughter escaped for a week of golf in the Algarve.

Judging by the photographs on Mrs Langton's Facebook profile and Instagram account, there was no evidence of bad blood between her husband and daughter, quite the contrary. So why had Kelly painted her father as a monster?

Instagram proved useless, almost defunct apart from a couple of photos of Mrs Langton's chihuahuas and a Portuguese sunset. It was while trawling through Kelly's Messenger conversations that Tom struck gold because way down at the bottom, he found a very interesting exchange with someone called Dee.

After reading the thread it became clear that Kelly was defending her own honour and denying any wrongdoing with the boyfriend of someone called Lucy. It appeared that Dee was a go-between, attempting to get to the truth or smooth things over and it didn't take Tom long to access her Facebook profile and then track down poor, cheated-on Lucy.

After unfriending and blocking Kelly from her life, and dumping her boyfriend, Tom noted that Lucy got on with the task of posting obvious memes about cheats, back-stabbers and boyfriend-stealers. In particular, there was an interesting group photo that included Kelly with her face circled in red, plus an arrow pointing to the word BITCH in bold, and it told Tom plenty.

They tracked Lucy down to her local pub – her Facebook page had told Tom exactly where she'd be that Friday night, and here, a chatty bloke called Aiden treated her to a few large vodka and Red Bulls. Lucy said she was excited to be interviewed by a real-life private investigator, it was a first apparently, and in between Aiden's shameless compliments and 'go on then, just one more vodka', her scarlet lips became extremely loose. During a shouty conversation, wedged between some rowdy football fans as they watched the match on the big screen, Lucy dished the dirt.

It became clear she had no time for Kelly and couldn't stand the 'manipulative tart' and was glad to see the back of her, even if some of their mutual friends didn't have the bottle to tell her to piss off. It seemed that the BITCH 'had been having it off' with Lucy's fickle boyfriend, now ex, and after a showdown, a slap around the face and a pint of snakebite over her head, Kelly finally got the message.

On a roll and whilst munching a packet of salt and vinegar crisps, Lucy had plenty more to say on the matter when Aiden enquired after Kelly's personality.

They'd been friends since school, not bosom pals though, more part of the same group. Lucy remembered Kelly as being a trouble-causing attention-seeker who could cause a row in an empty house. And there was a nasty side to Kelly because Lucy recalled her attacking another girl at school in a row over some boy, or had she tried to split two best friends up? It was probably both but the memory was hazy.

'It was a proper catfight, half the school were there to watch and if it hadn't been for the PE teacher sprinting over and splitting it up someone could've been really badly hurt. Kelly was a proper snapper and had a handful of Liz's hair in her hand, it was gross. And just before the teacher turned up Kelly stamped on Liz's phone. She never got away with it though, because Liz punched her in the face and gave Kelly a massive black eye, served her right as far as I'm concerned.' There was clearly no love lost between Kelly and Lucy who had no reason to lie – spread gossip, definitely, yes.

For example, she couldn't wait to mention the accusation Kelly made about one of the lab technicians at their all-girl secondary school. He was in his early twenties, nice-looking but geeky and kept himself to himself. As is usually the case he was lusted after by many but in a giggly schoolgirl way, whereas Kelly insisted he had the hots for her, much to the derision of her friends. When Kelly accused him of trying to kiss her, after she went back for her pencil case, the one she reckoned must have fallen under the science lab desks, none of the girls believed her. Unfortunately, the teachers did. In the end it came down to Kelly's word against his but her dad kicked up such a fuss, threatening all sorts, the poor guy resigned under a cloud of suspicion.

Aiden kept buying the drinks because Lucy was the gift that kept on giving. It turned out her cousin had a friend called Helen, who worked part-time in an Asda café. Helen had been at the same college as Kelly when they did their A-levels and as far as Lucy knew, there'd been a bit of man-related trouble there too.

A few days later, a member of Aiden's team spent a leisurely morning reading the paper and eating an all-day breakfast while keeping an eye out for Helen. After agreeing to chat to him during her break and thanking him for the twenty-pound tip he'd left on the tray, Helen spilled the beans all over Kelly.

The second accusation centred around a weekend residential trip in the Lakes. Here, Kelly pointed the finger at one of the adventure training staff, saying he'd touched her inappropriately while he was showing her how to use the abseiling ropes. Again, it was when she'd been alone with him, waiting on the top of the crag, with no witnesses. But later that night after swigging vodka, Kelly became distraught and told the other girls what he'd done.

'Oh yeah, Kelly couldn't half tell a tale but she could also turn on the waterworks like that.' Helen clicked her finger. 'She was really convincing and we all believed her at first, after all, she was on her own up there so anything could have happened. But when the instructor denied it and kicked up a fuss I started to feel a bit sorry for him cos there's two sides to a story and like I said, none of us saw anything.'

This time though, the staff at the centre closed ranks and supported their member of staff who refuted the allegations and was prepared to defend his unblemished reputation to the last. Consequently, Kelly got a bollocking for sneaking alcohol into camp and underage drinking and was summarily asked to leave, along with her foul-mouthed father who came to pick her up.

After that, the trail went cold so Tom had a rummage into her employment history, working his way backwards from the dental firm where she remained after the attack. Straight out of college, Kelly found a job at a local doctor's surgery as a filing assistant and stayed for around two years and then moved next door to the chemist where she worked in the dispensary and on the counter. This lasted a matter of weeks and when she left, there was a big gap, six months to be precise, where Kelly signed on. Eventually, she began working at the dentist and trained as a dental nurse.

His curiosity piqued, Aiden rang the chemist posing as a prospective employer seeking a reference for a Miss Kelly Langton and was given short shrift by Mr Macey, the pharmacist and owner of the shop.

'No, Mr Davis, I *would not* be prepared to vouch for Miss Langton, now or ever. That woman left under a cloud and caused considerable trouble so if you don't mind, I have customers and need to get on.' Mr Macey refused to expand further. Aiden refused to give up.

The following day Mr Macey was about to slide the door sign to *closed* and he sighed as the last-minute customer begged to be allowed to buy some cough mixture for his son. Rolling his eyes and standing to one side, he let Aiden in. Twenty minutes later, after Aiden assured the suspicious pharmacist that he wasn't from a local rag and whatever he said would be in strictest confidence, Mr Macey vented his spleen about Miss Langton and her antics, and none of it was good.

There had been a discrepancy with the takings, the second time it had occurred and after discussing it with his manager they concluded the culprit was Kelly. When they brought the matter up in the privacy of the small office, both were fully prepared to consider human error, rather than theft, thus offering Kelly extra training. Instead of admitting to any mistakes, Kelly had an almighty meltdown and became enraged, storming out of the office, grabbing her bag and coat before heading onto the shop floor. Blowing the situation out of all proportion, she accused Mr Macey of being a pervy old letch, workplace bullying and sexism, in full view of staff and customers then stormed out, screaming obscenities and threatening legal action.

Thankfully, Mr Macey never heard from her again but the shame of Kelly's vicious and wholly false allegations, along with his public humiliation, still stung. It wasn't until a few weeks later during a stocktake that they noticed a number of items were missing.

'It was nothing medicinal, you understand, otherwise I would have contacted the police immediately; it was make-up and toiletries but totalling a good few hundred pounds. We suspected Kelly, of course, but had no proof and rather than rattle her cage, I put it down to experience and for want of a better term brushed the whole matter under the carpet.'

Aiden presumed Mr Macey had concluded his character assassination of Kelly so thanked him for his time and made his way towards the door. As they shook hands, Aiden spotted that look people have when something occurs to them but they're not sure if they should say. Thankfully, after minimal encouragement from Aiden, the devil in Mr Macey won hands down, allowing him to relate one more juicy bit of gossip.

About a year after Kelly left, a very unpleasant woman called into the shop looking for her only to be told that she'd left, the circumstances not disclosed. It turned out that the woman was the wife of the man who delivered the stock from the pharmaceutical company and she was hunting down the tart he'd 'been at it with'. One of his mates let slip he'd been friendly with a girl who worked at the local chemist, and the trail led said angry wife to Macey's.

Mr Macey wasted no time passing over the name of the driver, Denny Cole, and as he did, Aiden recognised a hint of mischief in his expression. It took Tom no time at all to track

Denny the driver down and once again, his thoughts on Kelly were illuminating.

Aiden found him at the loading bay of his new firm. At first Denny thought Aiden was from the CMS or the social. He was doing a bit of cash-in-hand work, just to earn enough for Christmas pressies for his kids. Once he was reassured and pocketed fifty pounds towards the fund, Denny took a break and told him about Kelly.

'Yeah, we'd been having a dabble on the side but it was nothing serious, or so I thought until Kelly started demanding more and more of my time. Then she came up with a plan to line our pockets and suggested I should liberate some of the stock I carried in the van, and then she could sell it on eBay and split the difference. No way was I going to risk getting nicked so I gave her the elbow, she was becoming a bloody liability.'

The thing was, Kelly wouldn't take no for an answer and gave Denny an ultimatum – supply her with what she wanted or she'd tell his wife. Denny told her to piss off, not thinking for one minute that she meant it, but she did. As a result, Denny now lived in his mum's caravan in her back garden, saw his kids every other weekend where he had to grin and bear pleasantries with their new stepdad. He was on the sick after having a nervous breakdown and now suffered from severe depression and had to pop pills to get him through the day. He fucking hated Kelly.

18

Billie placed the drinks on the table and took her place opposite Aiden. She'd told him he deserved another pint after his report, and she'd been very tempted to treat herself to a large glass of Malbec but refrained simply because afternoon drinking sent her loopy.

'I ordered you a pudding too. My way of saying thank you for digging up all this dirt on Kelly.'

'Well thank you kindly, ma'am, but you didn't have to... so what did you get me?'

'It's a surprise.'

'How do you know I'll like it?'

'I think you will. Let's call it a test, how good or rubbish I am at judging someone's character.'

'Ah, I like tests, and I'm intrigued, but I haven't finished yet so you might end up buying me an Irish coffee when you hear the rest.' Aiden rubbed his stomach and smiled. 'I've always got room for a bit more; nobody can ever accuse me of being shy.' He winked and gave Billie a wicked smile, receiving a tap on the hand in return.

'I'm still not sure how to take you or how to work out if

you're being serious or rude.' Billie was laughing, having far too much fun under such serious circumstances but Aiden had a way of putting her at ease. It suddenly dawned on her that that was how he managed to extract so much information out of complete strangers. Clever, very clever.

'Ah, don't mind me, I'm teasing you. So do you wanna hear the rest?'

'I do, for my sins. So go on, get on with it.' Billie shuffled to get comfy and sipped her drink as she listened.

At that point, Luke arrived with a bowl of dessert and placed it in front of Aiden who looked at it, then Billie, and smiled. 'Jam roly-poly and custard, clever girl.'

Once Aiden had the background information, he decided to put a tail on Kelly and spend some time observing her. It was a long shot because for eight hours a day she was holed up in the dental practice, or so they thought. The team watched her over a two-week period and each Tuesday, her extremely supportive boss allowed Kelly time off to attend a women's group support session at a nearby community centre. It was run by volunteers, for victims of abuse and violence. The thing was, on Thursday nights, Kelly then drove across town to another centre where a similar group was held and even more bizarrely, the following Saturday, she attended a wellness clinic, run by a women's charity. When Tom reported that Kelly had set up a secret Facebook group for victims, that was growing quicker than her friends list ever had, faint alarm bells rang in Aiden's head.

He already knew from her email history that Kelly religiously kept once monthly psychiatric appointments at the hospital where she saw a counsellor, so why did she go out of her way to attend so many group sessions? Tom thought he had the answer when he explored her Google browsing history. Apart from holiday destinations around the world – a particular favourite topic of hers that fed into a Pinterest account festooned with exotic locations – Kelly had developed an interest in psychology, to be more precise, the procurement of online counselling courses and certificates.

Had Kelly stumbled on a world where she was the centre of attention, visiting centres where other women would listen to her experiences? Was she, owing to the distinct lack of bosom buddies in the real world, hoping to make new connections with kindred spirits? What if Kelly had identified a niche, a vulnerable section of society that she hoped to exploit? With distance courses for £190 that guaranteed a certificate by the end of the week, if she was as wily as Aiden suspected, Kelly could soon be coining it in.

Aiden had met all sorts during his time on the force and nothing really surprised him anymore. In the case of Kelly, that old copper's instinct told him she was a bad 'un. It was clear from her Facebook posts, telling of her appearances on radio phone-ins and frequent contributions to chat rooms, that she wasn't shy or backward at coming forward.

'It was a long shot but I got in touch with an ex-colleague, a police profiler and asked her to take a look at what I'd found and give me her opinion. When she sent me the report the pieces started falling into place and now I'm convinced that Kelly has a histrionic personality disorder. Here, I'll read you some of it.' Aiden opened the file on his desk and after flicking through, found what he was looking for.

'In a nutshell, the sufferer is characterised by long-standing patterns of attention-seeking behaviour where they desire to be the centre of everything and feel uncomfortable if they are not. Interestingly, people with the disorder are prone to self-dramatisation and have a theatrical and exaggerated way of expressing emotion. They may also be perceived as shallow and, engage in sexually seductive behaviour to gain the attention they crave. They sometimes act out a role within a relationship, taking the part of a victim and may attempt to control a partner through emotional manipulation, seductiveness or in some cases, great dependency. Even more telling, is that those with the disorder have difficulty forming relationships with same-sex friends because their sexually provocative style may threaten relationships. They also alienate people with demands for attention, becoming difficult, bored and depressed when they are not in the limelight. They crave novelty and are frustrated by routine and have a tendency to move from one relationship in search of a new, more exciting proposition. Finally, Histrionic Personality Disorder is more prevalent in females.'

Aiden leant forward and tapped the folder. 'My full report is in there, perhaps you can read it in detail when you have more time. I have a feeling that like me, you will find some startling similarities to Kelly.'

Billie put her head in her hands, trying to gather so many thoughts before looking up and asking Aiden a really important question. 'But how is all this' – she pointed to the file – 'going to help Stan? Surely it's all circumstantial and supposition or whatever they say in court. None of it proves a thing.'

'I know, but it's given me something to work with which is better than nothing.' Aiden didn't appear to have taken offence that she had dismissed all his investigative work as worthless and for this she was glad.

Then another question popped into her head. 'So where do we go from here? Because I have no idea.'

'Well I have, but I'm going to need your help.'

'ME! What can I do?'

Aiden sighed and leant in closer, his face serious now. 'One of my team, Josie, has buggered off to Australia to start a new life. Working for me was a means to an end and once she had her nest egg she booked her seat on Kangaroo Airways. It leaves me without a female detective to do the stuff a bloke can't.'

Billie held up the palm of her hand as if to silence Aiden. 'Why am I feeling nervous right now? Please don't ask me to go snooping about! I'm a mess. My nerves won't take it and anyway, I'd be rubbish at it, I was a rubbish bobby.' Billie had already broken out in a sweat and felt slightly panicky.

Aiden simply shook his head and carried on. 'I don't think you're a mess at all, far from it, and I knew as soon as you'd finished explaining about what happened on your little paradise island that you were what we needed. Look Billie, you're a fighter and a survivor, you got through a tough time and see' – Aiden swept his hand towards Billie – 'you are back here in Manchester, ready to defend the honour of the man you love. Our very own warrior princess.' Then he smiled, giving Billie time to protest.

'No, no way. I'm not any of those things you described, you've got me wrong.'

'I doubt it. I'm a good judge of character but hear me out... then make up your mind.'

Billie swallowed down nerves and told herself it would do no harm to listen. 'Okay, go on, but I'm still not saying yes, I'm just being polite.'

Aiden had definitely gone all serious on her now and hadn't cracked a smile. 'This is what I propose. I need someone to get close to Kelly, befriend her, really find out what makes her tick. If there's the faintest hope, it lies with you, Billie, because we're running out of time. Unless we can get another angle, prove she's lied or discredit her in any way, we won't have a chance. It will take time for me to recruit another female team member. But you're here, a trained copper, and it's a no-brainer.' Aiden's gaze was locked onto Billie's.

'Bloody hell, Aiden, no pressure there then... what exactly will I have to do?' Billie was now trapped in his headlights and as much as she wanted to run, knew she had to stay and face her fate.

'I'll explain all that over the next few days. Tom is making a few more enquiries and putting stuff together but I'll need you back in the office on Monday so we can go through everything with you. For now, trust me and know that you won't be in any danger whatsoever. I'll guide you through it all, I promise. So, it's in your court. Is that a yes?'

Billie sucked in air and then held her breath for a moment. She threw the ball back to Aiden. 'One more question.'

'Okay, fire away.'

'I asked you earlier why you hadn't given up on Stan, but I sense there's more to it than "just a hunch", so come on, tell me honestly, why are you going the extra mile?'

Aiden didn't miss a beat. 'Right from the start, when I was a beat bobby, I loved that feeling of catching the bad guy, or woman, knowing I'd done something good, got them off the street and away from decent members of society. There were some, jeez, they were bad, especially when I made detective. I saw the lowest of the low, the blokes who beat their partners senseless, abused kids, stole from pensioners, even beat them up, murderers and rapists, you name it, I met them. But when I went home at night, I was fulfilled, for want of a better word. Yes, some days were shite: too much paperwork and not enough hours, putting up with verbal abuse, taking the odd fall or punch in the line of duty, but I thrived on it, it was all I knew. Justice, that's what I cared about, right and wrong, protecting the weak, making my bit of Manchester safer. I met people like Kelly every day of the week, the wrong 'uns, those you just know are bad, shifty, compulsive liars who couldn't lie straight in bed at night or the blamers, those who reckon their deeds and situation are the fault of others.

'There's just something about Kelly, call it intuition, that tells me she falls into one of those categories and the thought that she might have put an innocent man away doesn't sit right with me. Stan's not the first and won't be the last bloke who's behind bars because a woman has accused him, like there's women out there right now who are living with the horror of being raped, but too scared, for too many reasons, to report it. If I'm right about Kelly, and Stan's version of events is true, I want to prove it.

'Women like Kelly do rape victims no good whatsoever and they make the job of the police even harder. The resources that go into just one victim, the man-hours, the support network et cetera are vitally important but stretched. When a woman or man asks for help, reports a crime, they should be believed but so many don't take the first step for fear of what happens next. The impact on their lives apart from the initial attack is immense. It makes my blood boil that while someone could be going through hell, others use the system for their own ends, maybe petty revenge, I don't know. It has to stop though, and then the real victims can be helped and the real abusers will get what they deserve.

'So, in answer to your question, the reason I haven't given up is because on the outside, I'm not a copper anymore, but on the inside I always will be and if I never solve another case again, I will do everything I can to solve this one.'

Aiden picked up his glass and drained it while Billie, wide-eyed and awash with admiration more than anything, could only think of two words to say in response. Reaching over and placing her hand on his she simply said, 'I'm in.'

19

Stan waited as patiently as he could for his solicitor to stop fannying around with his files and get on with it. The small windowless room that they'd been allocated only added to Stan's growing number of neuroses, claustrophobia being the latest to join the queue. He was just about managing to cope with the conditions in his cell, owing to a glimpse of the outside world that the small barred window afforded him. But being trapped in an air-conditioned box seated opposite a nervous, perspiring solicitor was making Stan even more anxious and fidgety.

Finally, Mr Hargreaves appeared to have reorganised his life and looked up, pausing a moment before he began. 'This isn't the news I'd hoped to be giving you but after reading the report from the private detective you hired and meeting with your barrister, my advice is that we should withdraw your appeal application.'

Silence descended on the room and even the prison officer standing guard seemed to be holding his breath.

'This better be a sick joke... I don't understand, why?' Stan's foot was tapping and his hands had started to shake.

'It's a damage limitation call and the fact that we have to

abide by certain protocols of law, and work within the respected areas of argument.'

'For Christ's sake, speak English will you! What protocols and arguments? Stop dicking about. And for the record, as far as I'm concerned respect is a dirty word, nobody bothered to give me any. Instead they treated me like muck from the minute I was arrested. Still do.' Stan had had his fill of listening to the bollocks they spouted in court and being looked down on by everyone, especially greedy solicitors. He wanted plain speaking and answers.

Hargreaves sighed and looked decidedly unnerved by Stan's impatience and aggressive attitude. 'Right, plain speaking it is. There are three argumentative appeals: logical, ethical and emotional and the strongest case has a balance of all three. All that we have, at the moment, is evidence of bad character. And we still need to secure witness statements to support it, and that might not be as easy as you imagine. There's no other substantial evidence and I've already explained why going ahead could be risky for you if we fail. That's even if they agree to hear the appeal in court.'

Hargreaves swallowed, clearly not enjoying being the bearer of bad news.

Stan put his head in his hands and puffed out his cheeks, exhaling, trying to stay calm. 'You have to have something... for fuck's sake I'm paying Aiden a fortune, and you. Surely the stuff he found out about that bitch proves she's a nutjob, not to mention a petty thief and a born liar.'

Hargreaves fiddled with his pen as she spoke. 'Yes, I agree it casts Ms Langton in a bad light and I do regret that we didn't have knowledge of the previous allegations against her to hand at your trial. But that's to be expected: they were private matters and not reported to the police. That said, we may not have been allowed to use it. The whole process of disclosing and having evidence agreed by both sets of counsel is a tricky business.'

'No kidding! It's a load of fucking bollocks as far as I'm concerned, but I'm not lying down and being walked over. I mean it, I want to fight on.'

'But–'

'No buts, I'm paying you and half of Manchester to get me out of here and I say we go ahead. So while you're on the meter, you can explain to me how it works, this bullshit you call the law. What exactly is evidence of bad character?' Stan was raging inside and had to clench his fists together to stop his hands from pummelling the table.

Hargreaves sighed and referred to his notes before answering Stan. 'Basically, bad character evidence could be an undisclosed criminal conviction but in a wider definition, can incorporate poor disciplinary records at work or even school, or show that a witness was not credible due to something in their past that suggests we shouldn't believe them. It would be directly relevant to the facts in the trial if, using previous records of violence, one can prove that the victim was actually the aggressor as you suggested in your testimony. Should this be the case, the witness can then be questioned further about their character or previous conduct, such as reprehensible associations or way of life. To that end, one could infer the witness was not worthy of belief and not a credible person.'

Stan smiled then sat back in his chair, holding out the palms of his hands towards Hargreaves. 'Well there you go then... that's her bang to rights. You've ticked all the boxes. Get what everyone told Aiden down on paper, then it's job done.'

'As I said earlier, it's not going to be easy, persuading the informants to make statements. Some people don't relish the idea of going to court no matter how noble the cause and this is precisely why we are erring on the side of caution.

'No, it sounds like you're giving up.'

Placing his hands together then resting them on the desk, Hargreaves looked Stan in the eye as he spoke. 'On the contrary, Stan, that's the last thing we are doing but as your counsel we are duty-bound to explain all of the facts as we see them. I urge you to take twenty-four hours before you instruct me further. Please believe me that whatever we say or do is in your best interests – even that last piece of advice.'

'And please believe me when I say that I don't need twenty-four minutes never mind hours. I have to get out of here.' Stan sighed and reined himself in. 'You know who's coming to see me next visiting day?'

Hargreaves shook his head.

'My daughter who I've never even met thanks to that piece of shit Kelly. So no way am I festering here for years while my girl grows up without her dad. That's why I want you to go back to your fancy office, ring that swanky barrister in his golden bloody chambers and tell him to get his finger out, okay?'

Nodding as he straightened his notes and closed the file, Hargreaves then stood and silently offered his hand which Stan shook. 'For what it's worth I do understand your desperation and continued frustration at the process, so rest assured, I'll do everything I can. I know we solicitors get a bad press but I am trying to help. You have my word.'

'Yeah, I get that and I'm sorry I lost my rag. Thanks for coming in. Keep me informed, okay? The thought of people on the outside trying to sort this shitstorm is the only thing that keeps me going, and my family, obviously.'

'No apologies necessary, Stan. I'll be in touch and in the meantime, keep your head down and stay out of trouble. And watch that temper.'

Stan nodded and watched as Hargreaves was shown out by the prison officer, wincing when the door slammed shut behind them. While he waited for someone to escort him back to the wing, Stan closed his eyes and blocked out the painted white bricks that surrounded him and instead, focused on his breathing, keeping it regulated. It occurred to Stan as he listened for footsteps and to the pulsing, swooshing sound in his ears, that Hargreaves was right about one thing and wrong about another.

He really did need to keep a check on his temper that sometimes verged on uncontrollable, but as for understanding, Hargreaves had no idea what it was like in there, no idea at all.

20

Billie had gone from almost flatlining to super-charged within the space of a few hours and now her brain was buzzing with ideas and her heart allowed itself a smidgen of hope. Thank goodness she'd accepted Aiden's invitation and given him the opportunity to talk her through his off-the-record hunch. They might not have written proof that Kelly had lied about Stan, but Billie was in total agreement with Aiden. Something didn't add up about her; something was off.

As she drove towards her second hurriedly-arranged appointment of the day, Billie kept an eye out for a florist because she wanted to take Carol a little something and maybe a bag of treats for the kids too. It would be the first time she'd seen them since that night and their last image of her hadn't been exactly pleasant, more like something from a horror film.

PC Billie Kenyon had been working a two-ten shift and was feeling hopeful that she'd get through the last hour without inci-dent and actually be home on time for a change. All she had to do was take a witness statement from a shopkeeper who'd caught some yobs pinching his stock, then she had a date with a stuffed-crust pizza. It was all going so well until she'd responded to the call on the radio and headed towards the address literally seconds away, where neighbours had reported sounds of a disturbance.

Billie did everything in her power not to think about that night. But it came into her head unbidden, like the trailer for a television drama, a slideshow of events that could not be deleted from her memory. She couldn't even change the channel.

The neighbour, a woman in her dressing gown clutching a miniature terrier to her chest like a cuddly toy, was waiting at the gate when Billie arrived with sirens wailing and blue lights flashing.

'Bloody Nora, you took your time! He's been in there about ten minutes now. I saw him come marching up the path. Look, that's his bottle of vodka. He chucked it in my flower bed after he opened the gate, the scruffy bastard.'

Billie interrupted. 'Can you tell me what you heard Mrs...?'

'Jones, Ida Jones. He's smashing stuff up from the sounds of it and screaming obscenities, I can hear the foul-mouth get through the wall, clear as anything and them poor kids are in there too. He's an evil bastard that Gary and I reckon he's giving Carol a good hiding again so you'd better get in quick.'

Billie approached the door and rang the bell persistently and then crouched, pushing open the letterbox and there sure enough, sitting at the bottom of the stairs were two little girls huddled together. One was sucking a dummy. She was no more than two years old. The other was slightly older, maybe four. They both looked terrified and Billie knew there was no way either of them could open the door even if she could coax them off the stairs. True enough, when she turned her ear to the letterbox, she could hear the sounds of a man's voice shouting,

'Get up, bitch, get up.' It appeared to be coming from the end of the hall, probably the kitchen.

Calling for backup, Billie told Mrs Jones to remain where she was and then made her way along the side of the house towards a small gate that led into a grassed back garden. A swing and children's toys were scattered on the lawn that was partially lit by the glow from the kitchen window. Reaching the back door, Billie stayed out of sight, paused and listened.

'Are you going to get up or do I have to drag you? I want you out, you slag, right now.'

The next sound was a woman's cry and Billie winced. Her intuition told her the woman had been kicked. Placing one hand on the door handle, she removed her baton with the other. There was no time to wait for backup. Billie knew she had to go in now otherwise Carol would suffer even more and she needed to get the two little girls somewhere safe. Pressing down on the handle, Billie pushed it gently, feeling a mixture of relief and fear when it moved and the door inched open. She had no idea that the next six minutes and twenty-seven seconds would set in motion a series of events, shifting her world on its axis, changing her life and Stan's forever.

In the moments preceding her intervention, Billie gathered every scrap of courage she possessed, putting the woman and children on the other side of the door, first. In the moments that followed, when fear wrapped itself around her heart and her brain knew the sensible thing would be to back off, or run, Billie stood firm and faced up to a man with hate in his eyes and a knife in his hand.

'Step away from Carol, now, and drop the knife,' Billie's voice commanded.

Gary turned his head and smirked. 'Get fucked.'

Billie's mouth had gone bone dry and her lips felt numb but

she spoke again. 'Gary, I'm asking you once more to step away and drop the knife.'

'Make me, bitch.'

There was a groan as Carol tried to push herself upwards, then a frightened voice.

'Mummy.'

A second. That's all it took. The plaintive cry of a terrified child, Billie's eye darting in that direction, taking in the little girl with the tear-streaked face and bedhead hair, holding her little sister's hand. When Gary lunged forward and punched Billie in the face, as her hands flew upwards in defence, from somewhere, her training kicked in and she attempted to restrain and defend.

When Gary responded, he plunged the knife deep into her groin.

There followed the weirdest moment, when their eyes locked and she stared into the crazed blue irises of a sneering, elated man. Billie had never forgotten that look. It had haunted her ever since. The trance was broken by screams, Billie's and that of a child, then another. Next came the pain, searing cold, like when your fingers stick to ice in the freezer, causing her to look downwards and register the steady flow of blood oozing down her black trousers and onto the tiled floor.

Instinct kicked in. It hadn't deserted her, though she had ignored its earlier message to flee. It told Billie to stem the bleeding: *Brain to hands, move now.* Clutching the wound before forcing her eyes upwards, Billie staggered backwards, her legs giving way no matter how much she wanted them to stay upright. Sliding down the wall, aware now of a dull throbbing, not the severe pain she expected, the adrenaline and endorphins in Billie's body acted as a natural sedative, but not on her brain. It was still functioning, just.

The girls were really screaming now. Billie was confused,

panicked yet transfixed by the sight of her own blood, cherry-red liqueur, like her grandma used to drink at Christmas, sticky and sweet, all over her fingers and hands. *What a mess. Mum get a cloth, Mum...*

Billie's sight was going all fuzzy, but she could still see Carol's legs curled into her chest, a discarded pink slipper, Gary's dirty white trainers, one set of laces hanging loose, very close, splattered with blood and as her head lolled backwards, resting against the wall, she felt muzzy and tried to focus on the knife in his right hand, dripping with liqueur. He was looking down on her and seemed oblivious to the distress of his daughters but also, the movement close behind him. Carol.

As she watched, felt, listened, Billie tried to make sense of what was happening, still desperate to prioritise, save life, hers, Carol's... *Oh God, the kids.*

In her last moments of consciousness, her brain took a snapshot of the scene. Two little bedheads in their *Frozen* and *Cinderella* nighties, snotty noses, tear-filled eyes, hiccupping and sobbing, holding hands. Carol on her feet, holding the table for support, staggering slightly, moving out of sight, behind Gary. Then he sensed it, movement, maybe heard the shuffle of one pink slipper as it came his way. When she averted her gaze from the approaching feet, Billie raised her head and saw Gary sneer. That's when Billie knew, he knew. Gary had evil in his eyes, wild abandon. He had nothing to lose, not now. Who though? Who would he choose? When he turned, Billie felt relief and then shame. It wasn't her, not this time.

The screams came next. Gary lifted his knife arm, ready to strike. There was another scream, of rage, from Carol, two of terror from the kids, then a boom, perhaps the front door, faraway voices, male. Her view, previously obscured was now clear as Gary's legs buckled. The girls were being scooped up and away by swift black-clad figures. Carol, the ashen, swollen face that went with the name, was frozen, one slit-eye purple and bruised, the other bulging. Her bloodied lips made an O shape while both arms dangled by her side, a steel meat tenderiser in one hand.

Gary fell backwards and Billie felt the weight of his body slam into hers. The pain that pulsed under her hands now seared red hot, and the blood that dripped suddenly exploded and gushed through her fingers. Giving in to the flow of cherry liqueur, Billie's world went black.

21

They had survived, both of them. Although what Carol had endured during the course of her marriage to Gary – prolonged, violent attacks, sexual and mental abuse – was nothing like the assault he'd carried out on Billie, they were both his victims. It tied them together and had in some ways sealed their friendship.

If they'd thought it was all over, that night in the kitchen when Gary turned and wielded his knife towards Carol and she smashed the meat hammer into his forehead, they were wrong. The wheels of justice were set in motion and while Billie spent weeks recovering from her injuries, first in hospital and then at home, Carol suffered an entirely different fate. After she was treated for numerous cuts and bruises, instead of going home to her children she was taken to the cells and later, wept through her interview with the police. The two little bedheads were spirited off into the night and placed in emergency foster care.

The news of this rocked Billie's world far more than the stabbing. How could a woman in that situation, who had clearly suffered so much at the hands of a despicable man, end up being questioned, a charge of attempted manslaughter hanging over her head? Once again she was at the mercy of Gary who, despite his crimes, was cared for by nurses who Billie imagined might want to pull the plug, or make good use of a squashy hospital pillow when nobody was looking. Billie knew she'd have been tempted. She also prayed he wouldn't die and the CPS would go for self-defence.

Billie was tormented by the image of Carol, whose babies were in a strange home, missing their mum after witnessing such a horrific scene and she could not comfort them. Worse, after being kicked around the kitchen and in fear of her life, while Billie bled out onto the floor, Carol thought Gary was going to turn the knife on her so acted in self-defence and ended up in a cell.

The whole thing messed with Billie's head. She thought she was going to die that night. That the bloodbath was going to fill up and overflow if Gary got his hands on Carol and those two, frightened little girls would lose their mummy. What if he'd gone for the girls too? When the flashbacks started, then the random, indiscriminate panic attacks that struck during the day or sweaty sleepless nights, Billie's life turned upside down. She was smothered by fear and self-doubt, saw danger everywhere and became riddled with such terrible anger, that swelled and bubbled over in bad-tempered exchanges with anyone who didn't understand, listen or seem to give a shit about how truly fucking awful life was out there. Not just on the streets and inner-city estates, but between four walls, care homes, everyday homes, A&E, shops, doctors' surgeries, where low-life scumbags made other people's lives a misery.

Billie couldn't cope with the injustices in the world, the imbalance, the unfairness and downright cruelty of human being on human being. Stan had tried his best to understand, be patient and accommodating whereas her mother, well that was like pouring petrol on the flames every time they met. Claudia reverted to tried and trusted sayings or 'bullshit', as Billie called them. She had no intention of getting back on the horse *or* bike that she had fallen from. She had no best feet to put forward: hers were staying firmly inside the house. Socks wouldn't be pulled up, neither would her chin and there was no bright side to look on.

Billie did not care that she had a decent wage and respectable job with prospects. As far as she was concerned she'd seen enough gore and grime, scumbags and sinners to last a lifetime. Billie wasn't prepared to put her life on the line so happily left cleaning up the city streets to the much braver, dedicated, determined men and women of Greater Manchester Police.

When her daughter resigned, Claudia was horrified and ashamed, although she'd never have openly admitted it. But Billie knew. Her dad was stoical and supportive, preferring a whole, free daughter to one in a coffin, or psychiatric ward.

Stan was relieved because he thought that Billie's decision was one less thing to deal with and given time and therapy for what they now suspected was PTSD, their life would get back to normal. So when Billie announced that she wanted them to go travelling for a year, get away from the humdrum of life and see the world, become a backpacking duo and hit the hippy trail, Stan's refusal hit hard. It was like Hiroshima of the brain.

Billie railed against his attempts to make her see sense. Stan said that his businesses were flourishing so he couldn't walk away now. And why couldn't they take holidays? Anywhere she wanted, he'd pay, his treat, no problem. What about his mum and Darren? It was tight, clearing off, he'd miss them, they'd miss him and her. Stan said running away wasn't the answer and they would find the solution together, step by step. But Billie didn't want to take steps, she wanted to run as far and as fast she could.

Billie finally gave Stan what sounded like an ultimatum. She was actually calling his bluff. She was going away whether he came or not. He had to make a choice. Stan dug his heels in and although it later turned out he was calling Billie's bluff too, their poker faces held firm. In a fit of rage and desperation Billie told Stan it was over then packed a bag and went to her parents' house. Once there, Billie didn't get the comforting words of approval she'd hoped for, mainly because her dad was at the garden centre buying compost and instead, she copped for an unsympathetic Claudia.

'Always running away, aren't you, Billie? When are you going to grow up and realise that you have responsibilities? And as much as I sometimes wish Stan didn't fall under that category, you can't expect him to drop everything because you're having a wobble. Now sort yourself out and book an appointment with your therapist, or a careers adviser, whatever, and find something you can stick at for once in your life.'

'Well thanks so much, Mum, very nice I must say! Do you forget that I could've died? Your only child was stabbed. Does that not scare you? Do you not worry it could happen again? And I have always paid my way, ever since I got my first job and have never asked you and Dad for anything so don't make out I'm a scrounger or layabout. The jobs I've had might not be up to your standard but I'm not a shirker!'

'I'm not saying that, Billie, what I mean is that you need to put your life in order and think of the future and of course I haven't forgotten. How could I? It was a dreadful time, terrifying, for all of us but you've recovered now and thousands of people suffer much worse than you and then get back on their feet. That's all I'm saying, Billie... you've been given another chance so should make the most of your life while you can, not spend it bumming around bloody Marrakesh or wherever the fancy takes you.'

Billie held her hands up in despair. 'That's it. I give up. I really, really give up with you, Mum. Just for once I needed you to understand and take my side instead of thinking about your own pride and what the bloody neighbours will say!'

'That's not true, Billie. Believe me, I *am* thinking of you but as usual you twist my words and use them against me.'

'Oh God, here it comes. The pity party, hold on while I get the violin out.' Billie shook her head in disgust.

Claudia responded with a tut and sarcasm. 'I think the only person holding a pity party is you! And if you can't be civil then I suggest you find somewhere else to sulk or – better still – go home to Stan and sort your life out.'

The whole village of Thurlstone probably heard Billie's screech as she stormed back down the path dragging her wheelie case, then raced off in her car, vowing never to speak to her mother ever again or listen to her stupid selfish advice.

No way was Billie going home so she headed further north and holed up in a small, remote village on the east coast as far away from scumbags, her mother and Stan as she could get. After burrowing down, Billie festered for a few days during which time she either ignored Stan's calls or repeatedly told him it was over. He had let her down, like everyone else, her dad not included. But by day six she was starting to calm down, miss Stan a lot, and was starting to see his point. Maybe they could compromise and a nice holiday might be what they needed. By day eight she was bored out of her head, sick of reading and pretending to enjoy the windswept, craggy beach view, and the nosey owner of the hotel was doing her head in, so Billie went home.

Relieved to find the locks hadn't been changed and her stuff wasn't in the hall in bin bags, Billie waited for Stan to come home and in the meantime made him his favourite curry, smiling at the notion he would smell it as soon as he opened the door and be pleased she was home. They could work it out she was sure, taking baby steps through their fragile relationship, not giant leaps across the globe in flip-flops and kaftans.

Stan didn't come home that evening and by the time he did, in the early hours of the following morning Billie had fallen asleep on the sofa and the madras was a dried-up problem for the dishwasher to solve. It didn't take a genius to work out what he'd been up to. After Billie wore him down with her relentless interrogation, wanting to know who he was with and where he stayed and why he couldn't have got a taxi straight home, Stan confessed to a one-night stand with a total stranger he'd picked up in a club. He really did think it was over, that she was never coming back so got pissed and found solace in a stranger.

It didn't matter to Billie what she looked like, her name, if she'd made his betrayal worthwhile because the faceless woman could have been anyone – even gorgeous Rachel Green from Central Perk, who met Stan bloody Geller while he was on a break.

What did matter was that Stan had let her down and the chain of events linking the moment she opened a kitchen door and faced up to a psycho with a knife to the moment when she found out her boyfriend was a cheat was coming to an end.

No matter how much Stan begged for forgiveness, for her to stay, Billie packed her bags then went to her cousin's. She sold her car on eBay, said goodbye to her parents by phone from the departure lounge at Manchester airport and buggered off to Greece. As Billie closed her eyes to hold in the tears and the plane took off, she told herself her mum was wrong. Running away was Billie's speciality – at least she was good at something.

Pulling onto the quiet suburban estate of new builds, Billie decided it was time for a quick chat with the face in the rear-view mirror, the one with pink hair and a nose ring. Rain began to splatter the windscreen but she wasn't going to let that ruin her parade. This was supposed to be a happy meeting.

'Right, stop it, stop it now. You're here for a good reason, not to drive yourself bloody insane. Being one step away from a psych ward was enough, so pull yourself together, woman.' Scanning the street for number twenty-nine, Billie realised that if anyone spotted her she'd look mad anyway, talking to her reflection.

'Ah, here we are. Now, paint on a smile and stop being a big, fat depresso.' Parking up outside the semi, Billie turned off the engine then grabbed the carrier bag and flowers and hoped she wasn't going to get soaked in the sudden downpour.

She hadn't even set the car alarm before the front door opened and Carol appeared at the door, waving like mad. The sight of her, physically healed and free, made Billie smile and as she walked up the path, any lingering dark thoughts quickly skittered away, washed down the gutter by the rain.

22

Billie shuffled in her uncomfortable plastic seat, trying hard to look interested in Jude, the support worker who was passing around leaflets giving details of a women's march taking place the following month. The group members were a nice bunch and Billie didn't mind spending time in their company. It was one person in particular that made her skin crawl and now that person was seated immediately to the right.

While the others discussed if they could make it or be bothered to head into the centre of Manchester for the protest, Billie's mind focused on the task in hand, all the time staying in character. Her legs were stretched out in front, ankles crossed over mud-splattered UGG boots, her arms folded onto her chest, semi-sullen face avoiding eye contact with the others.

While she waited for the session to begin proper, her mind wandered back to one morning in Aiden's office when he explained her mission. It had been a pivotal day that led her here, to a tatty community centre in Gorton.

Billie was trying to get her head around everything that Tom, Aiden's super-geek, was telling her. On the desk was a second-hand, half-decent iPhone that was part of her new identity. No matter how simple Tom and Aiden made it all sound her stomach was churning and her brain was on overdrive, trying to take it all in.

Aiden had explained that two of the groups Kelly attended were government- or charity-funded and required a referral from the police or another agency. However, the third was run on a volunteer basis by an ex-victim who, with the support of a local councillor and MP, had secured some funding for a women's drop-in centre. The only criteria needed to attend was that you were female and had been the victim of violence. Billie ticked both boxes.

'But I'd feel like a fraud because what happened to me isn't technically the same thing... Don't you think it's wrong to attend a meeting under false pretences? And what if they find out?'

'There's no way they will find out because you don't neces-sarily have to speak about your experience, just listen. And you're not a fraud, you still suffer from PTSD, so you might even learn something from the sessions – apart from what makes Kelly tick.'

'It seems wrong but if it's the only way, I'll have to do it. I can't exactly make an appointment at the dental practice where Kelly works, lean across the dentist and say "Hi, do you want to be my friend?" and I'm certainly not into having extra fillings. Anyway, it's hard to talk when someone's got one of those squirty water things in your mouth so it looks like I'm off to the community centre.'

Aiden smiled and gave her the thumbs-up. 'Right, so let's go through it one more time. Never ever take your own phone into a meeting with you. Leave it hidden in your car just in case it falls out of your bag. Anyone with two phones is seen as dodgy and you have to come across as legit, okay?'

Aiden was leaning across his desk looking intense. Billie nodded and then Tom took over.

'I've loaded your contacts with plenty of fake names and numbers. You'll never have to ring any of them. They're for show, like Mum and Dad and imaginary family members. The Chinese takeaway, local pub, taxi firm, are real and located close to where you are supposed to live on the estate, just in case.'

'Just in case what?' Billie had to ask.

'I don't know, but I thought it better to have a few real numbers. It's a fail-safe. The only two you will really need are mine and Aiden's in case of emergency and they are down as Andy and Trev. They can be your cousins, if you like. I kept our initials as a prompt. Any problems, ring or text us.'

'Okay, I get it.'

'Now, Facebook. I've created an online profile for you from the photos you sent. If Kelly has a nosey you will come across as really boring. There's only a couple of your cat, and some of your beloved boyfriend over there and his souped-up car.' Tom looked up and nodded towards Aiden who smiled and waved. 'And a few selfies of you, like I asked. Apart from that you mainly post cute animal pictures and cringy memes that hardly anybody bothers to like.'

Billie nodded and began flicking through the photos on her phone, stopping and squinting at the one of her pretend boyfriend then laughing when she realised who the unshaven lout wearing a grey tracksuit and regulation black hoodie actually was.

'Oh my God, is that you?' Billie looked up at Aiden who was also laughing.

'Yep, that's my alter ego. Jed absolutely hates it.'

Billie raised her eyebrows, imagining Aiden strutting about

at home in his unlikely get-up. Then she thought of something else. 'But won't it look odd that I don't get into conversation and talk about what I'm having for my tea and *Love Island*? And how the hell did you make it look like I'm mates with people I've never met?'

Tom smiled. 'Billie, you wouldn't believe how easy it is. Honestly, anyone could do it. All you need is an email address, then it's plain sailing to set up a Facebook account. All you do next is lift a photo off the internet, send a friend request to someone who has more followers than they know what to do with and probably hasn't a clue who half of them are anyway. Once they accept you, trawl through their friends list, find a similar target, and friend them and so on. Very soon you have lots of mutual friends which then makes it easier to add more. This profile took me less than forty-eight hours to create. It's that simple and hey, who can resist a cute cat wearing specs?'

'I see. But I won't have to actually engage with any of them, will I?'

Tom shook his head. 'Not if you stick to the story we created for you. Remember, your lovely boyfriend Davey over there controls most aspects of your life so doesn't like you chatting or sharing too much info online, after all he's a *very* small-time drug dealer who has to watch his back. Your friends on Facebook tie up to a few of the names on your phone, ones he would approve of. Their photos are fake, but if Kelly checks them out – which I doubt she will – she'll see that they have shedloads of friends elsewhere and think nothing of it.'

'Are you sure she won't be suspicious?'

'I'm ninety-nine per cent positive but that's why I've been careful and tried to think outside the box. Honestly Billie, this woman is desperate to make friends. From what I have seen over the past few weeks, Kelly has no life apart from her parents, going to self-help groups and the one she's inventing for herself.

I reckon if you play this right, it won't be too hard to worm your way in.'

It was Aiden's turn to reassure her. 'As long as you stick to the personality and background we've invented for you, it will be fine. Be shy, nervy, a touch defensive but in all things you have to refer back to Davey, your scary control-freak boyfriend who's handy with his fists and from whom you are desperate to escape. If we are lucky, Kelly might just take you under her wing but if not, just keep an eye on her.'

'Okay, I can do that.' Billie put the phone and charger in her bag.

Aiden was twiddling his pen, like a majorette, spinning a baton but in his case all focus was on Billie, not the marching band. 'This is our last chance, Billie. If we don't get something on her soon Stan hasn't got a hope in hell with his appeal. We have to cast doubt on Kelly, something that will stack up with all the other dirt we've found on her but that relates directly to Stan.'

'I know, I know, but I just can't help thinking it's a risk, and how long will it take? Time's running out and it makes me ill thinking of Stan in there while she's running around talking crap to anyone who will listen. I think I might end up smacking her one.' Billie's heart was racing, sometimes the whole situation made her rage inside.

'You're right, we are running out of time but let's focus on the job in hand and let the barrister worry about all that. So, are you set? I've got every faith you can do this, Billie, so let's give it one last shot for Stan and remember, me and Tom are always a phone call away.'

With that, Billie stood and hooked her bag onto her shoulder. 'Yep, I'm ready. Let's do this.'

That was two weeks ago and Billie was now in her third meeting, seated right next to Kelly who, just as Tom had suggested, was very eager to make friends, lend an ear and give advice out like sweets from a paper bag. At the first two meetings Billie had sat right opposite so she could observe Kelly, who had already introduced herself while everyone helped themselves to tea and coffee, before the meeting began.

'Hi, I'm Kelly. Nice to see you here. I take it you're new or have you been away?'

Billie concentrated on filling her cup from the urn. 'No, I'm new.'

'Try not to be nervous, I know I was the first time I came but everyone is so helpful and supportive.' Kelly hovered and took a digestive biscuit from the plate.

Again, Billie kept it simple. 'Right, thanks.'

Kelly persisted. 'Do you live round here?'

Sticking to the brief Billie gave away a snippet. 'Yes, on the bird estate.'

'Bird estate?' Kelly looked confused.

'Yes, all the streets are the names of birds. Everyone knows that.' Billie was being snippy, she couldn't help it.

'Oh, I see, sorry. I'm not from Gorton so I wouldn't know. Right then, looks like they're ready to start.' Kelly was still holding her biscuit which she replaced. 'And what's your name, by the way, you didn't say?'

'Beth.' There: she'd said it without slipping up. Billie felt relieved.

'Pleased to meet you, Beth. And don't forget, no need to be shy or nervous. We are all more or less in the same boat here and don't judge, okay?'

Billie nodded and tried not to flinch when Kelly squeezed her arm in a supportive way.

At the end of that first meeting Billie had lingered, perusing the rack that held self-help and information pamphlets, keeping one eye on Kelly who was chatting away to the group leader as she put on her coat and collected her bag. It was no coincidence that Kelly headed for the exit at the same time as Billie who was rather pleased to see it was raining, just for a change, when they stepped outside.

'Shit,' Billie said loudly as she zipped her green parka and pulled up the hood.

Kelly was also sheltering under the canopy at the entrance to the centre. 'Bloody weather, I swear it's not stopped raining the whole of November. Haven't you got a brolly either?'

Billie was being friendlier, the harsh tone from earlier had softened slightly. 'No, I didn't expect it to rain. I'll just have to get wet. Never mind, I'm not going far.'

Kelly took the bait. 'Do you want a lift? My car's just over there so if we leg it we shouldn't get soaked. I really don't mind.'

With raised eyebrows and a surprised yet grateful tone, Billie feigned relief. 'Are you sure? That would be great. I'm only round the corner.'

Kelly pushed her arm through Billie's. 'Come on then, before it gets worse.'

Billie cringed, then headed for Kelly's car.

At the second meeting Billie had waved back when Kelly, who was in the middle of a conversation, acknowledged her arrival. She was running late after dropping Iris off with Sue, who was slipping into the role of super-gran very nicely. Thankfully, she was just so happy to be spending time with her granddaughter that she didn't question where Billie was off to, and accepted the half-fib that she was attending a therapy session.

Aiden had been pleased that Billie had made contact during

her first encounter and had allowed Kelly to drop her off at the flats on the bird estate. They had chatted about the weather during the short journey, and Kelly asked if she'd enjoyed the group. Billie replied that it had been interesting but she'd felt too shy to take part. There wasn't much time for anything else. After she'd waved goodbye and ran up the steps at the side of the block, Billie waited for a good five minutes before emerging then walked across the estate to Asda, where she'd left Stan's car.

But all this had proved nothing and Billie had spent a whole week since feeling frustrated and deflated which was why she was much chattier when Kelly approached.

'Nice to see you again, I wondered if you'd come back. Are you okay?'

'Mmm, so-so. Had a bit of a do with my other half last night and wasn't sure I'd get here today. He can be a total knobhead sometimes and when he's on one I have to stay at the flat. Does my fucking head in.'

'Oh no, I'm sorry. Does he not go to work?' A look of concern accompanied Kelly's question.

Billie snorted. 'Don't make me laugh. He's never done a day's work in his life, nothing legal anyway. The lazy get stays in most of the day watching shite on telly then goes out at night with his so-called mates. I spend most of it hoping he won't come back.'

Both of them had sniggered and then the sound of the meeting being convened interrupted and caused Kelly to remove her hand from Billie's arm, then she headed towards the other women. By the time Billie had hung her coat on the rack, the seats next to Kelly were taken but that suited her fine. She wanted to sit opposite and look her straight in the eye.

It was during this session that Billie had studied everything about Kelly. As a lady explained how her one-to-one therapy sessions had helped sort through the mangled mess in her head, a subject that the other women were eager to hear about, Kelly often stared into space or pulled at the threads on her jumper. There was a point when the support worker asked if anyone would like to discuss something and three hands shot up, but when Kelly wasn't picked, Billie was sure she spotted a flash of annoyance in her eyes.

That was it, though. Sod all. And when Kelly had shot off after the meeting, any hope that Billie might wangle a lift and the friendly chat she'd been planning all week, disappeared with her.

That was why it was imperative that progress was made today, just something of use. A way into Kelly's life was all she needed.

They had been discussing the after-effects of violence and one lady described how she'd been attacked by her own son, which led to the feelings of isolation one experiences during abusive relationships. While the other women shared, Billie remained silent, so absorbed in their stories that she forgot about Kelly and focused on them instead.

It was heartbreaking to hear how they had been abused physically, but mentally too, their identity and liberty slowly eroded until they felt stripped of self-worth. They lived in fear, trapped with nowhere to go and without support, just like Carol had been. Billie was beginning to feel really uncomfortable, like an intruder on such a private and serious conversation but when Kelly raised her hand and asked if she could tell them her own story, things were about to get a whole lot worse.

'Hearing everyone's experiences has made me realise that I'm not on my own, but I feel stuck at the moment, in a dark hole I suppose, and over the past few weeks I've been trying to pluck up the courage to tell you why I'm here. I think today is the day, now or never I suppose, if you don't mind listening.'

The group leader nodded. 'Of course we don't, Kelly. That's

what we are here for. But if you need a break at any time just stop. We understand.'

Billie's whole body had frozen but she forced her head to turn sideways, just in time to see Kelly give a nervous smile. This woman, sitting centimetres away was about to talk about Stan and tell a room of strangers lies about him. Billie's insides trembled and she clasped her hands together so nobody would know they were shaking. When she heard Kelly inhale, Billie silently sucked in air too, desperate to keep her composure, dreading what she was going to hear.

'Last year, I was raped by my boyfriend.' Kelly paused as the other women gasped.

Billie thought she was going to be sick.

23

Kelly had reached the part where she'd gone to collect her belongings from Stan's house, the home Billie used to live in, the one that she could picture in every word and sentence of this fantasy story.

She had turned slightly in her seat because she wanted to take it all in, this performance. Billie was incredulous because Kelly had more or less turned every single bit of Stan's testimony on its head. It was like reading his letter but holding a mirror in front of the words and twisting them to suit herself, make her the victim.

Her whole version of events directly contradicted Stan's while staying close to the facts. It wasn't her that was controlling and pushy, it was him! Apparently, Stan encouraged Kelly to hang out with his mum – bollocks! Then there was the rugby incident where she was humiliated and abandoned and never on this God's earth would Stan ever tear up clothes, daub the bathroom mirror with obscenities or throw a kebab at someone in his car. Christ, he was obsessed with the bloody thing and had it valeted every week, inside and out! Kelly was talking utter rubbish.

No wonder the jury believed her because God, she was good. The tears and occasional catch in her throat, seconds before her eyes swept the room looking for sympathy from the nodding heads of unsuspecting women showing understanding and giving encouragement. Billie wanted to cry out 'STOP' but instead dug her nails into her palm and reminded herself why she was here: to look for clues.

Kelly had been offered a tissue by the woman to her left that she now twisted in her fingers as she spoke. 'I was looking for my stuff in the wardrobes and found a bag with it all in, so I yanked it out and made my way towards the door. He blocked my way, grabbing my hand which I pulled away but he held on tight and squeezed hard. He wanted us to go downstairs and have something to eat, he said he'd bought my favourite curry and wanted to discuss our relationship like adults. There was no way I was staying and told him so.'

Someone had a coughing fit so Kelly paused and waited for them to stop. She obviously wanted silence and centre stage. Billie, on the other hand, wanted a hole to appear under Kelly's chair and swallow her up. No such luck, the diva was on a roll.

'That's when he started pacing, saying it was happening again, just like before and he couldn't let me go. I didn't understand what he meant and focused on the bags but then he slipped up and I got it. While he was rambling on, saying that he was sorry, he's made a mistake and I had to let him fix it, he called me Billie. Then I remembered. He'd told me once that when his girlfriend left, they had a huge row because she'd cooked him an Indian meal and he stayed out really late and it got ruined. That's when she dumped him because he'd had a one-night stand. I think he was re-enacting that night but taking it out on me. Whatever it was, he just flipped when I picked up the bags and headed for the door.'

Kelly paused and as she did, glanced at Billie who could do

no more than stare back, stunned. There had been no need for the dramatic pause because little did Kelly know that Billie wasn't enthralled, more like trapped, listening with horror to this completely twisted version of events.

'When Stan grabbed me and blocked the doorway I tried to push past him. I wish now I'd taken a different tack and maybe agreed to go downstairs then made a run for it, but I didn't and I'll regret it always. I shouldn't have struggled because I think it turned him on, like I fuelled the rage. He totally lost it and started to slap me, really hard, one of the blows marked my cheek with his handprint. I was in shock and as I backed away I tripped on the foot of the bed and fell, banging my head on the bedside cabinet. The next thing I knew he was on me, pulling my coat and clothes off, pinning me face down on the floor until I was naked. I won't go into any graphic detail because it might upset some of you, but my injuries were as a result of trying to get away. I had carpet burns on my body and face, a cut on my head where I fell and bruises on my wrists where he held me down.' Kelly dabbed away her tears with the tatty ball of wet tissue.

'I thought it was over because he stopped, then stood and pulled back the sheets and told me to get onto the bed so I did, I was terrified. I will never forget the wild look in his eyes. It gives me goosebumps even now. I pleaded with him and said I didn't want to but he just stared and waited. It was at this point I knew I couldn't get away, so instead I gave in. I did as I was told and lay there and just let him get on with it. I didn't move or make a sound. I just closed my eyes and prayed for it to be over. Afterwards, he just got up like it was normal, then went into the en suite and took a shower. I was still paralysed with fear so stayed where I was. He dried himself then put on some tracky bottoms and went downstairs.'

There was silence in the room and as Kelly opened her

mouth to continue someone's phone began to play *The X-Files* music and there was a mad scramble inside a bag, the owner flushing red and apologising. Kelly simply waited, watched by the others but even more intently by Billie.

'I could hear him humming and the sound of plates clattering and then he called my name and told me to hurry up, the curry was going to get cold. I thought, *Oh my God, he's going to eat. How could he?* I was shaking like a leaf, trying to work out what to do. My phone was in my bag in the hallway so I couldn't call for help so instead I lay there and waited. I'm not sure what for, but I was too scared to move. I was dreading him coming upstairs. Apparently, he ate his curry and got pissed, watching the telly. I stared at the clock on the side for two hours, every single minute, waiting for the numbers to change. I hadn't heard him moving about for ages so pulled on my coat, I couldn't find my shoes, and crept down the stairs. When I got to the bottom I couldn't see him, just a plate and some empty beer bottles on the floor by the sofa, then I heard him in the downstairs loo, so I ran to the front door.'

There were sighs of relief from the gathered women, some muttering 'Thank God' before Kelly got on with her finale.

'When I dream about it, this part is always in slow motion because I had to turn the lock slowly and my hands were shaking so bad I didn't think I could do it, and all the time I kept looking behind, checking he wasn't there. It must have been literally seconds but it felt like hours and even now I wake up screaming, because in my nightmares he gets me, grabbing my hair and dragging me back up the hall.

'In reality, I flung open the door and ran, straight down the drive, across the street to the nearest house and banged on the door, over and over again until someone came. After that it's all a blur. I remember a nice lady taking me in, her husband called the police and the rest is just blue lights, words, statements, hospital and examinations. The thing is, it didn't end there. The nightmare went on, for months and months, going to court, giving evidence, how it affected my mum and dad, and it's still going on now. I just wanted you all to know that it can happen to anyone, and I understand how easy it is to be taken in, not see the signs until it's too late. It's not our fault, though. It's theirs. We are the victims; they are just animals who deserve to be locked up and punished.' Kelly burst into tears when the women began to clap.

Billie remained motionless, aware of the tears that leaked from her own eyes, but they weren't for Kelly, were they? No, it was incomprehensible that she would feel even a glimmer of empathy for a heartless liar who had ruined Stan's life, and his family's. It was just very emotive and reminded Billie of the women she had come into contact with during her time on the force. She'd seen some terrible sights and heard distressing accounts of women living trapped in an abusive relationship. Where being raped by the man you lived with, or beaten black and blue, or driven to the brink of despair by mental torture had become the norm. So many women endured it because they had no escape route, women just like Carol.

It was impossible not to feel empathy even when it was Kelly on the stage. But Billie's gut instinct told her Kelly wasn't one of these women. The way she had related her story, methodically with added drama, felt like an act and Billie could just imagine Kelly sitting in front of the mirror rehearsing her lines, practising the sad looks and the trembling hands. Or was she being sceptical because she'd been swayed by Aiden's take on Kelly, and unequivocally believed Stan's no-holds-barred letter?

The thing was, the woman seated on the other side of Kelly had her arm around her shoulders, giving comfort and Billie knew she had to snap out of it and show support or she would seem out of place. Leaning forward she placed her hand on

Kelly's knee and gave it a gentle squeeze. When the gesture was reciprocated and Kelly reached out and grabbed Billie's hand tightly, the snotty wet tissue squashing against her skin, it felt like an act of betrayal. How could she comfort a woman she despised, who had lied, telling a parallel yet warped version of Stan's story?

Reluctantly, Billie told herself she had no option other than to play along and stick to the brief, even if it meant holding hands with the devil.

~

They were in Kelly's car driving towards the estate where Billie supposedly lived. She had stayed close after the meeting, playing the concerned new friend, telling Kelly how brave she'd been to speak out about such a terrible experience so when she was offered a lift home, Billie gratefully accepted.

'I'm sorry if I upset you or the other women back there. You looked like you were really shocked by my story and I felt bad when I saw how pale you'd gone. Did it touch a nerve?' Kelly was concentrating on the road and appeared to be fully recovered but not completely ready to forget her traumatic afternoon.

'No need to apologise. I'm sure it's helped some of them and it sounded like you needed to get it off your chest but no, it didn't touch a nerve, you know, the rape part, but the control did. I'm even further down that road and I have no idea how to escape it.' Billie really couldn't bear to hear any more of Kelly's lie so tried to steer her in another direction.

'Oh no, that's awful. So what's your situation then? Or would you rather not talk about it?'

Billie was more than happy to explain but they'd reached the flats and there was no time. Then she had an idea. 'No, I'm fine about talking, just not to a group of strangers, well not yet anyway. Look, have you got time for a coffee? There's a Costa at the next roundabout. We could go there and I can explain properly. If Davey sees me here with you he'll start asking annoying questions and it's not worth the hassle.'

The engine was still running as Kelly smiled and indicated. 'Of course I've got time and I know where it is, so let's go. Then you can tell me all about this Davey and what's been going on. My treat.'

Billie gave her very best grateful smile and nodded and weird as it may seem, felt glad to be away from the prying eyes of her imaginary boyfriend. This roleplay malarkey was getting easier by the minute. Being nice to a woman you could cheerfully strangle, not quite so simple.

24

The first time Stan saw his baby daughter he had watched her intently, soaking up every single feature, how her lips formed a perfect bow shape, the long eyelashes that rested on tired dark eyes that mirrored his own and stared intently at him when she was awake. Now she was asleep. Her fingers twitched slightly and Stan wished she'd wake up but reminded himself that having her to hold was enough.

The second time he'd controlled his emotions, not crumbled into a trembling wreck who very nearly broke down and had to cover his mouth to stop the sobs from escaping, wiping away tears before they were shed, desperately trying to hold it together. Billie had been a rock and even though it was obvious she was experiencing some of the same, had jollied the reunion along and kept them both together. According to his mum, Iris was the spit of Stan when he was a baby, a point she had kept mentioning throughout the visit, nerves taking over as usual but at least this time she hadn't cried for the duration. For that Stan was grateful.

He couldn't believe Iris was nearly one and he'd missed out on so much of her life but that was by the by. It was coming to terms with the notion that he would miss out on so much more in the future that brought him untold pain, panic and near hysteria. Already she seemed to recognise him – or was he imagining it? Perhaps it was down to her placid nature and willingness to be held by a virtual stranger and she hadn't a clue who he was. Again, his mum insisted it was because they had a bond and Iris just knew he was her daddy. To be honest Stan didn't care, as long as he could make her giggle and give her a cuddle.

His other gorgeous girl was also coming back to him, Stan could tell, although she was far too big to sit on his knee and it definitely wasn't allowed. But their brief moments of contact lingered as much as they dared and her eyes and smile told him that Billie still loved him; that and her letters and phone calls. Any talk of her activities regarding Kelly was off limits during visits. They were about family not the family-wrecker so they saved their fortnightly meeting for happy talk, leaving progress reports for the phone.

Stan was also relieved to hear about the change in his mum and Darren. Sue had had her hair done and put on a bit of weight too and Darren was getting stuck into college and being super-uncle. Stan knew it was the Billie-effect, and Iris, and, even though he'd made massive mistakes in the past, he'd done the right thing when he begged her to come home.

While Billie told him about the first birthday party they were planning for Iris, he put on a brave face, knowing that she'd feel guilty for even mentioning it but was obeying his request that they talked 'normally' – whatever that was these days – during a visit. The images of his little girl having fun kept him going. And he was determined more than ever that he would be there for her second birthday. He had to be.

There was something else he was trying not to think about and that was the imminent release of Doog, his cellmate and protector. Stan was dreading him going. He knew it was selfish but the prospect of not having a six-foot bodybuilder onside – and God only knew who for a replacement – was just another worry to keep him awake at night.

When the bell rang Stan's heart lurched and knowing that they had literally seconds left, his resolve broke. Billie as always stepped in and quelled the storm that was being whipped up inside him.

'Hey, come on now... Don't give up, Stan, please be strong. I'm doing everything I can, I promise. Just hang on in there. I hate seeing you like this.' Billie rested her head on Stan's chest, just for a moment.

'Sorry, sorry. It's just so hard to let you go. It seems like a life-time waiting to see you and a fortnight might as well be a year.'

'It's the same for me, Stan but I'm not in here so I can't imag-ine. Will you ring me later and then we can talk more? I feel closer to you even when we are on the phone. Now I'd better go, the guard is giving me evils... And that creepy bald guy was staring again. I feel sorry for his girlfriend being with someone like that. I hope he isn't giving you any trouble.'

It was pecking Stan's head that Doog made Billie feel uneasy and he was just about to come clean and say that the bald-headed, nosey bastard was actually his cellmate and too vain to wear glasses, so stared a lot. But then the guard told everyone to clear the room so the moment was lost.

'Love you, Billie, take care going home.' Stan kissed Iris on the forehead then Billie on the lips.

Backing away, Billie wore her usual brave smile. 'Love you too Stan, be strong, okay?'

Stan made his way back to his cell, two inmates behind Doog who was having a bit of banter with the guard. Stan knew why Doog was giving Billie the evils and if he ever got the chance to explain, he knew it would be best to omit why he acted like a psycho. Doog thought it would spur her on, make her more determined to find some dirt on Kelly and secure Stan's release. There was no point in mentioning him to Billie, not yet anyway, because by the end of the week Doog would be gone, a free man. How Stan envied him.

Stan watched as Doog gathered his belongings and placed them in the cardboard box. Anything that he thought edible or useful he threw onto Stan's bed. The atmosphere was weird because while Doog was probably itching to get out the door, he was clearly playing it down out of respect for Stan's feelings which were at rock bottom. It didn't stop him giving some advice though.

'And don't forget what I told you. Make sure you keep your head down when you're out of the cell. Now they've moved that nonce off the wing, the gobshites will be looking for someone else to keep them occupied so stay out of their way.' Doog paused and gave Stan a stern look.

'Yeah, yeah, I get it. I'll watch my back. I'm more worried about who I'll end up sharing with, to be honest. It was bad enough getting lumbered with a twat like you.' Stan managed a smile and had a Twix launched in his direction in response to the jibe.

'Yeah well, at least I didn't want a cuddle in the middle of the night so remember what I said, keep yer arse facing the wall after lights out.'

'For fuck's sake, Doog! Why don't you kick a man when he's down? Anyway, less of the advice. You know what to do when you get out, who to go and see?' Stan was wired. It was like he was feeding on Doog's suppressed energy, living another man's dream of freedom.

'It's all in here mate... don't worry.' Doog tapped his shiny head.

'Right. Good. And if you hear anything on the grapevine, if you think anyone is trying to shaft me, let me know. I'm not so green that I don't expect people to be taking the piss and making the most of me being in here, so from now on you're the man, okay?'

'Fine by me, mate, but give me time to get home and sort the missus out first, then I'll be straight round to see this Aiden bloke and get my feet under the table.'

Stan laughed and then quickly wiped the thought of Billie and being home in bed with her, from his mind.

'Kenny will have your unit sorted out by now but he's no idea you know me. As far as he's concerned you're just another punter. It's a shame you're not handy with the tools because I wouldn't mind someone on the inside at the plumbing firm. Fuck knows what's up with Eddie. He's left me right in the lurch... bloody depression my arse. After all I've done for him an' all. Him and his wife have been going through IVF, costs a bloody fortune to pay for it private so I lent him the money for the first lot and made sure he got plenty of overtime in. And now he's on the sick. I reckon he just fancies swinging the lead and having a cheeky break while I'm out of the picture. So if you hear owt on that score, give me a bell.'

It pissed Stan off that one of his most reliable employees had let him down. Still, it kept him occupied, although keeping tabs on his business was a ball-ache when your office was a cell but now he had Doog on side.

Doog had finished his packing and sat down on the bed opposite Stan, leaning against the wall, arms crossed. A serious expression preceded his question. 'And what about this Kelly slag... how long are we gonna give Billie before she gets what she deserves?'

'I dunno, mate. We need to see how it pans out. But if Aiden and the barrister pull the plug and I end up stuck in here, then you know what to do.' Stan eyed Doog. Doog just nodded. Enough said.

The Kelly thing had been plaguing Stan for weeks, ever since Billie had befriended the woman who put him inside. It was a gamble and would take time and even then could come to nothing. Stan almost expected it, but he was, all the while, praying for a miracle.

He was touched though, that Doog referred to it as their problem. It told Stan that his new mate was a bloke he could trust. Sometimes you just knew. Doog did okay on his own and had plenty of lucrative irons in the fire so wasn't particularly in need of Stan's money or for that matter, a nice secure lock-up where all manner of knock-off could be stored. They were ten a penny. Doog wasn't bound by any oath of allegiance and could have quite easily walked away in the morning and left Stan to rot. Instead, they'd decided to go into partnership.

Stan was sick of playing it by the book and if he did end up festering in his vermin-infested cell, he was going to make sure that when he got out there was a nice pot of tax-free cash waiting for him. As for Kelly, she wasn't going to get away with landing him in here. It was becoming clear that the law wasn't likely to bring Stan justice so he'd just have to take matters into his own hands, or place matters in those of one of Doog's cronies.

He'd never forget what Kelly had whispered in his ear when he'd finally plucked up the courage to confront her. It had been a pointless exercise apart from showing him exactly what he was up against. Well, come what may; be it from the inside or when he finally got out, Kelly would regret what she said and did. One day, Stan was going to have his own revenge.

25

Kelly had arrived at the pub early to make sure she bagged one of the large booths in the corner. There was plenty of space for all the women she'd asked along for the impromptu midweek get-together but she placed her bag on the end to save a space for Beth.

They'd only known each other for a few weeks but despite Beth's annoying boyfriend, Kelly had struck up a great friendship with her. It was based largely on texts back and forth but that was okay. It was good to have someone to chat to and their girly conversations and hilarious GIF exchanges sometimes lasted well into the night. Beth's boyfriend sounded like a complete pain-in-the-arse scumbag who, apart from being a self-centred control freak and too handy with his fists, was getting in the way of Kelly having some fun with her new best mate.

She wasn't really looking forward to Christmas apart from the two days she'd spend with her mum and dad who spoilt her rotten. It was the rest of December and the New Year that resembled a barren wasteland. The works Christmas do had been shite. What made it worse was that while the other girls made the effort during the meal Kelly could tell they didn't want her tagging along to the club. So she'd left them to it.

Women didn't like Kelly. They never had and she'd got used to it, telling herself she wasn't a girl's girl and they were just jealous. The works do hadn't been a complete waste of time, though, because after her colleagues had sloped off, she'd spent it with a tasty bloke she'd met on Plenty of Fish. It was how she preferred things these days, no-strings sex with men who were only after the same thing as her. Relationships weren't worth the hassle. Stan had taught her that.

All was not lost, though, because after Beth had let slip that Davey was going to be away for the night – some jolly over to Dublin with his other scummy mates – Kelly had an idea and was going to put it to Beth when she arrived. Checking her watch she saw it was five past. After scanning the empty car park she felt her heart sink and prepared to be let down. *Once a loner, always a loner,* she thought. It was nothing new but she'd hoped the women on her Facebook group would fancy a break from their humdrum lives and be up for a laugh and a few cheeky drinks.

She was expecting at least five definites and hopefully a few stragglers. After all, some of them owed her. It had been an awkward moment, the previous week at the drop-in when Beth had stumbled on her and Lynda in the toilets and yes, it must have looked and sounded dodgy so no wonder her face was a picture.

Lynda had been searching through her bag trying to find her purse, apologising as was her way, a trait that had probably been beaten into her. 'It's in here somewhere, honestly. Sorry for taking so long, I didn't mean to make you wait for it but you know how it is.'

Kelly didn't, but had nodded her head. Her patience was

running out and she wished Lynda would get a move on otherwise Beth might get bored and set off without her.

'Here, found it.' Lynda pulled out her purse and then with trembling fingers unzipped the top and extracted a roll of twenty-pound notes. 'Like I said, sorry I made you wait.'

Literally, just as Kelly's fingers wrapped around the money, Beth burst into the toilets and caught the women red-handed. Their shocked expressions must have told a tale all of their own and it wasn't surprising that she reacted with suspicion.

Looking from one to the other Beth asked the obvious. 'Oh yeah, so what's going on in here then? You two look very dodgy... should I turn round and pretend I didn't see?'

Although Beth's tone was jokey, Kelly spotted suspicion in her eyes and Lynda's propensity for behaving like a timid mouse wasn't helped by her stuttering and stammering over something really quite straightforward.

Kelly just said it how it was. 'Nope, nothing dodgy going on here, mate. Just Lynda repaying a little loan, that's all.'

Lynda nodded her agreement then found her voice as Kelly listened. The words that came tumbling out of Lynda's mouth were no doubt a result of being used to thinking on her feet to swerve the fist. 'Our Patrick wanted to go on a school trip but his dad said he couldn't, so I slipped him the money and told him not to let on but then our Rachel needed some new shoes cos some little bastard pinched hers out of the changing rooms, so when the gas and leccy bill came I was short so Kelly here lent me the money till I got straight. She's an angel, she is.' Lynda took a breath then reached out and squeezed Kelly's arm, a grateful smile accompanying her words of thanks.

'Honest, Lynda, it's no trouble and if it happens again, just say. You've got enough on your plate without worrying over money, too.' Kelly gave her a wink and a smile.

Lynda hitched her bag over her shoulder then slipped past Beth who stepped aside to let her pass.

Once she had gone, Kelly raised her eyebrows, laughing as she spoke. 'What's with you, Detective Inspector Beth? For a minute I thought you were going to arrest me for crimes against the sisterhood. Since when did you get all suspicious?'

Beth coloured but seemed to take the jibe well. 'Mate, if you lived with a shady bloke who does most of his business in loos, you'd be suss too, and less of the detective shit, that's all I need. Now, are you giving me a lift home to paradise or not?'

Kelly had snorted a laugh and pocketed the money before pulling open the door. She had followed Beth towards the exit, waving to the other women as they went. It felt good to be part of a group regardless of the reason they were all there but most of all, it was nice to have a friend again, even the slightly scruffy, pink-haired, tattoo-freak up in front.

Kelly took a sip of her spritzer and tried to ignore the spark of annoyance that her solitary status in the pub ignited. She was starting to feel like a right pillock, sitting in the huge booth and just wished one of her ragtag Facebook group would turn up, especially Beth. Kelly was getting the hump which was ironic and apt, seeing as it was Wednesday.

Little did Beth know that the incident with Lynda wasn't the first time she'd helped some of her growing army of lost waifs and downtrodden wives, or that lending them money wasn't a problem. She had a nice little nest egg tucked away and if dipping into it meant she was needed, liked even, then all well and good. Kelly was honest with herself at least, because she was never going to be Mother Theresa and her benevolence was in the most part self-serving. Gaining the trust of women like Lynda, jolly meet-ups like this and getting to hear their stories first-hand was going to be invaluable when Kelly began her new venture. She was sick of her job as a dental nurse, of looking into the mouths of people who didn't know how to use a toothbrush and working alongside women who shunned her so it was time for a change.

After plenty of research, and now she had the funds, enrolling on a few online courses wouldn't be a problem. The internet world was her oyster and all being well, in the new year she would be on her way to becoming a relationship counsellor, or whatever dedicated solver of personal problems one required. She'd even been practising her concerned face in the mirror, that doctorly way of nodding your understanding while focusing on the client, as if your scholarly brain is working it all out as they speak.

Along with her credentials, Kelly was banking on the fact that her tragic experience and understanding of police and court proceedings would be an invaluable plus, like a cruel but useful job reference. The tentacles of her 'situation' and those in similar circumstances, wrapped around the lives of extended family members and Kelly understood this. She could see herself now, doing the nod, passing the box of tissues. Her survival status would show the victims that there was hope and something good could come out of all this: after all, she had risen from the ashes.

Kelly had it all planned out and kept her eye on social media and the many groups she had joined where she was a popular regular, commenting on issues and lending support from behind her laptop screen.

She was also honing other skills like public speaking because who knew where this could take her but until the opportunity presented itself, she would make do with radio phone-ins. Kelly enjoyed it, giving her side of the story even though she had had to learn to curb her descriptive tendencies rather than upset or offend anyone. This new, sensitive side to her personality was actually borne out of regret because Kelly's own parents had suffered too, not only when they heard of her ordeal but in the months of investigations and court appearances, those tentacles constantly squeezing joy out of their lives. It was at times like that when she had questioned many things, like her decision to report the attack. The thing was, in the end, Kelly couldn't alter the past or what her parents had heard in evidence. They'd been advised by the liaison officer to leave when Kelly's video interview describing the rape was played, but decided to stay so now they had to live with it. After that, all Kelly did was tell her side of the story. That's what the barrister wanted, and that's what he got.

Kelly was getting impatient and furiously texting Beth when she felt a tap on her arm and there she was, with Paula and Nicki in tow, all three looking frozen.

'Hey, you made it, now sit down and I'll get the drinks in. My treat.' Kelly watched as they unravelled scarves and removed hats and coats, placing their orders before shuffling around the booth.

Beth hovered by Kelly's side. 'Sorry I'm late. That prat was taking ages to get ready so I had to linger until he was well out of sight. Do you want a lift with the drinks? I'll just have a diet Coke. I feel a bit rough today. Think it might be a bug.'

'Bloody Coke? Well you're gonna be a barrel of laughs. Just have one with vodka in it. Might settle your stomach.'

'Nah, honest, mate, it won't and I don't have to get mortalled to have fun, so chill. Now lead the way, these ladies are parched.' Beth gave Kelly a hard push and pointed to the bar.

'Okay, I know when I'm beat but you'd better not let me down on our big night out I've got planned.'

'What big night out?' Beth was leaning on the bar, focusing on Kelly.

'I'll tell you later on when the others have gone but I think you and I deserve a treat. It is Christmas after all.' Kelly tapped the side of her nose and winked, then turned away and waved at the barman.

As she ordered the drinks, all plans for career changes and doom-and-gloom memories of the past got shoved to the back of Kelly's mind and instead she concentrated on her new friend and having some fun. The thought of her empty flat and dire Christmas card list made her even more determined that next year would be a complete new start and, if she played her cards right, she'd have a brand new, pink-haired flatmate into the bargain. Carrying the drinks while Beth held onto the bags of crisps, Kelly allowed herself a smug smile. Maybe, regardless of the consequences for all concerned and especially now her ordeal was over, she had done the right thing.

Kelly and her new best friend were seated by the window, eating KFC and watching the other customers shuffle along in the queue. The meet-up with the other women had been a success, in that Kelly had laughed and chatted about normal stuff, not the depressing subjects they covered in the group. They seemed to appreciate her generosity too, especially the platter of sandwiches and chips she'd ordered as an extra treat.

The best part was that once the others began to trail off, stressing about putting kids to bed and getting an ear-full from their other halves, Beth said she was feeling better and had suggested they went for a bite to eat while Davey was at the match. Beth certainly had hollow legs and Kelly envied her svelte figure that she said came naturally. Or maybe she lived on her nerves that were frazzled thanks to her waste-of-space boyfriend.

Once she'd finished her popcorn chicken, Beth asked Kelly a question. 'So go on then, what's all this about a big night out? You know what Davey's like and the only time he lets me party is when I'm by his side and even then it's not exactly a barrel of laughs. In fact I'd rather stay in and watch *Countryfile*.'

Kelly laughed out loud. 'Sodding *Countryfile*, you sad act! I bet you watch *Doc Martin* too.'

'I do actually, I fancy that gormless policeman and fantasise about him handcuffing me to the bedpost and reading me my rights.' Beth took a huge bite out of her drumstick and ducked the French fry that was thrown at her.

'Well I have the answer to your prayers. You said Davey was going to Dublin for a lads' weekend. Well why don't you and me have a night out while he's away?' Kelly was excited already and Beth hadn't even said yes, but going by the expression on her face, the answer was going to be no. Kelly's mood nosedived.

Beth sucked in her breath and gave a pained expression. 'I don't know, mate... if he finds out he'll go spare and I'd be shitting myself that someone would see us. But don't get me wrong, I'd love to. Believe me, I really would.' Beth sipped her Coke then wiped her greasy hands on the napkin.

Kelly leant forward and dipped her chips into the barbeque sauce as she spoke. 'I've already thought of that. We could go out in Didsbury, well away from East Manchester and I'm not being funny but I can't see any of Davey's crew hanging out around there. Surely it's some other drug dealer's turf. And anyway, won't they all be on the fun boat to Dún Laoghaire?'

Beth looked a bit less mithered. 'Yeah, I suppose so.'

'And if you're worried about someone seeing you all dressed up, you could get ready at mine and stay over afterwards, we'd have a right laugh. Come on, this is the perfect opportunity to have some fun so what do you say?' Kelly held her breath. She'd been thinking of nothing else since Beth mentioned Davey's trip in a text.

'I've got nothing to wear though... seriously I haven't, this is the best I've got and anything that's remotely going-outy isn't suitable for the wine bars of Didsbury.'

Kelly raised her hand. 'That's not a problem, I'll treat you to a new outfit as long as you say yes... go on, I know you want to.'

Beth folded her arms and looked pouty. 'I'm not a charity case and anyway, since when did you win the lottery? I've noticed you always seem flush?'

Kelly tutted and rolled her eyes. 'I know you're not, so stop being a touchy cow... see it as a Christmas present if it makes you feel better. And don't worry about money, let's just say I've had a little windfall and there's more where it came from.'

'Ooh, that sounds interesting. Tell me more.'

'Not until you say yes and then I might just let you into my secret.'

Beth sucked on her straw which made a loud, embarrassing slurping noise that attracted an amused stare from the man seated close by, making them both burst into fits of giggles. 'Okay, go on then. You're right, I'm due a bit of fun and I'm sick to death of sitting in that flat while he's gadding about so it's a deal.' Beth looked at her phone and checked the time. 'Right, we'd better go otherwise knobhead will be home before me and then he'll kick off. So come on, where's all this dosh come from? I didn't have you down for betting on the horses.'

Kelly narrowed her eyes and took out her phone. 'As if! I don't even play Foxy Bingo. I'll tell you while we wait for the taxi. Just let me order one then we'll go.'

Beth joked. 'I reckon you've got a sugar daddy.'

'You've got room to talk, I reckon Davey's old enough to be

your granddad... I still don't know what you see in him, or have *you* got daddy issues?'

'Oi, you cheeky cow! Actually, he looks fit when he makes the effort and I'll have you know I like the more mature type of bloke and he likes having a trophy girlfriend. Well, that's what he said when he chatted me up. Now I think he just wanted a young dogsbody to look after him in his old age.'

'Urgh, you mean wipe his bum and feed him mushed-up food when he's past it?' Kelly feigned horror.

'Oh God, that mental image is so gross. I think my popcorn chicken's on its way back up but nah, I'll just stick him in a home.'

Both of them were tittering as Beth made disgusting sick noises.

'Stop it or I'll wee...'

'Anyway, enough taking the piss out of me. Who's this bloke? You still haven't told me about your daddy issues.'

Kelly sighed. 'I'll have you know I don't have daddy issues, mine's perfect. But you're a right nosy parker aren't you? I might start calling you Miss Marple, or Agatha, yep, that suits you much better. Come on, Aggie.' She swung open the door and grimaced when Beth punched her, harder than was necessary, if she was honest. But the fizz of happiness at having fun and a laugh with someone she regarded as a proper friend, cancelled out the pain.

Once they were on the street and the Uber was ordered, Kelly told Beth about her source of tax-free cash, just the bare bones because before she could say too much, the taxi appeared and the conversation was closed. Instead, they made plans for their big night out.

26

Aiden sipped his coffee while Billie ranted on. They had met in Sainsbury's café where she was supposed to be buying nappies and a packet of muffins for lunch. Sue was looking after Iris and still oblivious to Billie's mission. *My mission impossible*, thought Billie, because if she was honest, that's exactly what it felt like.

'Seriously, Aiden, I don't know how much longer I can keep this up. It's not just the sneaking about that's getting to me and having to tell fibs to Sue. It's *her*. Kelly's doing my head in.'

'Well you're all we've got. The barrister is adamant that a statement from Mr Macey at the chemist and our randy van driver, Denny, won't be enough to prove bad character on Kelly's part. If I were a betting man I'd say Stan's appeal is dead in a ditch.'

Billie put her head in her hands. 'Oh God! He's going to be devastated. But I am trying you know, I really am, but meeting her face to face once a week and talking bollocks by text isn't enough time to get under her skin, even though she's getting under mine.'

'What do you mean?' Aiden took a bite out of his chocolate muffin.

'This is going to sound weird and I'm not being a traitor, okay? The thing is, the way she told her story in the meeting, well, I could understand why the police and everyone believed her. Even though it is different to Stan's, it's sort of the same... like there's a fine line between the two versions. Maybe I'm too close to it all but I could picture everything she said, and it made it too real. Not only that, it was creepy.'

Aiden flicked crumbs off his suit. 'What do you mean, creepy?'

'Well this might sound daft but the night of the attack reminded me of when I left Stan and it did make me wonder...'

'What? Come on, Billie, you know you can trust me. What you tell me stays here between us. I promise.'

Billie lowered her voice a notch. 'It was the curry, and then her saying she was leaving and the row they had. It reminded me of the night I made Stan his favourite meal and he didn't come home because he'd cheated. And then the next day, we had a massive argument and I left. So... do you think it could have triggered something in his head, you know, like a spark of anger that made him snap?' The moment she said the words, Billie felt dreadful and, yes, like a traitor. She instantly wished she could take them back. But Aiden's answer eased her conscience slightly.

'Those thoughts are perfectly normal and good because it shows you are working things out and taking a step back. I like that. It's only by looking at things from every angle that you can build up an accurate picture and consider all scenarios.'

'Well that's made me feel better. Christ, I felt like a complete shit saying that but while I'm on a roll, I might as well tell you the rest, otherwise I'll never sleep again.'

Aiden opened his packet of biscuits and offered Billie one, which she declined.

'Go on then, let's have it.'

Billie took a breath and got it all off her chest. The thing was, Billie hated Kelly before she'd even met her and wouldn't have even contemplated the notion that Stan's version of events wasn't one hundred per cent accurate. That was why she had gone to the first meeting despising Kelly. It had been hard to look at her without wanting to punch her, and even while Billie listened to the emotional and often uncomfortable telling of her ordeal, she'd silently heaped scorn on every word.

It wasn't until she had the opportunity to spend time in Kelly's company that the cracks in Billie's armour started to show. As each layer of Kelly's self-preserving veneer began to flake away, and a more vulnerable woman appeared, things started to make sense to Billie, and to bother her.

Kelly was quite honest about herself and her situation and didn't mind telling you she was, for want of a less cringey and uncomfortable phrase, 'a Billy No-Mates'. Kelly also came across as a really nice person if, perhaps, a bit desperate and borderline bossy. But Billie understood why her female friends had begun to exclude her. Mud sticks.

Maybe a true best friend would have stood by Kelly but as it was, she was a loner and those in her limited circle had their own lives and problems. They didn't want to listen to her banging on about her neurosis, or feel obliged to lend a friendly ear, or go out on the town with a woman who was scared of her own shadow and men in general.

It was a shame though, because Kelly went out of her way to help. The moneylending thing for a start. Billie had also learned from some of the other women how kind she was in private, always willing to listen either by message or on the phone. It was so frustrating because the woman Stan painted as a complete and utter fruitcake and bitch, came across as the complete opposite in real life.

This was why Billie's head was mashed and the juxtaposed testimonies of that awful night didn't help either.

Then there was the 'daddy's girl' thing. How could Stan have got that so wrong? Why would Kelly make up all that stuff about her dad being a narcissist? It didn't make sense. Then Billie remembered what Aiden had said about blamers, describing them as 'those who reckon their deeds and situation are the fault of others'. Maybe when Kelly lost control and behaved badly, like the body-art incident, she resorted to fantasy and made up a nasty dad who was responsible for all her problems. It was an easy way out and impossible to disprove, and clever, very clever.

When it came down to it, Billie was beginning to wonder if, somewhere in between two different versions of an event that there wasn't a common theme running through and in the middle lay the truth. She'd heard it said many times before, 'there's no smoke without fire' and, 'only two people know what really happened that night'. So one of them was lying, or at best, telling a half-truth.

To make matters worse, if they possibly could be when someone you loved was going to be in prison for Christmas, Kelly had well and truly latched onto Billie and saw her as a friend. During one round of the late-night messages Kelly had used the word 'best' and it had made Billie feel so bad, despite her loyalty to Stan.

'So do you see now why my head is mashed? I feel like I'm living a lie. The clock is ticking away and everyone sees me as their last hope or sodding best friend and now, Kelly wants me to go on this big night out. I can't do it, Aiden, it's too hard. I'll have to lie to my mum and dad and Sue about where I'm going... like a blooming teenager. Shall I say I'm staying at yours then you tell your mum you're staying at mine?'

Aiden laughed, then became serious. 'I suppose you could tell Sue the truth, if it would ease your conscience.'

'No way. I don't want to get her hopes up and she'd ask too many questions. It's better to keep it simple and contained.'

Aiden leant on the table and looked serious, his hands clasped together doing the twiddly thumb thing. 'But you need to go out with her, Billie, because you're right, the clock's ticking for the appeal but at the same time, we have to be sensible and decide how long we can keep this up for, regardless of Stan's morale.'

'I know, don't you think I've realised that?' Billie was studying the dregs of her tea and wishing the tiny specks of black at the bottom of the cup would tell her the future, or at least what to do.

'The thing is, Aiden, I don't think she will ever confess to lying about what happened... why would she, why would anyone? And as much as I wanted her to be the devil's spawn, she's not, is she? She's just a mixed-up, lonely woman who has now unwittingly befriended her attacker's girlfriend. With every day that goes by I feel like I might as well bang my head against the wall for all the good I'm doing. And the irony is, I'm not actually helping Stan, I'm really helping Kelly.' Billie flung herself back against the booth and shook her head. 'What a bloody mess!'

Sighing, Billie rubbed eyes that desperately needed a good night's sleep, like her brain, which needed to switch the fuck off and wake up sometime after Christmas and New Year.

'Billie, I get it, I really do and, like I told you when we met, I'm not a shark who's after Stan's money. I will call time on this soon. I have a feeling it's inevitable but before I do, let's give it one more shot.'

Aiden took Billie's hands in his and gave them a squeeze, continuing. 'I agree that it's unlikely she's going to come out and confess because if she does, she's in deep trouble. But then again, it'd be your word against hers and your connection to Stan would pour cold water on all of it. The only hint of something suspicious is this windfall she says she's had, so let's focus on that. It could be bullshit but it's worth following up on. That's why I want you to go on this night out, get her paralytic drunk to see if it loosens her tongue. Let her buy you a new outfit too... and when you are in her flat you can have a mooch about. It's the only place Tom can't get to, so you can be our girl on the inside.'

'But what will I look for? A signed confession written in blood?'

Aiden laughed. 'That would be perfect but I was thinking more about a diary, letters, maybe even a spare mobile, you know, a cheat phone... anything you think is suspicious. You said she'd had a windfall, so look for bank statements that show a large deposit or maybe a paying-in book. If she lives on her own it's unlikely that she'll be privacy-conscious and might leave stuff lying about.'

'Okay, I'll do it, but if I don't find anything and she won't tell me what she's up to, I'm not carrying on indefinitely. It will kill me having to tell Stan because he'll see it as giving up, and then he'll have to face serving out his sentence...' Billie felt herself welling up at the thought of Stan's face and that dreadful prison.

Aiden intervened. 'No, I'll tell him. It will be my call. I'd rather it came from me. I'm detached. Well, I'm supposed to be, but you know what I mean.'

Billie gave him a grateful smile. 'So, you really are a big softie on the quiet. Who knew?'

Aiden shrugged, the corners of his eyes betraying a smile.

'Can I ask you something though and I need you to be honest?' Billie watched Aiden closely while she spoke. 'Do you believe Stan, still, after everything I've told you about Kelly?' She held her breath.

'Yes, I do.'

Billie felt her whole body relax. Then another question. It had to be asked. 'Why?'

Aiden turned slightly to retrieve the carrier bag of shopping that lay on the seat beside him. 'Because I just don't believe that the Kelly you know is the real one. I don't like the person I heard about from the various witnesses who knew her before but most of all, there are always two sides to a story and in this case, I'm inclined to think that Stan's version is the truth. And I am a betting man by the way, and my money's on him.'

There was something in Aiden's tone that told Billie the conversation was closed, that he'd passed judgement and that was enough, no need to expand. So she followed his lead, shuffled along the bench seat then stood. The meeting had drawn to a natural close. As they made their way to their respective cars and passed the kiosk selling lottery tickets and scratch cards, Billie averted her eyes. No way was she going to buy one because – unlike Aiden – she wasn't quite so confident that she could choose a winner.

27

Stan winced as he lowered himself onto the bed and tried not to grimace otherwise his lip would split again. With one arm wrapped around his ribs for protection he tried to get comfortable and prayed the paracetamol the doctor had given him would kick in soon.

Kick, now there was a word. Stan had known since the first day that a good kicking was inevitable and the odds were further stacked against him as soon as the nonce next door and a few other sex offenders were moved to another wing or jail. And now the other inmates had nobody else to pick on or amuse themselves with, their attention soon turned to him. He'd done everything to avoid it. He never lingered in the bathroom; he was quick when he took his bedding and clothes to the laundry and kept himself to himself when he queued up for meals or walked around the yard during his thirty-minute break. Every second spent outside his cell was fraught with danger and the thought of it was enough to bring on a panic attack, but Stan forced himself to do it, he had to otherwise he'd starve, stink and seize up.

They got him on his way back from speaking to Billie. At

least in the moments before they jumped him, Stan had felt marginally happy and pain-free as she described, under duress, how much Iris had enjoyed the Christmas markets and seeing the giant Santa on the town-hall roof. After that it was a blur. He preferred not to think about the feet that kicked and the fists that punched or the names he'd been called because that sliver of sanity, that fragile thread that he held onto was about to snap.

During his nightly periods of sleeplessness, when a blanket of gloom began to slowly suffocate him, Stan lay in the darkness of his cell and swallowed down hysteria, avoiding the temptation to scream out his frustration. Oddly enough, it was during the day when tiredness and boredom enveloped him that Stan managed to sleep, even amongst the noise out on the landing that competed with the screams in his head. When he day-slept it was like a drug-induced coma, total oblivion, and probably the only thing that kept Stan borderline sane. That and having The Professor for a cellmate.

The bespectacled slip of a man who had shuffled into the cell one afternoon, barely making eye contact and saying almost nothing for twenty-four hours was as unlike Doog as it was possible to be. He was unassuming, polite, and for want of a better word, a bit of a boffin. When they finally managed a conversation Stan learned that Quentin (there was a name he needed to keep to himself) was in for growing cannabis with intent to supply. It seemed that amongst his friends, many had creaking bones, or other age-induced ailments that responded well to the poultices Quentin made in his kitchen from the plants he grew in the cellar. Stan could only assume that being in his eighties was responsible for Quentin ending up on the vulnerable wing and all things considered, they'd both got lucky.

A slight cough and the sound of paper scrunching broke into

Stan's thoughts, a minor irritation and one he could cope with, the lesser of all evils.

'Still no better then?'

Stan groaned as he turned tentatively on his side. 'Nah, mate. To be honest I think it's getting worse because I'm stiffening up now. I could do with some of your magic cream though. I reckon that'd sort me out.'

A chuckle from Quentin. 'Oh without a doubt. I'd have you right as rain in no time, young man.'

Stan smiled. Quentin spoke so well, like the useless barrister that had told him, via a twitchy, nervous solicitor that his appeal was a non-starter unless some earth-shattering piece of new evidence came to light. So that was that. Billie was his last hope and after a brief and to the point conversation with Aiden the previous day (lingering on the phone was to be avoided now), it was looking like the plug was about to be pulled on their investigations. Stan appreciated his honesty though and the fact that Aiden was also looking out for Billie who, it seemed, was running out of steam too. Dragging his mind away from his family who he would be seeing later that day for their last visit before Christmas, he focused on Quentin who he found even more fascinating than anything on telly.

It seemed that before he'd walked the corridors of Strangeways, his new cellmate had spent most of his life walking the hallowed halls of Oxbridge, both as a student and professor of mathematics and philosophy but in between times, had broadened his horizons travelling the globe; Borneo, Cambodia, Yucatan, then the Galapagos and Antarctica, the list went on. Quentin was a political activist, environmental warrior, peace protester, rabble-rouser and in his own words an old and wrinkly specialist in recalcitrance.

Stan had had to look the word up but after hearing many a tale from Quentin, was forced to agree. 'So go on then, tell me where you learned to be a witch doctor. Was it on one of your hippy adventures... and how does it work, you know, how does wacky baccy stop people having fits and tremors and stuff like that?'

Quentin sighed, placed the bookmark on his current page and closed the book. 'I sense that you are in need of distraction from your pain and the anticipation of your young lady friend's visit this afternoon so, I shall indulge you. Now are you reposing comfortably?'

Stan saw the skin at the side of Quentin's grey eyes crinkle – they twinkled when he was amused and the old warrior loved to tell a tale. Giving him the thumbs-up, Stan prepared to hear the ins and outs of whatever chemistry and alchemy was involved in curing the grateful arthritic masses. And just as Quentin said, Stan sought to pass the time until he saw his mum, Billie and Iris.

He'd considered cancelling but knew that it would cause a right hoo-ha and upset them all so there was no other option. Instead, he'd forewarned Billie. There was no point in bullshitting about slipping on soap in the shower or tripping on the stairs, so he'd told her a watered-down version. It consisted of a bit of pushing and shoving where the other guy got more than he bargained for. Now all he had to do was act like he wasn't in pain and pretend that a cut lip and black eye was all he had to show for a punishment beating.

Zoning in on Quentin, Stan concentrated on the merits of the Cannabaceae family, along with the origins of *Cannabis sativa* and an insight into its indigenous home in Asia. This was going to be interesting, and it would take a while but Stan didn't care because he had all the time in the world. Actually he had two hours, seventeen minutes and approximately thirty-four seconds – not that he was counting or anything.

~

Stan squeezed Billie's hand really tightly and held onto Iris with the other as he jiggled her up and down on his knee. She was playing with a set of plastic rings, her chubby fingers attempting to hoop each one on top of the pole. Most of them had ended up on the floor, but at least that kept his mum occupied. The clock on the wall told him that it was almost time to say goodbye and as his focus returned to the faces around the table, he caught his mum's look and the ever-present knife twisted in his gut.

She had definitely aged in the past year but religiously painted on a mask to hide her feelings. The blusher and lipstick didn't conceal the greyish pallor that lay beneath or the fear in her eyes when they dared to glance around the dismal, room. The guards were making her nervous too, he could tell. His mum wasn't used to scrutiny or talking privately but the sombre, straight-backed men were probably listening in to their conversation and Stan sensed it upset her.

In some ways it reminded him of the day of his dad's funeral, when his mum looked to her sons for strength and away from anything that caused her distress, like the coffin and the flowers, the church and a deep dark grave. Maybe it was a mum's inherent nature to look for danger, be one step ahead, and have those big lion paws at the ready to fend off any predators that might attack. But Stan wasn't a cub and this wasn't the jungle and there was sod all she could do for him in here. Perhaps that was what made her cry, that feeling of impotence. He knew it so well.

Stan saw his mum check her watch and straighten before she spoke. There it was, that mum resolve, putting her own feelings last, that innate sense of knowing what to do when it mattered, a strength she didn't even know she possessed. *God, I love her so much.*

'Right, young lady, give Daddy a big kiss and then we will go and wait for Mummy over there. Look, I can see some toys and I've got some chocolate buttons we can share, chop-chop.' Sue was standing now and holding her hands out to Iris who had recognised the word chocolate and was looking with interest at her gran.

Stan gave Iris a hug and was rewarded with a sloppy kiss, more of a chew of the cheek than anything but her willingness to be cuddled by a man she hardly knew still meant the world to him.

Trying not to wince as Iris leant against his ribs, Stan gave her one last squeeze before letting her go, hugging his mum tight and giving her a peck on the cheek. He couldn't speak so allowed her to ferry Iris away and turn his attention to Billie, who, he noticed, was flicking away a tear.

The nearest guard stared, unmoved and vigilant.

'That's the bit that always kills me, when you say goodbye to Iris. Even though she has no idea what's going on I think her innocence makes it all the more sad, like this is all normal when it's not. And it seems like forever, waiting for two weeks to see you, which sounds selfish when you're the one in here.' Billie was flushed and teary.

'It's not selfish at all, Bill, but I know what you mean. And the time goes so fast when you visit and then you wouldn't believe how it drags in between. But let's not dwell on stuff like that. I need to talk to you about something quickly so I'm glad Mum's gone.'

Billie interrupted. 'And I need to talk to you about something too... this supposed tussle with some hardman. And don't give me the innocent look, Stan, I saw you wince a few times and you could barely sit down earlier without grimacing, so, what really happened?'

Stan sighed. 'Okay, okay I give in... it was more like five or six hardmen and I didn't exactly get a few slaps and a telling off. So now you know, can we move on? There's no point in going over it and before you ask, no, I won't be telling the guards who did it, end of.' In contrast to his opening gambit of looking innocent, Stan went for the firm glare, hoping it would shut down the discussion.

Billie held both Stan's hands in hers as she replied. 'I knew it, and even though it pisses me off I get why you won't grass so there's no point in banging on. I wanted to know, that's all.'

'And I wanted to shield you all from it but I knew if I cancelled this visit you'd have a meltdown and think all sorts so I tried to conceal what I could. Don't let on to Mum, though. Ignorance is bliss, eh?'

Billie nodded. 'So what did you want to talk to me about?'

'Your night out, with *her*. It's pecking my head.'

'I thought it might but as much as I'd love to get out of it, I have to go. This is probably the closest I'll get to her and her flat so it has to be done. Just think of it as a cold-hearted surveillance, but with the personal touch. And Aiden is going to be in contact with me all night and if I feel uncomfortable we have a backup plan so don't worry.'

The bell rang and caused Stan to jump slightly. His reaction to loud noises was getting worse and a sure sign of where his head was at.

Billie wrapped her arms around Stan and gave him a gentle hug. 'Listen. Why don't you ring me tonight and we can talk about it more if you want but honestly, it might be better if we don't. It will only stress you out.'

Reciprocating, Stan pulled her close despite the pain. Then, as he let her go he looked into Billie's eyes and as the others began filing past, gave her one last panicked instruction.

'Just don't let her get into your head, will you, Billie. She's warped and I'm scared she's going to suck you in. I need you to have faith in me, Billie. I need you to believe me. Promise you'll be careful and you won't fall for her lies.' Stan felt Billie's fingers fall from his as they backed away from one another but before he turned, she said the words he needed to hear.

'I promise, and I believe you so don't worry. Love you, Stan.'

28

Billie had given up on wiping Iris's mouth and fingers so left her to mash up what was left of her chocolate muffin which she was now smearing across the highchair table. Instead, she admired and stroked the soft baby wool of the cardigans that Carol had knitted for the horrid little chocolate monster.

They were sheltering from the rain in the M&S café, sitting in a quiet corner away from prying ears and diners who might be put off by prison talk and baby mush.

'These are absolutely gorgeous, thanks Carol. I love hand-made clothes especially knitted ones and she will look fab in these, just not right now.' Billie glanced at Iris who grinned and showed off black teeth and a lot of dribble.

'Aw, I'm glad you like them. Knitting is one of my favourite things, and reading, so I do as much as I can now that my life is my own. You'd be surprised how easy it is to have the things you love, simple stuff really, stripped away. Eventually, you become someone who functions, getting through one day at a time, hour by hour. So every time I finish a book or a jumper, I see it as a major triumph. It's like a symbol of freedom, or does that sound daft?'

Billie placed her hand over Carol's. 'God no! Not at all. Lately I've come to understand more and more what it's like being in an abusive relationship and it's so complex and utterly devastating. So I get how these are symbolic. All those stitches you knitted mean a lot to you, and me now. So thanks again, I'll treasure them.' When Billie looked up she noticed the quizzical look on Carol's face.

'What do you mean, you understand what it's like? I'm worried now. What's going on?'

Billie waved away Carol's concerns. 'No, it's not what you think, honest, it's just that...'

'Just what? Go on, you can tell me.'

It was then that Billie realised she wanted to tell Carol all about Stan but it was a tricky subject. Billie had explained about Stan's arrest, during their constant exchange of emails back and forth from the UK and Greece, during which Carol had remained neutral and supportive. But how would she feel about Billie defending a convicted rapist?

To be honest, Billie was mentally exhausted with it all. The constant battle with her conscience as it churned over every decision she made and each disloyal thought she had. There was also the task of boosting Stan and Sue's morale, ignoring her mother's sullen disapproval, and then being a fake friend to Kelly who, up to now, had stuck to her story and seemed like a nice person to boot.

It would be a relief to get it all off her chest and have another opinion, a female one who might see things from both sides, or not. There was a chance that Carol would be disappointed and then the bond they had forged since that dreadful night, the support they had given each other through respective hospital visits and court appearances, could be snuffed out.

Despite her reservations, Billie knew she had no choice. She had to explain to Carol about her mission to exonerate Stan, otherwise, when it all came out, she'd feel like a fraud. 'If I tell you, I want you to promise to say how you feel. It's important and if you don't hate me afterwards I need your honest advice because if there's one person I trust, it's you.'

Carol looked wary. 'Okay, I promise, although you really have got me worried now. Go on, I'm all ears.'

Billie took a deep breath, passed Iris her bottle of milk and once she was occupied, told Carol everything.

When Billie returned to the table with more tea and coffee, she felt lighter than she'd done in ages and relieved that Carol hadn't stormed off in disgust. If anything she'd listened attentively as Billie worked her way through events and evidence and now it was her turn to listen.

'The first thing I want to say is that I understand why you are doing this, so there's no need to convince me of your motives. You believe Stan and I respect that but I can also see why you are confused. Not only is this woman sticking to her story like glue, but no matter what Stan says, the police, CPS and a jury thought otherwise.'

Billie nodded. 'I swear that sometimes I feel like my head is going to explode. If it wasn't for the stuff the detective dug up I'd probably have given in, but even *he* is suspicious of Kelly. That's why I have to see this through to the end, wherever and whenever that may be.'

'Well I admire your determination, I really do. The sad and scary thing is that only two people know what really went on that night and one of them is lying. Unfortunately, twelve men and women of the jury looked at the facts as they saw them. Nothing will change that but you never know, something might turn up and you could get lucky.' Carol sounded hopeful which lifted Billie.

'That's all I want, just the chance to cast some doubt on Kelly but apart from that, you don't know how relieved I am to have someone to talk to about this. And that you didn't judge me, you know, for standing by Stan. I wish my mum was like you. There are no grey areas with her and if she knew what I was doing she'd have a fit.'

Carol grimaced. 'I take it she's still not a member of Team Stan then?'

'No chance. I doubt she ever will be. But you, on the other hand, amaze me, you really do. After everything you've been through, you manage to look at things from another angle. You're so calm and self-assured, wise I suppose.'

Carol gave a small laugh. 'I'm not wise but I do look at life differently now and I'm determined not to let the past control my future. You know, I had plenty of time while I sat in that cell to think things through, that was when I wasn't going half mad with worry over the girls. It wasn't being arrested that nearly tipped me over the edge. It was knowing they'd been taken into emergency foster care. What a family, eh? Not one person stepped up that night. Nobody offered to take them and I still can't bear to think how frightened and upset they were that night. The irony is that even now we are safe we still feel the ripple effect. The girls are nervous in their own home, albeit a new place far away from where we used to live, and they both used to wet the bed and have nightmares about their dad. I sometimes wonder if our lives will ever be classed as normal or if there's too much baggage that we'll carry around forever.'

Billie had a sudden urge to hold Iris, so took her from her highchair and began to clean her up. Carol's words also reminded her of Sue and Darren and how what happened to

Stan had affected both of them, ruining their lives too. The bloody ripple effect.

'I can't imagine how you felt... if that happened to Iris, it would destroy me. Thank God they let you out on bail.'

Carol nodded. 'And thank God Gary didn't die! Otherwise I'd have been up on a murder charge and on remand for months. It didn't end there, though, because social services got involved and it felt like I had to prove I was a good mum and jump through hoops. I was terrified that the girls would be taken away permanently. I still blame Gary and he deserved that smack on the head, more so for what he did to you. I'd have never forgiven myself if you know... you didn't make it, all because I met him and wasn't strong enough to stay away.'

Billie took Carol's hand in hers. 'Stop it right now. We've been through this before and I've told you, what I did that night was my job, I wanted to protect you but it went wrong simply because he was... is evil. That's the end of it. And you could see it as a blessing because when he stabbed me, along with what he'd already done to you, he booked himself a nice long stretch inside. Now, you and the girls are free of him.'

Carol stirred her tea as she spoke. 'I should never have gone back, though, not after the last beating but it was impossible. Whichever way I turned it was a dead end. I remember sitting at the bus stop ringing round and almost begging for help. Nobody really wanted to put us up and after two nights sleeping on my cousin's sofa she said we had to leave because her boyfriend had been complaining. Me and the girls spent all day at the housing office and just before it closed they got us into a mixed homeless shelter, but it was more like a hellhole. There were men with tags on, drunks, youths hanging about outside and during the night the mice came out, I could hear and see them and the smell in the room was horrendous. Me and the girls had to share a single bed and the bathroom was communal and filthy.

'I stuck it for a week but I was running out of money and the girls were hungry and scared. I endured another interview at the housing department who wanted me to prove I was homeless, which technically I wasn't. The shocking irony was that if I did declare myself homeless I stood the risk of having the girls taken into care. It was like being backed into a corner. There were no women's refuges available and I couldn't bear to go back to that shelter so we went home. Living with Gary was my only option, or that's how it felt at the time.'

Billie knew all this, Carol had already explained her circumstances but maybe, like the women at the meetings, it did her good to talk about it.

'I've heard similar stories to yours, Carol, and they are truly awful and it's hard to believe that so many women are going through horrific abuse in their own homes because they have nowhere to go and nobody to turn to. It seems to me that even when they pluck up the courage to speak out, or run, or ask for help, there are so many hoops to jump through and walls to break down.'

Carol nodded. 'That's exactly it. I'm in touch with lots of women now through online forums and we support each other that way, like those at the group you go to. It's like there are so many stages before you escape or report a crime and for me and others, the hardest thing was the fear of not being believed, your voice not being heard. Bruises tell their own story but the stuff that goes on up here' – Carol tapped the side of her head – 'the mind games and mental cruelty, well, that's a tough one to prove. And who wants to tell a stranger their most personal thoughts? I certainly didn't. How can you put into words that, even though it makes your skin crawl and you don't want to, having sex with your husband or partner prevents a beating. It's like rape of the body and the mind, your last barrier has been broken down and in that moment you are nothing. He's taken everything, your dignity and free will. I often wondered if I spoke out, would people think I was mad, or making it up to get rid of Gary. Especially his relatives who thought he could do no wrong. It's a lonely place to be.'

Billie was rocking Iris gently on her knee and could tell she was ready for a nap so spoke softly. 'I feel such a fraud you know, attending that group. It was never intended to be a long-term thing and yet as much as I want to leave because I don't consider myself a victim, part of me wants to stay and help somehow. The stories they tell and the discussions we have can be hard to listen to, but it's like I connect with them even though I haven't been a victim of domestic violence or sexual assault.'

'But you are a victim of violence at the hands of a man, because of what Gary did. You know what it's like to be attacked, feel helpless and the worst thing of all, to know fear, during and after the event. That's the invisible bond. You and I have faced what we thought was the end, that moment when you hover between holding on and giving in, letting it happen, allowing the inevitable. I did. I remember once thinking it would be the easy way out, an end to it all, but I couldn't do it. I had to survive for the girls.'

Billie wiped a lock of hair from Iris's face as she spoke. 'You are so right, and when I've listened to the women, it's like their experiences reignite my own and I have to swallow down the panic. Even though each of their stories are different it doesn't matter, I get it.'

'That's what I mean. You have PTSD... so do I. We both suffer flashbacks and nightmares. If you've experienced violence I'm convinced it bestows a deeper understanding of another's pain. Some people deal with it by switching off, or by listening or by sharing or by being proactive. You just haven't worked out which one you are yet but I have a feeling you will. For now though, even if it is for an unusual reason, you have a place in that group. If you can hold someone's hand or listen to them cry it out, all well and good. It might help you, too.'

Billie wasn't convinced. 'Mmm, that's what Aiden said, but I'm not so sure. If any of them find out my real motive they'd string me up. It's a bubbling pot of emotions in that room and most of them are borne from anger so the last thing I want is for them to turn that on me. The thing is, that desperation and rage some of the women feel is rubbing off on me. I might be turning into a man-hater. Don't you feel bitter and hate, you know, for men like Gary and Stan?'

Carol nodded. 'Yes, I do feel a lot of negative emotions but you know who I feel the most anger towards?'

Billie shook her head.

'The system. They know this is going on and it's getting worse yet there aren't enough resources and funding to even skim the surface. Out there, right now, women are being abused in every way imaginable and for the majority there is nobody to turn to. Escaping mental and physical abuse is hard enough when you are single but imagine if you have children – the choices you have to make for them, putting yourself last. I stayed for the girls, so they would have their own bedrooms and a place to call home. I put up with him for them and because it was easier than being alone in poverty or one of those shelters.'

Billie shook her head. 'I remember when I was on the force, the paperwork was ridiculous when we would rather have been out there, on the streets. But with so many cutbacks it was impossible, despite the rising number of domestic incidents we were called to. Most of the time our hands were tied. I suppose the frustration and what happened to me was why I quit... but sometimes I feel like a failure because if I'd stayed, I could have helped. That pecks at my head a lot but I simply went to pieces and had to leave. You see that, don't you?'

Carol held up her finger and pointed to Billie as she spoke.

'Of course I do, so stop it right now. You had the right to choose, Billie, it's your life.'

'It's a pity though, that so many women don't seem to have just that, a choice.' Lately, Billie managed to feel guilt for the most random things and today it was having free will.

Carol began stacking the empty cups and plates onto the tray as she spoke. 'I know, and the heartbreaking thing is that once they do summon the courage, or whatever it takes to run or make that call, it's only the first step and there's no guarantee of a solution. While social services struggle to meet demand, all the police can do is follow the leads, put together the evidence and let the CPS do the rest. The end result can sometimes be down to luck, like a perfect storm.'

'And in Stan's case, the perfect storm landed him in prison. Sometimes I still can't believe it. It's like a nightmare.'

'I can imagine, and I do see it from both sides, Billie, I promise. I'm sure there are many men who slip through the net for loads of reasons and deserve to be behind bars. Like others are in prison for things they swear they didn't do, but they haven't the resources to investigate like your private detective has done. Like there aren't enough refuges and social housing for women who need help. It's wrong and things need to change but until then, all people like you and I can do is fight for justice and make our voices heard, wherever and however we can. That's why I'm doing my Open University degree, so I can make a difference.'

Carol crumpled a sugar packet between her fingers. 'One thing I will say though, is that in my opinion any woman who has a man sent to prison because she's lied about something as serious as rape, does true victims no favours whatsoever. I believe that one of the biggest hurdles for a woman or a man to get over is belief. Will the police listen to me? Will I have to go through hell over and over, reliving what happened, giving evidence, telling my family? The list goes on. And I imagine that in reverse, the same terror applies to a man who is desperate for people to believe that he has been falsely accused. So if you believe Stan, fight on. And I pray you are vindicated because I can see how much this is getting to you... and if he is innocent, shame on this Kelly person.'

'I will. I have to.' Billie glanced at Iris who was fast asleep now, her mouth sucking on her dummy, long lashes resting on rosy cheeks.

As she looked upon her daughter, Billie was thankful for her oblivion. Iris was still innocent and trouble-free and not affected by the big bad world out there.

Carol checked her watch. 'I'm going to have to make a move soon and collect the girls from school but will you bring Iris round during the holidays? They love babies and will make a big fuss of her and it'll give us a chance to catch up again. I need to keep an eye on you now, Miss Marple.'

'Of course I will. She needs to be with other children. I'm going to look up some mum and toddler groups in the new year.' Billie placed Iris in her pushchair, gathered all her bits and bobs and then turned to give Carol a hug. 'Thanks for listening, I feel so much better now.'

'My pleasure, but I want you to promise you'll keep me informed and don't be scared of ringing me if that head of yours gets in a muddle?'

Billie smiled. 'Promise.'

Carol asked one more question. 'Are you meeting Kelly this weekend?'

Billie answered with a nod of the head. 'And I'm dreading it but if it comes to nothing, I think we'll call it a day, so fingers crossed.'

'Well take care and text me when you can, just to let me know how it went and that you're okay.' They'd reached the exit and once outside Carol shivered. 'Right then. Now give me another hug and I'll see you very soon, and don't forget that text.'

Billie said she'd let her know, before setting off towards her car and then home to Sue's. The notion that the idea of home was more connected to Sue and Darren than her own mother's house wasn't lost on Billie and that swell of irritation rose again in her chest. Why did her mum make everything so damn difficult? But on a more cheerful note, her heart did feel a bit lighter, surer. Her head had managed to untie some knots and let go of the guilt it had been carrying for a while. All she had to do now was keep the faith; her own, Carol's and most of all, Stan's.

29

Sue sipped her sherry as she watched Billie wrestle with the giant roll of wrapping paper that she was using to disguise a pink, fluffy rocking horse. During their prison visit, Stan had told Sue to transfer enough money to buy the whole of Argos, not just the list of things he wanted Iris to have. Billie thought they should have waited for spring to buy the huge plastic Wendy house that was waiting to be erected by Darren, but the doll's pram and little cart with coloured bricks were already under the tree.

Whenever they visited Sue, Billie had taken to staying over with Iris, rather than drive back to her mum's. It was an arrangement that suited everyone and had given Billie some free time to carry out her 'undercover work' that remained a huge secret. The thought of her upcoming big night out caused her stomach to roll so she pushed it to the back of her mind and listened instead to Sue who was taking one of her frequent walks down memory lane where as usual, the subject was Stan.

'He was a little sod, you know, our Stan when he was little and it became a battle of the wits every Christmas to hide his presents because no matter how hard me and his dad tried, he'd always find them. Used to drive me mad and I couldn't understand why he wouldn't wait to have a surprise on the day. And you should've heard him swearing on Father Christmas's life that he hadn't opened them – but I knew. You could see where he'd wrapped them back up again.'

Billie chuckled. 'Oh I know, he did that to me on our first Christmas so after that I'd leave them at my mum's until Christmas Eve. That really drove him mad and you're right, Stan is an expert when it comes to looking innocent and swearing on things... like Agüero, or David Silva. It's a wonder the whole of Manchester City hasn't been cursed the way he goes on.'

As soon as she'd said the words Billie regretted them. Not because she was being disloyal: the conversation was meant in fun. But it didn't sit right and had made her feel uneasy. Sue's next comment didn't help.

'Believe me, if I had a tenner for every time our Stan swore on something when I knew he was fibbing I'd be living in Alderley Edge right now. There was one time, someone climbed through the domestic science lab window and pinched all the fairy cakes that were cooling off. Nobody would own up and school sent a letter home to the parents about stealing, there was a right hoo-ha. I put it down to high jinks and suspected Stan and his mates who looked a bit cagey. Then I found a pile of those paper cupcake cases in the bin in his room. I thought I'd solved the mystery but he blamed Pete and said he couldn't dob his mate in.' Sue tutted and shook her head.

Billie was listening but trying not to take it seriously. It was nothing like the 'blamers' that Aiden despised so much. It was lads being lads. She set about wrapping some books, nice and easy compared to a horse.

Sue, on the other hand, was off with the fairies. 'And then there was the toilet paper incident. Someone had stuck or knocked a whole roll down the loo. Our Darren was only two and hadn't been upstairs, so I accused Stan who flatly denied it. I made him stay in his room all morning till he owned up but it was a battle of the wills. He lay on his bed and brazened it out until *I* gave in because he made me feel bad. Can you believe that? I was too soft, that's for sure, but he could be very stubborn when he wanted to be. And then there was the cheating.'

At this Billie's head snapped up. 'What cheating?'

'In his exams and tests, at school. Haven't I told you?'

A shake of the head from Billie.

'Well, he'd been getting really good marks and while he wasn't stupid, Stan was no child genius so I had a little chat about it and you know what he said? That he had developed a photographic memory!'

Billie managed a smile. 'Oh I know, he was always saying that to me... he didn't need to take a shopping list because he could remember it all, stuff like that. He does talk rubbish sometimes.'

'Mmm, well in the case of his exams his top marks were due to the rolled-up piece of paper he shoved inside the back of his tie, not his amazing party trick. It made a right bloody mess of the washing machine, bits of mushed-up paper everywhere. Photographic memory, I ask you.'

Sue chuckled but Billie hadn't found the conversation remotely funny. Not because of loo paper and cakes, or cheating, but while Sue had been telling her tales, Billie had remembered many more. Incidents from back in the day when Stan the Man was the leader of the gang, the proverbial cheeky chappie who thought up crazy schemes and pranks, then always managed to talk himself out of trouble and emerge unscathed. Like when the park-keepers hut burned down, and someone turned over moany Mr York's Reliant Robin onto its roof. But it was the time when they lived together that pecked Billie's head the most. Silly things really, minor tiffs over Stan's fibbing that were now hammering into her brain like Woody bloody Woodpecker. Who ate the last Kit Kat, drank all the milk, couldn't remember her telling him to put the bins out, load the washer, and he definitely booked a table at the restaurant and her car in for an MOT. It wasn't his fault nobody ever wrote things down and *she* imagined telling him to do things!

By the time Sue had wandered off to check on Iris and make some crumpets, Billie had finished her wrapping and couldn't wait for supper to be over and get to bed, away from Sue's reminiscing and if she managed to sleep, her own irritating thoughts.

Two hours later Billie was still a fully paid-up member of the Wide Awake Club. While Iris slept peacefully in her cot in her daddy's old bedroom, her mum lay a few feet away in his bed. Billie kept telling herself she was being silly, that Stan's personality traits were what she'd fallen in love with. He meant no harm with his banter and propensity to gild the lily. Or was she being naive, like Sue who laughed off his mistakes and lies and consigned them to humorous family stories?

The thing was, Billie knew full well Stan could sell sand to the Arabs, and those sad, puppy-dog eyes that begged for forgiveness would melt the hardest of hearts. And after all, none of his past misdemeanours were all that serious. Who cared who had left the freezer door open? It was hardly the end of the world. Or was it? Had Stan got too used to getting away with it, did he still believe that he could talk or fib his way out of trouble even in the big, bad, grown-up world?

Billie turned on her side and watched the rise and fall of Iris's chest, her cherub face illuminated by the street light. She wondered if her daughter would inherit her dad's looks because for now, no matter what Sue said, Iris was the spit of Billie. Time would tell. She tried not to dwell on it too much but in moments like this, when the night demons messed with your head, all her worries came out to play.

She had to maintain regular contact between Iris and Stan, especially now it was looking less likely he'd get his appeal. It was important that Iris knew who he was. She would be missing her father for a huge chunk of her life, and it broke Billie's heart. It didn't matter who Iris looked like, what did matter was having bonds and role models because a parent's influence, nature and nurture, even between those not related by blood had a profound effect on a child.

There it was again, that question, a whisper of doubt that Billie tried to silence but failed. Were there aspects of Stan's personality that she'd rather Iris didn't inherit? It was best not to dwell on those. Though a photographic memory might come in handy.

Turning onto her back Billie closed her eyes and wished she had the patience for mindfulness and that the recording she had of the sea lapping on the shore actually worked. Instead, she went over Stan's letter in her head, dissecting the facts as he told them, imagining his face as he wrote the words, putting his heart into a plea that brought her home.

When she'd received that letter, Billie believed every single word, like they were the 'Gospel According to St Stan' so why now did she feel so... unsettled? Yes, that was the best word for it, *unsettled,* not disbelieving or suspicious, just mildly perturbed by Sue's stories and her own bank of silly squabbles. Surely they were nothing more than that, not lies, or truth-twisting. You couldn't compare the mistakes and flaws of a teenager to the man that Stan had become. He wouldn't lie about something so serious; he wouldn't *do* something so serious, it was incomprehensible. And Kelly's version was simply a warped version of a short relationship that went wrong and an opportunity to take revenge and wallow in the drama of it all.

Billie couldn't waver now, she had to hold firm, believe in Stan otherwise it would all be a waste, a terrible mess that would splatter mud all over everyone's lives, Iris included. Stan was telling the truth, she believed that and she believed him, and that was all that mattered.

Billie was exhausted when she waved goodbye to Sue the following morning. Apart from a sleepless night, she'd received an early morning text from Tom along with five laughing-face emojis. It seems that instead of uploading one of her perfunctory memes, Billie had inadvertently posted a photo of Sue's Christmas tree onto Facebook. It could have been a costly mistake but seeing as she was a complete techno-klutz, Tom let her off and advised her to concentrate. Billie bloody hated Facebook. She could also have done without her mother asking for a favour. Seeing as she was in Manchester, Billie had agreed to collect a parcel on her way home. This was why she was now waiting in a huge queue in Next. Iris was in her buggy, engrossed in a noisy toy that made very annoying sounds, but Billie thought, *Hey, it's Christmas so who cares... Most of the queue from the looks on their faces.*

It was as everyone shuffled along that she spotted a woman who seemed vaguely familiar and in that eye-catching moment as she passed by and fell into line behind Billie, the feeling turned out to be mutual. It was all a bit awkward really, but when the woman broke the ice and in hushed tones introduced herself, everything soon became clear. 'Hi, you probably don't recognise me but I've seen you at visiting.' The woman paused and looked hopeful, clearly waiting for the penny to drop.

Billie was almost at the front of the queue and desperately racking her brains, then it dawned on her: prison visiting. 'Oh, oh I see, sorry. My head's all over the place and yes, I do recognise you now.' Billie was talking rubbish but didn't want to offend the friendly woman who meant no harm, and had the decency not to blurt everything out.

'How is he doing then, your bloke? My Doog thinks the world of him, thick as thieves they are now, excuse the pun, but you know what I mean. I reckon he misses sharing a room with his best mate. Men, eh?' She nudged Billie playfully.

'Oh he's fine thanks, putting a brave face on it and all that. How's your...' Billie had to think for a second. 'Doog doing since, you know, he came home?'

'Oh, he's fine. Behaving himself, which is what matters, I suppose. Look, here he is now, my professional bag carrier.' The woman nodded towards the man heading their way who, when he clapped eyes on them, went a deep shade of beetroot, waved sheepishly then shot off.

Billie thought she was going to faint. The thuggish-looking bald guy who had stared her out and gave her the creeps was Doog, Stan's cellmate! *No, it couldn't be.* She'd asked Stan if he was in the visiting hall, and he'd never pointed him out. Why? The thug had been there a few times, giving her the evils. And even when she'd said the bald guy was freaking her out, Stan didn't bat an eyelid. And now, according to Chatty Woman, it seemed they were 'thick as thieves'. What the hell was going on?

Her mangled, manic thoughts were interrupted by the assistant calling out 'next please' so Billie had no alternative than to move along while at the same time, Doog's girlfriend went to the farthest checkout and paid for her things. Billie was too flustered to even consider carrying on the conversation so returned her departing wave then concentrated on Iris.

All Billie wanted to do was go home. The drive over the tops would give her time to think. She needed to process this information which, on top of the revelations about Stan's propensity for lying, as told by his own mother, brought her out in a cold sweat.

After she'd collected the parcel and with trembling fingers fastened Iris into her car seat, Billie settled herself behind the wheel, tilted back her head and sighed before turning on the engine. Her whole body felt weak from exhaustion and nerves, embellished nicely by a creeping sense of fear while disappointment hovered on the periphery.

Joining the queue for the motorway, the cars crawling towards the M627, Billie pictured Stan's face that day in prison when he'd held her hand tightly and looked at her with those sad, scared eyes and asked her over and over, 'Please, Billie, please believe me.'

As she sped down the slip road and onto the black tarmac, Billie said out loud, 'I want to, Stan, I really do.'

30

In a world where it is possible to contact each other with a click or a tap, via messages, emails, tweets and even photos, to have to wait by the phone for someone to ring you, at their whim, was sheer torture. While Iris slept and Claudia stomped and clattered about in the kitchen below, playing her own bad-tempered tune with the pans and doors, Billie sat on her bed and stared at her phone, willing it to trill.

This was worse than being a loved-up teenager who'd given her number to some gawky lad. This was real, game-changing stuff and whatever Stan said when he eventually got to the front of the queue, could potentially alter their lives. Billie had rehearsed what she was going to say and what she was going to ask. She wasn't going to rant or make accusations. No, she would simply mention her chance meeting and wait for him to explain why he allowed a thug to make her uncomfortable and omitted to mention said nutjob was his cellmate, oh, and his new thick-as-thieves bosom buddy.

In the meantime she listened in wry amusement to the voices filtering up through the floorboards as her dad placated her mum. The irony of how roles had been reversed wasn't lost on Billie. Moments earlier she'd put Claudia firmly in her place about Christmas arrangements, and then left her to have a mini tantrum.

There was no way that Billie was going to choose between Sue and Darren and her parents, so she'd suggested they all spend the day together at Sue's, who'd offered to do the honours. That way Iris would get the best of both worlds and Stan's family would have company. Billie was happy to drive so all her mother had to do was be the bigger person, for once in her life. The cacophony below was her way of coming to terms with being backed into a corner. Claudia wanted Billie and Iris to go for lunch with them at her aunt's, like they did every year. Billie had refused then thought of a compromise. Her mum and dad would see Iris open her presents there, then Billie would spend the rest of Christmas Day and night with Sue and Darren, that was final.

There was so much going on in Billie's head that her mother's meltdown was incidental, especially when the 'big night out' was looming and Sue's uncomfortable revelations were gnawing away, never mind Stan's tendency to be frugal with the truth!

The phone sprang to life, the vibration causing it to shuffle along the bedside table and make more noise than usual. Billie snatched it up quickly and swiped. Stan only managed to say hi and ask how she was before a red mist enveloped her.

She unleashed a torrent of questions and accusations that were nothing like she'd rehearsed. 'You want to know how I am, do you? Well I'm totally pissed off and you're bloody lucky I haven't blocked this number after what I found out today. Do you think I'm a complete mug or is this your way of getting your kicks and manipulating me?' Billie sucked in air and ignored how hot her cheeks felt.

'Bill, what the hell is wrong? Calm down and explain... I have no idea what you're talking about.'

'Don't you dare tell me to calm down!'

'Okay, okay, I'm sorry, bad choice of words. Let's start again. What have I done wrong? I don't understand.'

Billie was furious and she hated being told to calm down. It always made her angrier and he knew that, which annoyed her even more.

'I'll spell it out for you, shall I? Doog. You know, that ugly-looking baldy thing who used to stare me out on visiting days. Well it seems you omitted to mention he was your cellmate, you know, revenge-porn guy, nice bloke, easy to get on with?'

There was a deathly silence, then Stan found his voice. 'How the hell did you find out? Has he contacted you? I told him to keep his distance.'

'What the hell do you mean "keep his distance"? You'd better start talking, Stan, because I am so mad with you right now...'

'Okay, right, listen. Yes, the bald guy is Doog, my cellmate and it was his idea to give you the death-ray stare, not mine. I did tell him to pack it in but he's got a will of his own and thought he was helping. He didn't really mean any harm.'

Billie was dumbfounded, just for a moment. 'Helping, how?'

'He got it into his head that if you saw how intimidating some prisoners can be it would spur you on to help me... I know it sounds daft but that's the way his mind works and he took it upon himself. I swear I didn't suggest it. That's why I told you not to make eye contact with anyone. It was easier than control-ling him.'

'No, Stan, the easy way would have been to say: "See that nutter over there who thinks he's in a gangster film? Well that's my freak-show cellmate." Boom, job done.'

A sigh came down the line. 'Well now you put it like that, I suppose you're right.'

'Oh yes, I am right and I have a feeling that you played along with it because deep down you're desperate for my help and chose to put my feelings last. That's out of order, Stan, and you know it.'

'I'm sorry, Billie, I swear I am.'

'And don't bloody swear on anything and anybody because it's bollocks and I'm sick of it. I've trusted you. I've believed every word you've said and stuck my neck out to help you and I feel like a fool. Can you imagine what's been going through my mind? You know I hate it when you lie and this has rocked my confidence in you. It's made me re-examine everything and I'm actually beating myself up about that and I don't deserve it, Stan. I even questioned whether you'd really been beaten up or not, or were you faking that too?'

The shock and hurt in Stan's voice when he replied was plain to hear. 'Bill! How can you even think that, never mind say it? You saw my bruises! How could I fake that?'

'I don't know. Maybe you got your new cellmate to give you a good hiding? Right now I can imagine anything is possible just so you get what you want.' Even as she said the words she regretted them, but temper and anger and disappointment had taken over and she had to have her say, get it into the open.

When Stan replied it was more of a whisper, not quite a hiss but somewhere between being sorry and irritated. 'Billie, I promise, the bruises were for real and I am so sorry that you've ended up feeling this way but you are blowing it all out of proportion so please, can we talk sensibly about this because I'm going to have to go soon. I don't like being out of my cell for too long.'

This had an immediate sobering effect on Billie. She was acutely aware that their limited time together was always at the mercy of a ticking clock and, now, the thugs that had attacked Stan. 'Okay, okay. I was so shocked and I felt humiliated too. I have so much going on in my head right now and this was like the last straw.'

Stan's voice took on a softer tone. 'Right, I get it. I'm in the doghouse, just to make life a whole lot worse than it is already.'

Billie knew he was playing the sympathy card and while she felt calmer, she hadn't finished with him yet. So she ignored the image of his puppy-dog eyes and ploughed on, determined to get to the bottom of it and, if necessary, teach him a lesson. 'Yes you are, and after I bumped into Doog's chatty girlfriend in Next and caught a glimpse of the man himself, I'm now wondering if you've been brainwashed or something.'

'Eh?'

'What I want to know is why she said you and Doog are thick as thieves because it sounds to me like you two have forged a brotherly bond while you've been banged up... and from where I'm standing that's not good. So go on, explain.'

Stan blew air through his lips. Billie heard it whistling and she could feel his exasperation fizzing down the line.

'Billie, I can't explain on the phone, I'll tell you when you come in... do you understand?'

Silence followed while Billie processed his words then remembered that their phone calls could be monitored and recorded, so changed tack. 'Yes, yes I understand. I'll wait until I see you at visiting and then I want a proper chat, Stan. I mean it.'

'I promise, Bill, but until then will you promise me we're okay? It was a stupid thing to do and I really am sorry.'

'We're okay, I promise.'

'Oh, and as for Doog, will you believe me when I say he's a good guy deep down and there's nothing to worry about on that score. He's got my back while I'm in here, that's all. I trust him and that's all you need to know. You have to trust me too.'

The words hung in the air and ever mindful of where Stan was and what he was going back to, never mind the dangerous corridors he had to walk along before he arrived at his cell, Billie gave him what he wanted.

'I do, Stan. I'm okay now I understand so please don't worry. Will you phone me on Sunday and then I can tell you all about my night out with *her*. I'm dreading it so it'll be good to hear your voice. I can only hope I have something positive to report back.'

'Babe, just take care of yourself and watch your back. I'll be thinking of you and if it comes to nothing don't worry, you did your best. Look, I've got to go now. Love you, Billie.'

The prick of tears at the corner of her eyes were somehow scorning her, and she wished she could go back to the beginning of the phone call and handle it differently because now she'd spend the whole night wracked with guilt. At least she'd forgiven Stan and that made her feel slightly better so gathering her strength, Billie said her goodbyes. 'Bye Stan, love you too. Take care and I'll speak to you soon.'

Before her last syllable was uttered she heard a click and the line went dead. Wiping tears away Billie pulled the duvet over her body and blanked out any thought of what Stan was doing right now. She had to focus on the tasks in hand: getting through the night out from hell, and then the rigmarole of Christmas. No matter what she had to deal with on the outside, it was nothing like what Stan was going through in there.

31

Billie was so cold and that was before they'd even stepped foot out of the taxi that was heading towards their first watering hole of the evening, an upmarket bar where apparently footballers hung out. No matter how hard she tried, due to her unfamiliar surroundings and scanty, totally unsuitable attire, Billie couldn't relax and Kelly had picked up on it already.

'Mate, I wish you'd chill out. And stop pulling the hem down. You look bloody amazing in that dress so stop fussing. You're doing my head in.'

Luckily, Billie had a perfectly believable excuse ready to go. 'Sorry, sorry, I'm nervous, you know, if we see anyone or Davey rings. I'm dreading it in case we're somewhere noisy. If he finds out I'm here, he'll flip, I know he will.' Billie shivered, not for dramatic effect but for real. She was now one of those stupid women she used to roll her eyes at as they teetered along the street on a night out, wearing as little as possible, regardless of the temperature.

'I told you to have some more vodka before we left. Honestly, talk about being a lightweight. Now come on, forget about knobhead and let's have some fun. I've got some ace news so we need to celebrate.'

Billie's interest piqued immediately. 'Ooh, go on, spill the beans... does this mean we're having champagne or is it more Prosecco kind of news?'

Kelly laughed. 'I'd say Prosecco but it's still exciting. Guess who's going to be on the telly after Christmas?'

Billie looked over her shoulder and pretended not to know what she was getting at, which made Kelly squeal with rather annoying fake laughter before she answered. 'Me!!'

Billie felt duty-bound to play along. 'No way! But why?'

At this, Kelly settled back into her seat and spoke loudly enough for the driver to hear, thus extracting the maximum amount of attention as she explained. It seemed that Jude, the group organiser at the centre Kelly and Billie attended, was organising a Women's Day just before New Year. It was during the period where relationships are statistically likely to hit rock bottom and the highest rates of domestic incidents occur. Their local MP was fully on board and would be appearing too, but they needed a victim to speak out and spread the word about helplines and support networks. Kelly had leapt at the chance and was thoroughly looking forward to sharing her experience on behalf of women everywhere. According to Kelly, the national press would be doing a special report as were the local rags and radio. There was even going to be a reception at the town hall later that evening and Kelly had been invited, and a plus-one.

Billie was initially nonplussed because she'd hoped it was going to be something that related to Stan. Gathering her wits quickly she set about congratulating Kelly who clearly thought she was in line to be a UN special envoy and a rival to Angelina Jolie.

'Oh my God, that's amazing! You'll be brill and fancy being

on the telly! Can I come along and watch?' Billie couldn't think of anything worse but had to show some enthusiasm.

'Yeah, all the group are going to be invited along. Jude understands that some of them won't want to show their faces for obvious reasons, but the more the merrier. And I want you to be my plus-one for the mayor's reception, so you'd better think of an excuse to get rid of knobhead before the night.'

Billie grimaced. 'I'll do my best but it won't be easy and no way can I be on telly either. Someone's bound to see me and that's all I need.'

'Don't you worry about that, I'm sure between us we can figure out a way to get rid of Davey. Ooh look, we're here. Forget about all that for now, it's party time.' Kelly gave Billie a nudge and a wink then instructed the driver to pull over.

Billie watched closely as Kelly peeled off a twenty-pound note from the rolled-up bundle of cash inside her purse and then told the driver to keep the change. After leaving the taxi, Billie was eager to get inside the swanky bar, not because she was looking forward to the evening but because it *had* to be warmer in there. Otherwise she would die of hypothermia, or get frostbite in her nether regions.

Once inside and thawing nicely, Billie waited while Kelly bought the first round of drinks, observing her closely as she had done ever since arriving at her flat earlier that evening.

To say Kelly had behaved like an overexcited teenager hosting her very first sleepover was an understatement. Billie had tried to ignore the creeping unease as Kelly gave her a grand tour of the two-bedroomed flat, pointing out the matching pyjamas and fluffy socks she'd bought for when they got back later. They were laid out on the bed with a towel folded into the shape of a swan and by the side, brand new miniature toiletries. Billie couldn't decide whether it was tragic or manic so instead said they were nice but unnecessary. Kelly had waved it off, insisting she wanted to make her special guest feel welcome. Then when they entered the kitchen, the table was bulging with vodka and Prosecco and an array of buffet food. The whole set-up caused Billie's skin to crawl and, bizarrely, it made her think of Hansel and Gretel.

Billie was pacing herself with the drinks and when Kelly nipped to the loo, she chucked one glass down the sink and replaced it with tonic. It was also hard not to keep checking the fingers of the clock which never seemed to move, or to think about Iris who would've had her bath and bedtime story by now. It was the first time since her birth that Billie had stayed out all night and it was torture.

Her parents hadn't batted an eyelid when she asked them to babysit while she met up with one of her old police colleagues. Neither wanted her driving over the Pennines at night so seemed relieved she'd be staying over. Her mum said it would do her good and almost shoved her out the door. The only thing that kept Billie focused and from making an excuse to leave was the knowledge that Iris would be safe and sound with her grandparents, and that all this play-acting bollocks was for Stan.

Along with throwing drinks down her neck, Kelly also threw herself into getting glammed up, insisting on painting Billie's nails, fingers and toes. Her behaviour was cloying and creepy and the phrase 'space invader' would not leave Billie's mind. Kelly reminded her of the freaky housemate in a film she'd seen once, where a woman was obsessed with her flatmate. In the end, Billie was glad to get out of the flat without Kelly wanting to curl her hair and help her dress, or be suffocated by attention.

～

Billie tried to look elegant and aloof as she sipped her drink, perched on a ridiculously high stool in full view of the other customers. All the while, she eyed Kelly and had already noted two things. The first was that she was a subtle flirt and enjoyed being gawped at. Her supposed fear of men and noisy surroundings that she'd mentioned in the group certainly wasn't affecting her tonight. The second, was that with every drink, she became bolder and more, for want of a better word, cocky. The sheath that shrouded her damaged soul was beginning to fade and a woman Billie had not before encountered was blossoming into life. She took this as a good sign.

Kelly piped up. 'I'm so glad I persuaded you to come out tonight. Are you having fun? I am. Have you seen anyone you fancy yet?' Kelly scanned the room as she spoke, making no attempt to disguise her roving eye.

'Yes, I'm having fun but you need to slow down otherwise you'll be hammered and no, I've not seen anyone I fancy and have no intention of looking either. I don't have a death wish and my nerves can't take much more, so less of the flirting. Look but don't even think about touching, okay?' Billie raised her eyes knowingly at Kelly who smirked and gave a cheeky wink.

'Hey, if I'd wanted a lecture I'd have brought my mum out... and anyway, it won't do any harm to get a few phone numbers in case I need warming up at night. If you had any sense you'd do the same. Then you can ditch Davey. I might even get you a T-shirt with that printed on. It's a good slogan.' Kelly drained her glass and looked ready for another.

'If it was that easy I'd have done it yonks ago but he's like sodding superglue and I'll pass on the T-shirt, thanks. Right, it's my round. Same again?' Billie slid off the stool as elegantly as she could without showing her knickers and after getting the thumbs-up, set off for the bar.

It was busy so while she waited her turn, Billie checked her phone and saw a message from 'Davey', asking what she was doing. Replying that she was okay and watching telly, Billie felt a glimmer of relief. Touching base with Aiden and responding as they'd arranged helped her relax. He sent her a thumbs-up back, so if Kelly got a glimpse of her messages it would seem normal: an overprotective boyfriend checking in.

After ordering vodka and tonic for Kelly and an almost identical fizzy water for herself, Billie made her way back and as she did, saw her reflection in the window of the bar. Her too-short, ice-blue sequined dress – chosen and paid for by Kelly – made Billie cringe and she was glad Stan couldn't see her. But as she looked away from her reflection someone briefly caught her eye.

No, it couldn't be. He'd been and gone before Billie had a chance to look closer but she could've sworn the guy on the street who'd been talking on his phone was Doog. Billie never forgot a face, especially one that had made her so uncomfortable. He'd totally vanished now so she shrugged it off as a coincidence, and made her way back to Kelly, who was on her phone. When Billie asked what she was doing, the answer didn't surprise her.

'Looking for cute guys in the vicinity... I've got an app that tells me, but nobody takes my fancy so for now I'm all yours. Anyway, I know what I meant to ask you: how come you only joined Facebook recently? I was browsing your profile the other night and if you don't mind me saying, it's *so* dull.'

Billie's heart flipped so she took a sip of her drink before answering. 'And if you don't mind me saying you sound like a stalker, browsing my Facebook.' Billie added a cheeky wink then continued but was glad she'd made the point. 'It's because Davey made me delete my account when he thought I was flirting with some lad I went to school with. He had a complete meltdown and smashed my phone and told me I wasn't allowed on Facebook anymore. I eventually persuaded him to let me back on it when I got my new – or should I say second-hand – phone, but only if I added him and his family, and girls, no blokes.'

'What a prat. So who does he think the women from the group are? His long-lost aunties?'

'He thinks they're from 'fat club'… I said I go once a week so I don't get chubby and the arsehole reckoned it was a good idea. The cheeky get! But that's why I look at gossip and the news and post memes, it's less hassle.' Billie thought that was a flipping excellent answer and the change in subject proved she was right.

'Well he's a tit, that's for sure, and if you ever do ditch him there's a room waiting for you at mine. We can be flatmates! How much fun would that be? Two single girls living it up.'

'Thanks, mate, and I'll bear that in mind. Now drink up. We should go somewhere else. I can't hear myself think in here.' Billie grabbed her bag and more or less jumped off her stool and when Kelly did the same, she noticed she was less steady on her feet and well on her way to getting drunk.

Good, thought Billie, *let's see if I can't loosen that tongue a bit more before the night's out.* There was no way she was going through this torment again, one bar crawl was quite enough, and she was already missing Iris and desperate to ring her mum and check up, but she daren't use her fake phone. Her real one was in the glove compartment of Stan's car, parked four streets from her pretend flat. God, she hoped it would be okay and not get pinched, or broken into. With one hand under Kelly's arm, Billie guided her onto the street and when the fresh air hit their lungs, suggested they went straight to the pub across the road and then she could begin the serious job of interrogating her semi-sloshed 'friend'.

32

Two very long hours later, Kelly was annoying the taxi driver by insisting he joined in with Jingle Bells. She wasn't having much luck and she finally got the message when he slammed the Perspex hatch shut to drown out her wailing. It was the only time during the evening that Billie had really laughed.

Now she had a lot on her mind, little snippets of this and that, a verbal jigsaw puzzle that she needed to fit together and she wished Kelly would shut the fuck up so she could concentrate. It had started with the talk of holidays, and ended with curry, and in between there had been glimpses of the woman Stan said Kelly really was.

They stayed in the pub for the remainder of the evening. They'd found a decent seat in a quiet-ish corner, and Kelly was far too drunk to walk any further. She was adamant that they were going to a club because she wanted to dance the night away but Billie had other ideas. While Kelly behaved like a dog on heat and flirted outrageously with any bloke who caught her eye,

Billie gave them the evil eye, her dour look forbidding them to even approach the table. No way did she want to waste the night making small talk with randy chancers.

The pub was decorated in a Caribbean Christmas theme that prompted Kelly to suggest they went on a girls' holiday. 'Tenerife is warm all year round and we can go in the new year,' she'd said. Naturally, Billie had used Davey as an excuse, and added that she was skint.

Kelly had a solution to both. 'I've told you, I've got a nice little nest egg hidden away so there's no need to worry about money. And as for that pillock you're shacked up with, dump him and move in with me. You need to grow a spine otherwise you'll end up like that lot at the centre, whingeing on forever about their sad lives instead of doing something about it.' Kelly plucked the slice of orange from the side of her cocktail glass and flicked it onto the table.

As Billie listened, she'd noted that thinly-veiled bitterness that was in complete contrast to the caring side Kelly had shown to the women in their group so she decided to push the point. 'What do you mean, "sad lives"? I thought you liked the girls; you're always so kind to them.'

A snort from Kelly was accompanied by a roll of her eyes. 'They're okay, I suppose, but they are starting to get on my tits. You know, with their *poor me* stories and dreary downtrodden lives. There's only so much I can take and sometimes I want to tell them to stop whining and do something about it, like I did. No bloke is ever going to get one over on me, or use me, I can tell you that for nothing. From now on, I'm in charge.'

Billie's ears had pricked up but she played it cool. 'That's a bit harsh, Kelly. Some of the women have it tough and it's not their fault how they live. They have kids to think of and anyway, if you're so wise perhaps you should spill the beans. Kelly's secret to a perfect life.'

'Well if you must know I'm thinking of training to be a counsellor, I reckon I could impart some wisdom and make the whiners see sense, *and* it's money for old rope.'

Billie egged her on. 'Nice one, but I suggest you adopt a more softly-softly approach otherwise you'll scare everyone off, you know, less of the tough love and more understanding. But you still haven't told me where all this dosh is coming from and how you sorted your life out. Or are you bullshitting?'

Kelly stopped mid-sip and eyed Billie before answering. There was a flash of annoyance but she countered it with a smug smile. 'You cheeky sod, I'm no bullshitter and for your information, the money is coming from a guy I hooked up with who should've known better. Now he's paying the price.'

Billie laughed and leaned forward, faking admiration. 'No way! The dirty dog... so how are you making him pay? Oh, I get it. Is he married?'

Kelly's eyebrows raised slightly, then she winked. 'Now you're getting it. All it took was a few selfies of him passed out and naked with yours truly and bingo, my silence has earned me a nice little nest egg. Once he's paid me the last instalment he's off the hook... Or maybe not. I haven't decided yet.'

'So who is he, this guy?'

Kelly looked like she was about to answer but then her need for a top-up interrupted and instead, she grabbed her bag. 'Ah, that doesn't matter, and the less you know the better, apart from he's a big-time loser and cheat. I hate cheats. Stan was one, at it behind my back, so that's why I took my revenge. As far as I'm concerned all men are the same and deserve what they get.'

Billie was rooted to the spot, literally trembling, desperately trying to hold it together. Out of everything Kelly had said, it was the mention of Stan's name that had rocked her to the core. The way she'd spoken about the women at the group had made Billie feel sick and it had been hard not to lose her rag and defend them. But to hear that once again Kelly was up to her blackmailing tricks was pure gold. She had to find out who this man was. Surely, if they could prove Kelly was extorting money it would blacken her character. It was something, at last. And that word, 'revenge'. Why did she say that?

When Kelly returned with a bottle of wine and two glasses, Billie had already decided how to play it and waited for Kelly to sit before leaning over and placing a caring hand on her arm. It felt like petting a snake. 'Hey, are you okay? I'm sorry if I've upset you, talking about the past but this is the first time we've had quality time together, so I'm trying to pack as much in as I can and it's nice, getting to know you better.'

Kelly responded with a squeeze of Billie's hand. 'Aw mate, that's a lovely thing to say and don't worry about me, I'm tough. So go on, ask away. It's nice to have someone to talk to about stuff and I trust you; it's like we clicked, right from the start.'

Billie heard the words of an emotional drunk, then felt a twinge of guilt but brushed it aside, allowing her instinct to guide her. Flicking the good angel off her right shoulder, she listened instead to the devil on her left who was egging her on. 'You hardly ever mention this... Stan, which is good and I get why, but every now and then his name pops up. It's like he still bothers you and that's not right. I could've cried when you told your story in the group because it must be like hell, going through all that and not being able to forget. Does the therapy help?'

'Nah, the only reason I still go is because I get time off work. They feel sorry for me and I think they're a bit scared of saying no. I am a victim after all.'

Billie was going to ask another question but Kelly piped up instead. 'And as for him, I don't mention Stan because he's of no consequence and he certainly isn't making my life hell. I'd say it was the other way round. Revenge is sweet as they say, so it's ten-nil to me.'

Kelly smiled, a cocky smirk that twisted her face. Billie thought it made her look ugly on the outside and that, maybe, her inside was the same. 'But I thought you were still hurt over his cheating and you know, what he did. That type of thing can't be easy to wipe out. I know I couldn't do it.' Billie was choosing her words carefully since the ones she really wanted to say would call time on the whole fiasco.

Kelly shook her head in that patronising way that makes people feel stupid. 'Beth, Beth, you have got me very wrong. There's so much you don't know about me *and* what makes me tick.'

Billie smothered the words 'that's the truth' and instead attempted a look of shock and hurt. 'What do you mean? I thought I'd got to know you quite well over the past few weeks. So go on, enlighten me. How did you know he was cheating? I reckon Davey's at it with someone so maybe you can give me a few tips on how to get one over on him.'

It was like Kelly was playing a part now, trying to be tough and self-assured, method acting at its best. She reminded Billie of all the school bullies and cocksure, badass women she'd seen portrayed on telly. To be honest, it was cringey. The wine and vodka mix was definitely working so she sat back and waited patiently for Tracy Barlow's mad twin to spill her guts.

Kelly unscrewed the lid and poured the wine as she spoke. 'Oh I'd be happy to. I'm a pro where dealing with cheats is concerned and in my case it was easy to catch him out and then wreak my revenge.'

On hearing those words Billie felt the spread of something crawling over her skin, mingled with a barely perceptible pinch of hope. Billie held her breath and listened to Kelly who had dribbled wine down her dress and lazily wiped it away as she spoke. 'I'd known for a few weeks he was up to something after I found a text from his ex-girlfriend. He must have thought he was clever, deleting them as soon as they came but she messaged him one night while he was asleep and I read it. I used his finger to open touch ID on his phone.'

Billie's lips had gone a bit numb and she hoped her face wasn't betraying her. 'No way! And that's very MI5 of you. I'd never have thought of that, you clever clogs. So go on, what did it say?'

Kelly rolled her eyes. 'Nothing earth-shattering. The daft cow wanted to go for fish and chips at Harry Ramsden's when she came home. How sad is that?'

'Very! So who is she, this ex?'

'Well that was the big mystery because *he* never spoke about her. It was like he'd wiped all trace of her out of his life, no photos, nothing. She'd broken his poor little heart apparently. She was a copper and got stabbed on duty then lost the plot.' Kelly pulled a stupid face and made a circle motion at her temple with her fingers. 'Seems they'd been going through a rough patch and had a huge barney because he wouldn't go travelling, so she stormed off. Turns out that when she came back with her tail between her legs, you know, the candlelit meal thing and his favourite curry, he was out having a one-night stand.' Kelly snorted her derision.

Billie somehow managed to regulate her breathing and ask another question, even though she already knew the answer. 'And what happened then? Did she find out?'

'Oh yes, saw her arse big time and pissed off to Greece to find herself, or something wet like that. Never came back, until she decided to get in touch with Stan. She was hoping, from what I could tell, to rekindle the flame.'

'And you had other ideas?'

'Yep. Like I said. Nobody gets one over on me so I decided to dump Stan first. I was getting bored with him anyway and I already had my little honeypot on the side so it was just a matter of time. He was *so* fit though, Stan I mean, and it was hard to resist him, I can tell you.'

Billie watched as Kelly brushed more wine off her dress. She was really drunk and having trouble controlling her limbs, and her lips. Billie had never wanted to beat someone to a pulp in her life, but in that moment she would have cheerfully murdered Kelly with her bare hands. Now certainly wasn't the time because she still hadn't explained about her revenge. Did she mean by two-timing Stan, or the rather immature intention of dumping him first? It could be a simple case of either or both, but Billie needed to be sure. She was about to ask the million-dollar question when Kelly piped up.

'Right, I need to go for a wee. Here, get the drinks in.' Calling time on the discussion and passing Billie a twenty-pound note she stood, swayed, then set off for the ladies.

The problem was that when Kelly returned from the bathroom, it was clear she didn't want to talk about the past, Stan or the guy she'd ensnared. No matter how much Billie prodded, Kelly said it was history and insisted they had a good time. The conversation was closed. Luckily for Billie, the triple vodka shot that she placed before Kelly served its purpose and within minutes, gave her the excuse to call time on their outing.

Kelly could barely speak properly, let alone stand but managed to stagger on jelly legs into the street where they waited for a taxi. When two merry men passed by, eating curry and chips from a plastic tray, the aroma made Billie's stomach rumble, whereas it caused Kelly to retch.

'Urgh, I think I'm going to throw up, I hate the smell of curry.' She placed her hands over her mouth.

Billie couldn't resist saying the first thing that popped straight into her head, which was now alive with so many other unanswered questions. 'I thought you said you loved curry. I swear it was chicken tikka–'

'No, I hate it. Always have and anyway it reminds me of him and what he did, fucking curry and men and cheating two-timing bastards...' Kelly closed her eyes and slumped against the wall, mumbling.

When the taxi arrived, Billie began loading Kelly inside. It was as she waited for Jelly Legs to flop into her seat that flashing headlights caught her attention and she spotted the driver of the car parked a few feet away. It was him, Doog. This time, instead of the disappearing act, he raised his hand, smiled then nodded.

The light dawned, causing Billie to smile and return the gesture while her heart flooded with love for a man who, despite being locked in a cell, was still looking out for her. Climbing into the taxi, Billie swallowed the lump in her throat and gave the driver the address. Once they set off, Doog's car pulled out and joined the line of traffic. She spent the rest of the journey listening intently to Kelly's intermittent ramblings that were interspersed with moments of animated singing and lapses into sleep.

Now, as they headed towards East Manchester and Kelly's flat, Doog following on behind, Billie focused on getting Sleepy Girl home and to bed. Then she was going to take the flat apart and find that money, or evidence of it *and* the poor sod who'd handed it over.

At the entrance to the block, as Kelly fumbled with the lock and eventually managed to stagger inside, Billie turned and raised her hand in thanks, receiving a wave in return from Doog, who was pulling away from the kerb across the street. Shivering, she followed Kelly up the stairs, feeling abandoned yet wired. The next few hours were vital, her last chance before Aiden pulled the plug and Billie reluctantly threw in the towel.

33

Kelly had woken with a mammoth hangover. Billie did her best to be kind while hiding her own feelings of disappointment and frustration, exacerbated by mild panic. The first two were borne from a fruitless search that unearthed absolutely nothing of value.

Billie had put Kelly to bed immediately and placed a sick-bowl by her side, a kindly act that was preceded by a battle of the wills. In the end she decided that choking on vomit was too good a death for Kelly so before she left the room, Billie pushed her onto her side. Then got on with a methodical sweep of the flat.

It had been easy to locate Kelly's bank statements. They were stored in a cardboard file and showed nothing more than wages in, bills out. The drawers and cupboards didn't surrender an envelope stuffed with cash and the only suspicious item was in the kitchen drawer – an old iPhone with a flat battery and no charger. Was it a cheat phone, like Aiden mentioned? Billie had looked through every single contact and message on Kelly's iPad and phone after using the unconscious woman's finger to unlock touch ID, but there was nothing. She was either very clever or she had made up the blackmail and photos. Out of desperation Billie considered stealing the cheat phone, then bottled it.

It had been a long night after that, going over and over everything that Kelly had let slip but by morning Billie was none the wiser and had a list of unanswered questions that needed matching up to random clues. For now though, her main objective was escape.

Having listened to Kelly's plans, it looked like an intervention was necessary, which was why, when 'Davey' had texted and asked 'you ok, are you up, wot u doing?' she replied, 'yes I'm up, got headache, going Starbucks for breakfast.'

'I'm up' meant she had some news and 'headache' was their prearranged signal that Billie had had enough and was ready to bail out. 'Migraine' was the code word for 'help', just in case.

Kelly had suggested they went out for some fresh air and to grab a coffee. She needed to sober up and then they'd been invited by her parents for Sunday lunch. Apparently, she couldn't wait to introduce Billie and seeing as Davey was in Dublin they could make the most of being together. Not a chance was Billie going to visit Kelly's parents. She needed to escape the clutches of her desperate bestie and see Iris.

Rather than irritate Kelly in this mood, Billie played along and frantically worked on an excuse that would get her out of lunch and home. She sent a text saying 'got migraine, feel crap, need to go home'.

It was good to be outside and back in her jeans and jumper, not the ridiculous dress she'd left at the flat. They were heading towards the coffee shop, Kelly linking Billie's arm and sucking in fresh air to ward off nausea when a car shot past them and screeched to a halt at the kerb. The noisy, souped-up engine followed by the skid made both of them jump. When Billie saw 'Davey' jump out of the white Subaru, his black hoodie pulled over his head but not enough to hide his glare as he marched towards them, her mouth dropped open in genuine surprise.

Kelly looked from one to the other, a bemused expression on her face. Billie's next words solved the puzzle for her.

'Davey... what are you doing here? I thought you were in–' Billie didn't get the chance to finish.

'Yeah, Dublin. But surprise, Davey's home.' He spat the words, using a strong Manchester accent.

Billie stammered. 'B-but–'

Davey interrupted. 'The car broke down on the way to the airport and we missed our flight so we made other plans and went to Liverpool instead. Thing is, when I got back to the flat this morning guess who was missing?' Davey's voice was laced with sarcasm as he grabbed Billie's arm and dragged her away.

Aiden's unshaven face and unlikely get-up was really unnerving, never mind his attitude but Billie played along. 'I-I'm sorry, Davey. I just went out with... how did you know I was here?' Billie looked briefly at Kelly who was eyeing 'Davey', clearly pissed off with him.

'Find My Phone, dumbo... I can track you anywhere. Now get in the car.'

Davey pushed Billie towards his white sports car with tail fins and giant exhaust, and she tried hard not to smirk at his play-acting.

Then Kelly waded in. 'Oi, dickhead, let her go. I mean it. I'll call the police.' Kelly pulled her phone out of her bag and held it in the air, her finger poised.

Letting go of Billie, Davey turned and raced towards Kelly and before she could respond, he'd grabbed her phone and thrown it into the litter-strewn bushes that edged the street, snarling, 'Fuck off, Barbie, and mind your own business.'

With that he strutted back to the car, pointed at Billie and told her to get in, which she did. The second they were inside he started the engine and as they sped off, Billie turned and saw Kelly, foraging around in the bushes for her phone. Twisting forward as she fastened her seatbelt she looked at Aiden who glanced sideways and gave her a wink, and with that they both burst into fits of laughter.

Once she'd controlled herself Billie gave him a nudge. 'I think you missed your way, mate. You need to go on the stage cos for a minute you really did look the part and scared the crap out of me. And that accent! Have you been watching *Shameless* or something?'

'One of my favourites, and *Corrie,* of course. I think our Kelly bought the scumbag boyfriend routine and you looked so shocked it worked like a dream. I quite enjoyed playing a bad lad. Gave me quite a buzz especially when I threw her phone. Don't know what came over me.'

Billie laughed and looked around the leather interior of the car. 'And where the hell did you get this from? It's so not you but, actually, I think it's cool.'

'*This* little beauty is my brother's pride and joy, so don't get it dirty. He loves it more than his wife and kids.'

'Oh, I see. Nice.' Billie settled in and allowed the drama of the last few minutes to subside and relief to wash over her.

Aiden, however, wanted answers. 'So, come on, what did you find out? I've been awake half the night worrying. I'll take you to your car and you can tell me on the way, then if you've got time we'll get some breakfast. I fancy a fry-up.'

'Okay, deal, and I want to ring Mum and check on Iris. As for what I found out about Kelly, it might be something and nothing. She's definitely not the person she makes out to be in public and she's up to no good, that's for sure.'

Aiden glanced over and raised his eyebrows so while they raced through the sleepy streets of Manchester, Billie told him everything.

34

The radiators clunked and floorboards creaked as Billie lay on the bed with Iris who was sleeping soundly in the crook of her arm. She needed to feel the comfort of her daughter's warm little body.

She'd put her fake phone on silent because she was sick of replying to messages from Kelly. Seeing her name made her want to scream. There had been a stream of 'are you okay, I'm worried about you, he's a total psycho, you have to leave him' messages that Billie had fobbed off with, 'I'm okay, can't really talk, he's on one, will be in touch soon.'

Tears coursed down Billie's face which she wiped away with the sleeve of her cardigan and held in the sobs of frustration that accompanied them. Babies pick up on distress and Billie was determined that Iris was not going to be sullied in any way by the stain of Kelly.

No matter how hard she tried to think positive and give herself credit for trying, Billie knew she had messed up and hated herself for it.

After going through everything she had gleaned from Kelly the night before, to her dismay Aiden's prognosis was grim. Yes, all the evidence confirmed his suspicions that Kelly was an evil bitch but, unless they found some hard evidence, for example physical proof of this nest egg she had stashed, or they extracted a statement from the stupid bloke she'd been blackmailing, they were screwed. Even then it would only prove bad character in the present, but added to what they had from the past it might nudge them ahead.

Worst of all was that when she'd mentioned the old phone she'd found in the kitchen drawer, Aiden made it clear he thought she should have taken it. It was worth the risk for the potential information that was stored on it. She might have mentioned Stan or the offence in a message, given some hint that she'd lied in her evidence. Anything was better than what they had. It was clutching at straws, but he was going to get Tom to go through Kelly's text messages again, just in case he'd missed something but he had a suspicion that the 'cheat' phone was the key.

Billie had felt such a fool and still did, but at the time she was a bag of nerves and terrified Kelly would wake up and catch her. Even though it had occurred to her to take the phone, what if Kelly noticed it was missing? Surely she'd suspect Billie straight away. That thought didn't assuage the guilt and irritation she was feeling. Kelly had dropped so many hints and clues but no matter how hard they had tried to piece them together, Billie and Aiden were at a dead end.

There was no way she could sleep and she didn't want to wake her parents by going downstairs to make a brew. So instead Billie wiggled free of Iris and pulled open her bedside drawer and removed the first letter that Stan had sent her from prison. Maybe reading it again – even though she knew it almost word for word – would help make sense of the jigsaw puzzle in her head. Using the torch on her phone Billie began to read and as she did, imagined Stan writing it in his cell, pouring his heart out and asking for help.

It was when she reached the last part, the hardest bit to read, that Billie wavered but forced herself on. She wanted to compare Stan's version with the one Kelly told in the group.

I'd picked up a takeaway, plus extra for the freezer like always, then drove home and parked on the drive. When I got there I expected the house to be in complete darkness. I noticed a light on in the front bedroom, though I thought nothing of it. I presumed I'd forgotten to switch it off that morning. I let myself in and switched on the hall light. Then I heard footsteps overhead, heels tapping on the wooden floor, and knew instantly who was in the house. I froze for a second, totally shocked.

When I recovered I took the stairs two at a time and found Kelly lying on the bed, the sheets pulled back and let's say she wasn't wearing a lot apart from a sickly sweet smile on her face. Then she said, 'Surprise'.

Too right!

I know you are probably screaming at me right now 'why didn't you just throw her out?' but my head was mashed. It wasn't working properly. For a start I wanted to know how the hell she'd got in. Later on, I worked it out. At some point she'd had a key cut from my spare set because NO WAY had I ever offered her one. She denied it in court, amongst other things, like having a twat for a dad and being a second-generation psycho herself.

I could tell she was enjoying getting one over on me, you know, being in my home, mooching about. She must have parked her car further along the road and then snuck in and waited. It was dark outside and there were no witnesses to her arriving. You know what the garden is like, all those bloody bushes are great for privacy but also hide nutters lurking in the shadows. The next few minutes of madness will haunt me forever. It's like Groundhog Day or a never-

ending nightmare. Please try not to hate me when you read the next bit because the hatred I have for myself is swallowing me alive.

Here goes, this is what happened next.

I asked her again what she thought she was playing at and she shrugged it off and said she wanted to surprise me. I said she'd done that all right because she was early and I wasn't expecting her. I went over to the wardrobe and took out the bag containing her belongings and placed it near the door and asked her to get dressed and leave. Instead, she got out of bed and wrapped her arms around me. She said she was sorry for all the hassle and if we were going to split up, she didn't want any nastiness. She hoped we could stay friends, actually her words were 'friends with benefits, no strings and a bit of fun now and then', and if I didn't believe her, she wanted to show me what I'd be missing, for old time's sake.

That's as far as I'm going to go because you don't need me to tell you what happened next so I'll skip that part.

Afterwards, she nodded off so I had a shower then crept downstairs because I was starving. I left the carton marked 'tikka' on the side and transferred the jalfrezi and rice onto a plate. You'll think I'm mad for telling you this but it's important because she said I'd bought her the curry and wanted to talk about getting back together over a meal, but I didn't. Why would I? She doesn't even like Indian food. Anyway, while I waited for the microwave to ping I had a beer, then another with my meal. I didn't bother to wake her up and hoped that when she did, she'd take the hint and leave. I settled down in front of the telly and must have dozed for a while, that's until I was woken by a hard slap around the face.

It scared the life out of me and as Kelly punched and screamed at me, I was disorientated and to be honest really pissed off. She was calling me a cheating, two-timing bastard and said she hated my guts and was leaving.

When I managed to stand I chased after her and found her in the bedroom, pacing like a wild animal, pulling her hair, tearing her clothes and ranting, wanting to know how long I'd been shagging Billie the Slag behind her back. That's when I realised. She must have come downstairs while I was asleep and read our last messages and it sent her nuts. Remember – I said I missed you and was counting sleeps till you got back. You replied with 'Lol' and a five snoring emojis.

I told her to calm down and I'd explain but she wasn't having any of it and launched herself at me, clawing at my face, kicking and punching. Please don't hate me but she was hysterical so I slapped her across the face. It sounds daft but I'd seen it on telly when people were in shock. Maybe it was a mad knee-jerk reaction. The crack made me wince if I'm honest, but at least it shut her up, for a second. Then it was like she came to her senses – or not.

She picked up a statue, you know, one of the dolphins on the bedside cabinet. I realised she was either going to smash it in temper or use it as a weapon against me so I did the only thing I could and grabbed her and held her arms by her side and pleaded with her to stop.

That's when she went completely mental and struggled, causing us both to lose balance. We hit the floor hard. I landed on top, which winded me so I'm damn sure it did the same to her. I didn't realise at the time that she'd caught her head on the cabinet because after a second or two she continued to struggle but I didn't let go and because I was knackered, hoped that eventually she'd run out of steam too. Sure enough, after a few minutes she stopped moving and I could hear her breath was ragged, so asked if I let go, would she stop fighting. I heard her say yes so I let go and stood.

Her face was side-on so I couldn't see that her head was cut because if I had I'd have fetched a towel or something. She remained motionless and as I backed away I could see the rise and fall of her back as she breathed in and out. I was a bit shaky, really shocked and pissed off but I tried to keep her calm so offered to bring her a glass of water. She told me to fuck off. With that I went downstairs, out of her way. I know from past experience that it's best to leave her alone when she gets like that. All I wanted was for her to get her things and go.

Downstairs, I went into the kitchen and downed a glass of water then took another beer out of the fridge, drank half, went into the lounge and put the bottle on the floor, next to my plate from earlier, then went to the loo in the hallway. The flushing chain and running tap water must have masked the sound of her coming down the stairs but as I came out of the loo, I heard the front door close and knew she'd gone.

I cannot tell you how glad I was, so put the chain on, so she couldn't get back in, and promised myself I'd change the lock first thing.

I sat on the settee, flicked on the news and closed my eyes and tried to wipe the bedroom scene, and Kelly from my mind.

Thirty minutes later I heard the doorbell ringing and I remember thinking, Piss off Kelly. But it wasn't her. It was the police and the second I opened the door, my whole life fell apart.

No matter how many times I gave my version of events, nobody believed that it was Kelly who seduced me and attacked me afterwards, or that she was the one who ripped her clothes up and the external injuries she sustained were a result of me trying to restrain her. According to the experts the bruises to her wrists and body, the cut to her head and the internal physical evidence were conducive to a violent sexual assault.

Kelly said I'd tried to persuade her to stay and talk things through over a meal and when she refused I became aggressive, more so when she picked up her bag and attempted to leave, which is when I raped her. The statement given by the neighbours who opened the door to the hysterical woman dressed only in her coat nailed the lid on my coffin. I didn't stand a chance.

She's warped and I realised that when I confronted her a few months later. Yes, it was a stupid thing to do but I was so desperate I'd have begged, if that's what it took to get her to drop the charges.

I was on bail and waiting for the police and the CPS to make their move. I panicked because it was like waiting for an axe to fall. I sat in my car outside her parents' house one Sunday afternoon, hoping she'd be there and when she finally turned up I approached her, not too close but so she could hear me. When she saw me she looked amused. She actually smiled then looked around, probably to see if there were any witnesses or if she could make a fuss, but the street was deserted. I asked her why she was doing this and told her that she knew it was a lie and I hadn't done what she said. You know what she did? She threw her head back and laughed, proper laughing, like a nutter.

It stunned me a bit so I stooped to begging like some pathetic sad case. I asked her to drop the charges but her reply was 'Never. I'm going to destroy you.'

I asked her again, why she was doing this and do you know what she did? She marched straight up to me – no fear, just madness in her eyes. She pushed her face into mine, snarling almost, and said, 'Because I can.'

I'll never ever forget those words, ever. They made me go cold, like my blood actually froze.

Then she turned round and stomped off, shouting over her shoulder, 'Now fuck off before I call the police. See you in court, loser.'

My legs were shaking and I somehow managed to get back to my car and drive to mum's where I waited all night like a gibbering wreck for the police to come and arrest me. I knew I'd be on remand for breaking my bail. When they didn't, I realised she already thought she'd won and my begging was another trophy to add to her cabinet, and more than likely she was looking forward to her day in court, in the spotlight.

You know most of the rest, so there's no point going over the court case and everything else that happened as a result of her lies.

What matters to me now is that you believe me and if you do, you'll come back like you said you would. I need you, Billie. I need help and something to hold onto. One visit, that's all I ask.

I'll leave you in peace now to make your own mind up but before I go I want to tell you again that I'm sorry, for everything and while I can't turn back time, I can still love you, from behind these walls and forever. If nothing else, my heart will always be free.

Stan x

Folding the sheets neatly, Billie slid them back inside the envelope and laid it on her chest. A kind of peace had washed over her which was weird considering the rage she'd felt previously. Every time she'd read Stan's letter Billie had felt the same. Now it was different. She wasn't at the beginning of a quest; she was at the end, but it didn't feel like it. While all the doors had been slammed in her face and her back was firmly against the wall, another cliché popped into Billie's head, one that Stan always used when he was getting beat at Monopoly. The thought of him sitting at the table, fuming because he had to pay the taxman and only had five pounds and a house on the Old Kent Road to his name, made her smile, and she knew exactly what he would say in the situation. No matter how bleak things looked right now, Billie couldn't, wouldn't give in. Speaking into the darkness, she hugged Iris and said softly, 'Don't worry, Stan, I'm still here for you and it's not over yet, not till the fat lady sings.'

35

Billie breathed a sigh of relief as Sue went to the tea bar, leaving her alone with Stan at last. It wasn't as though she begrudged either of them mother-and-son time, but there were things she needed to discuss. Not just that, Billie was weighed down by the misery of her surroundings. Never in a zillion years would she have imagined spending Christmas Eve at HMP Manchester. But here they were, and they had all tried to make the best of it.

Play-acting aside, they all knew that this year, and a few more yet, it would be a day to endure for Iris's sake and perhaps their own sanity. Most of all it was out of respect for Stan's wishes that they had all promised to at least try to enjoy the day.

Billie had been weak and looked online, and now regretted reading the articles and accounts of what Christmas Day was like behind bars. From what she could gather, apart from rock-hard roast potatoes and piss-thin gravy over insipid chicken, sod all changed because prison budgets didn't run to extravagance or festive spirit.

There was no time for maudlin thoughts now, because Billie had too many questions to ask Stan, and first on the agenda was Doog.

'Thank you for despatching my very own bodyguard. Once I realised it wasn't a coincidence he did make me feel safe, not that I was in any great danger from *her*, but his presence made me feel close to you too. Will you tell him thanks?'

Stan smiled, dragged his gaze away from sleeping Iris. 'I couldn't bear the thought of you being with that freak show, and I knew Doog would take care of you. He got in touch with Aiden and they agreed he should tail you. He only made his presence known because you looked really miserable and on edge, apparently it's his bouncer's intuition. Oh, and he said you looked fit in your sparkly-blue mini dress which did surprise me a bit... Did you *really* wear something like that?'

Billie tapped his arm and laughed. 'Yes, I did and I never ever want it to be spoken of again because it was in the line of duty and I felt like a complete prat, so let's change the subject. Don't forget you owe me some answers.'

'Oh, oh... what've I done now?'

'Nothing, I hope, but what did Doog's girlfriend mean when she said you and him were "thick as thieves"? On the phone you said you couldn't talk about it, so come on, tell me now.' Billie gave Stan her best firm stare, with a hint of a smile to keep the atmosphere light.

Stan leaned closer and lowered his voice and explained that from now on, him and Doog were business partners, one of them silent for the obvious reasons. It was nothing illegal, more a case of making easy cash via cheap imported goods that could be sold on the internet. Doog just needed somewhere to store them. Not only that, stuff had been going missing from the plumbing yard and Stan suspected the lads were pinching materials and flogging them on eBay. The police suspected passing gypsies, especially when one of the vans went missing but Doog wasn't convinced so Stan had asked him to be his eyes and ears on the outside. They'd formed an allegiance during their time locked up together and Stan would always be grateful for the protection Doog had afforded them. Yes, it was an unlikely friendship but sometimes you clicked with the strangest of people, and that's what mattered right now because via their weekly phone calls, Doog made Stan feel useful and connected to the real world.

Billie was dubious but that damn clock was ticking so she let the subject of tacky fakes and cheap imports go. There were more pressing matters on her mind.

'Okay, I get it and I suppose you can't get into trouble from in here, as long as Doog can be trusted that is. But forget him. I need to ask you something.'

Billie noted Stan looked relieved at hearing this. She took a moment to think, putting off her question because she hated discussing Kelly and even saying her name. 'Some of the stuff *she* said has been bugging me and top of the list is the fact she knows a lot more about me than I expected. I read your letter through again and it said you never talked about us, or how we split up. I've gently quizzed your mum and she's adamant that family gossip or personal details were not divulged on the few times she met the witch. If that's the case, how the hell did *she* know that I was a copper and got stabbed? She knew all about why we split up, even the bloody meal I made you and that you'd cheated on me. Are you sure you didn't let slip while you were drunk?'

Stan was vigorously shaking his head. 'No way! Bill, I couldn't bear to talk about you. I was so cut up and pissed off with myself about everything so not a chance would I have told her. How the hell does she know?'

Billie sighed. 'I wish I knew because it kept me up all night trying to fathom it, but there was something else. You know this photographic memory you reckon you've got? Well you said you could remember all of the messages I sent you. You said the last one ended with sleeping emoji's – but it didn't.'

'Billie, it did. I can see it now.'

'No Stan, I checked my phone and I sent another, before I went to sleep telling you how much I missed our Friday night takeaway and that I was craving Harry Ramsden's fish, chips and mushy peas. I asked you to take me when I got back but you never replied. I think that's the message she saw on your phone and flipped. She told me about it and it wasn't until I read your letter I realised the messages didn't tally. She reckons she'd already sussed that you were cheating but I think she went to yours that night to get back together and when she saw my text, her plan crashed and burned and she lost the plot, big time.'

'That sounds feasible because up until then she didn't look like she was going anywhere fast but I bet you're right, that's why she went mad.'

'She's clever though and managed to put everything she already knew and saw that night to good use, like the sodding curry fib.'

'Curry fib?' Stan looked confused.

Billie explained. 'When she told the group her side of the story, she said that you'd bought her her favourite curry, tikka, and wanted a romantic make-up meal. Thing is, on our night out, she told me that she hates curry and the smell makes her feel sick. Little things like that irritate me and I know the police probably missed it or overlooked it, but it shows what a manipulator she is, like this ridiculous thing with her dad. One minute she's telling you he's vile and ruined her life, then when it suits her he's the best thing since sliced bread. She's an attention-seeking, pathological liar, that's for sure.'

Billie came up for air and noticed that Stan was quiet, examining his fingernails that were far too short.

'Hey, what's wrong, have I said something to upset you?'

Stan met her eye. 'No, I'm not upset, just riddled with hate and bitterness for that... piece of crap. The thing is, Bill, I know all this. I know she's a liar but nothing you've found out is going to get me out of here and if it frustrates you and Aiden, can you imagine how I feel? I swear it's driving me insane and if I ever get home in one piece, bodywise, up here I won't be.' Stan hit the side of his head with the base of his palm.

For the first time since she came to see him, Billie saw a different Stan, not only in his thinly-veiled actions that screamed out his temper and frustration, but the panic in his eyes, the pallor of his skin and the beads of sweat on his forehead and, now, the shallow breathing. His demeanour startled but didn't scare her. It snapped her heart in two because now she knew how close to the edge he was. The big smile at the beginning and end of each visit was a sham, like the jolly questions and selfless interest in their everyday lives. Her Stan was holding it together for them, swallowing down his fear and desperation while every day, with each tick of that blasted clock on the wall, hope faded and any hint of a reprieve simply evaporated.

Billie acted instinctively and grabbed his free hand, holding on as tightly as she could. 'Now you listen to me. This is not over, not yet so do not give up. I will not allow you to fall apart, do you hear me, Stan?'

He couldn't speak. She could see that because he nodded as tears plopped onto the arms of his sweatshirt.

'I've had an idea and I'm going to give it one more shot after Christmas. God, I'm wearing that phrase out but that's how much I love and believe in you. I think I know how to get it out of her where the money is, or who she's blackmailing and if she won't tell me I'm going to pinch that phone out of her kitchen because Aiden reckons it will have stuff on it that we can use.'

Stan looked up. 'No, Billie, leave it. It's over. We have to accept that she's been too clever and will never admit what she did. I don't want you getting into trouble with the law. You have to think of Iris. She comes first now.'

'I am thinking of Iris because she needs her daddy home and if I don't do this I'll go mad, then she's got two loopy parents, and a mad Granny Claudia, and that's more than any kid deserves.' Billie saw him crack a smile so carried on. 'Look, all I have to do is go round there and try to distract her so I can get the phone and while I'm at it, see if I can egg her on about this money. It's better than nothing and I swear, if it leads to a dead-end I'll give up.'

'You swear.'

'Yep, I swear. And then I'll send her fucking mad when her new bezzie mate disappears off the face of the earth. When she rings Beth's phone it will be dead, Facebook profile deleted, an empty chair at the group meetings, nobody at the flats will ever have heard of her, no such person as Davey Willis, either. That'll give her something to think about, and I might even come back and haunt her now and then, like the ghost who taps on your shoulder and whispers down your ear at night. See how she likes the taste of revenge.' Billie was fired up now, maybe from the surge of adrenaline that was pumping around her body after her inspired speech, and it looked like it had done the trick with Stan, too.

'God, I love you Billie, you know that? And I'm sorry I lost it a bit, but sometimes all this gets to me–'

Billie interrupted. 'Hey, I get it, you don't have to explain, and I love you too and whatever happens I will stand by you every single step, okay. Me and Iris are waiting for you however long it takes to get you home, I promise.'

In the corner of her eye Billie saw Sue approaching and sensed that Stan had too, because he quickly pulled himself together before she gave him a goodbye hug. As she watched the man she loved struggle to keep control as he handed back his daughter, Billie waged her own war, summoning that inner warrior princess that Aiden once joked about. Somehow they would all get through the next few minutes, then Christmas and as soon as she could get away, Billie would carry on the fight alone.

She was going to take the battle straight to the enemy, knock on their door and, once they let her inside, do whatever it took to claim victory. For Stan and Iris, for all of them.

36

Billie was seated next to Aiden in his car, the engine running to keep them warm while she smudged her eyeliner in the visor mirror. She looked a wreck. Greasy hair stuck to her scalp in patches, her skin was stripped bare of make-up and now, she had panda eyes, an after-effect of a tearful sleepless night – thanks to 'Davey'. She had even considered sniffing an onion to ensure it looked authentic but Aiden assured her it wasn't necessary. The huge bruise on her arm was a godsend, even though slipping on her mum's path and landing with a wallop had hurt like hell.

'So, do I look rough then?' Billie turned to face Aiden who grimaced. Result.

'Oh yes, I'd say dog rough.' Now he smiled and watched as Billie flipped up the visor. 'Are you sure you want to do this? You can still back out, you know.'

Billie shook her head vehemently. 'No way am I backing out. This is it. Last chance saloon. Kelly's not going to know what hit her today.'

Aiden sighed. 'Okay, if you're sure. I'm going to stay here until you come out. I'll take my lead from you but if you can't get that phone, just bail and then you never have to see her again. It might not still be in the kitchen, so don't freak out or feel like you've failed.'

'We could break in, or get someone to do it for us. I reckon I know someone who could help.' Billie was so fired up she would try anything.

Aiden nodded. 'Ah, the infamous Doog, I take it. Don't you worry, I've already been made aware of his willingness to help but for now, let's stay legal. I have a reputation to consider.' He winked at Billie.

'Yeah, I suppose so but let's face it, your interpretation of legal and mine are clearly poles apart. Right, I'm going before I bottle it. I'll post the cringey meme when I can, then stick to the plan after that.'

'Okay and good luck... and remember–'

'Aiden, I'm fine, I get it, stop worrying. See you in a bit.' And with that Billie got out of the car and headed up the street towards Kelly's.

It was bitterly cold outside and the wind was actually making her eyes water for real which was a plus. It was only a short walk to Kelly's, and Kelly was expecting her. Billie had sent a desperate-sounding text, asking if she could come round. She wasn't surprised when Kelly agreed at once.

It was the day of the television interview at the community centre and Kelly had talked of nothing else, in between counselling 'Beth' through a terrible Christmas with nasty Davey. She completely believed he'd been obnoxious throughout and had prevented Beth from going to see her mum and more or less kept her prisoner in the flat. As a consequence Beth had a massive alcohol-fuelled argument with Davey that left her battered and bruised and determined to leave him, which was why she'd asked good old Kelly for safe haven.

After much thought, Billie had dissected all she knew about Kelly's personality and realised where she may have gone wrong. Kelly liked to lead, be top dog and in control, when she wasn't playing the victim. So instead of stroking her ego and playing softly-softly, hoping for snippets and clues, Billie had decided to challenge her. Today, she was going to rile her a little and see if in defence, Kelly would come out fighting to prove she really was the master blackmailer. It might not work but neither had playing the wimpy best friend, so it was worth a try.

They had a good two hours before the television interview and the plan was that if Billie couldn't get anything of use verbally, or access to the phone, she was going to ask Kelly if she could stay at the flat. Naturally Beth was too scared of bumping into Davey and knackered after rowing all night, so fingers crossed, Kelly would agree and trot off in giddy expectation of becoming a media star, leaving Billie alone. Aiden had said to play it by ear and go with the flow. 'But,' he'd said, 'the minute you have the phone, get out.'

Billie pushed the intercom buzzer and waited. Hearing Kelly's voice telling her to come up and the click of the lock, Billie pulled open the door, took a deep breath and made her way up the stairs.

Billie had clearly interrupted Kelly's interview preparations and Dutch courage routine. There was make-up strewn across the kitchen worktop, accompanied by a bottle of wine. Kelly poured a glass for Billie and topped up her own. 'Here, get this down you, you look frozen. Why didn't you put a warm coat on? I'll lend you one of mine when we go out.'

Billie faked a shiver. 'Yeah I know... but I grabbed the first thing I could and legged it.'

'Mate, I hate that you were so scared and you look truly dreadful. Are you in pain? Let me see your bruises because we need to take some photos of them for evidence.'

'Yes, I am. I ache all over but can I pass on the wine? I wouldn't mind a glass of water, though.'

Kelly was playing the attentive nurse and immediately filled a glass and passed it to Billie who hovered by the all-important drawer.

'I'll show you my ribs in a bit. They'll look worse when they start to change colour like this.' Billie held up her wrist. 'I'm more bothered about this pounding headache. Have you got any paracetamol?'

Billie willed Kelly to head for the bathroom so she could pinch the phone when to her shock, Kelly opened the very drawer where it was stored. Billie saw it, exactly where she remembered and her heart began to race.

'Here, get those down you. So where is big hard Davey now?' Kelly tossed the packet of paracetamol over.

Billie took a seat at the table, removed her phone from the top pocket of her denim jacket and pretended to check it for messages. 'No idea, in fact I don't care. I hate him so much. He's ruined Christmas before but stopping me from seeing my mum was the last straw. Are you sure it's okay for me to stay here tonight? I didn't get a chance to pack anything so I might need to borrow some stuff, you know, clean knickers and a nightie.'

'Mate, it's fine and your pyjamas from the other week are all clean, so make yourself at home. You can stay as long as you want but I think it's time you made some tough choices and left Davey for good.'

Here goes, thought Billie as she posted the meme on Facebook, *it's now or never*. 'Well it's okay for you to say but everything in your life is rosy, you've got a job, a nice flat and all that. I've got sod all apart from Davey so I'm stuck. It's not going to be easy starting from scratch, you know.' Billie pressed the word *post* and smiled inwardly, knowing that Aiden would see it and get the message. When she looked up she saw Kelly glaring at her so asked, 'What's up?'

'You, that's what! Why don't you stop pissing about on Facebook like always and take control of your life. Stop whining for a start.'

'Charming, and for your information I've posted a meme that will give the arsehole the message I'm not pleased with him. Look.' Billie turned the screen so Kelly could see and listened as she read the words.

'I am a strong woman. No man can define me.'

At this, Kelly burst out laughing. 'Seriously, that's so lame. I'd delete it if I were you. Davey walks all over you and saddo memes won't bother him one bit. It'll probably give him a laugh.'

Billie made a fed-up face. 'Okay then, smart-arse, what would you put?' But before Kelly could reply, the phone began to ring. It was 'Davey'. Acting cocky, Billie swiped the phone and said, 'What do you want?' and was then treated to a foul-mouthed tirade that ended with him telling her to stop posting shite on Facebook and get home, now!

Billie cut him off in mid-flow, like they planned. They wanted Kelly to believe that Beth was too scared to go home. It looked like she'd taken the bait.

'Bloody hell, he really is pissed off. Please tell me you've switched off that app where he can track you... the last thing we need is the nutter coming round here.'

Billie winked. 'Already thought of that.'

'Good... so you're not entirely stupid after all.' Kelly was applying mascara as she spoke.

Billie decided to take umbrage as she scrolled through Facebook which seemed to irritate Kelly.

'For fuck's sake will you leave that sodding phone alone and make some decisions about your life. Take control for once.'

Instead of doing as she was told Billie held up the phone and took a photo of Kelly in her rollers.

Kelly pointed. 'Don't you dare put that on there... I'm warning you!'

Billie laughed. 'Well stop being a grump then! You've been a right narky cow since I got here. What's wrong? Are you getting nervous about this telly thing?'

Kelly put down her mascara and rested her arms on the table, looking stern and when she spoke her tone was serious. 'I want you to sort yourself out, that's all. And stop letting him pull your strings.'

'And I told you, it's not as easy as that. Don't you listen to anything at the meetings? If women like me could just walk away we would. I'd have gone to my mum's ages ago but I'd be bringing trouble to her door and I haven't got a wonderful daddy to protect me like you do.'

'Are you deaf or stupid or something? I've told you, you can move in with me and now is as good a time as any. I won't charge you rent until you get a job or the dole, but at least we can start having some fun rather than sneaking about when Davey's out of the way. And I'm not scared of that knobhead. I'll ring the police on him if he comes round here. What do you think? Have you got the bottle or are you going to limp through life like this?'

'Are you serious? You'd let me move in rent free? I'm not a charity case, you know. I need to get a job first so I could pay my way. I can't let you bankroll me, it's not fair.'

'Look, I told you, money isn't a problem and I don't mind sharing. I was going to ask you if you fancied going on a winter break, my treat. You do have a passport, don't you?'

Billie's mind was racing but she had to get this right, throw Kelly off balance when she least expected it. 'Yeah, yeah, you keep telling me you're loaded but how do I know you're not bull-shitting? You can't expect me to leave Davey just cos you reckon some bloke is going to keep giving you money. For all I know you could be making it all up and yes, I have got a passport – not that I ever get to use it.' Billie folded her arms across her chest and adopted a sullen expression, one her mum had been used to in her teenage years.

A flash of temper crossed Kelly's face as her eyes hardened. Then a sly smile crept to her lips. She'd accepted the challenge, Billie knew it.

'So you think I'm a bullshitter do you? Well, look at this. Then you can apologise and eat your bloody words.' Kelly pushed back the chair so hard it nearly went flying then stomped over to the sink and flung open the door below. She pulled out a giant box of soap powder which she slammed onto the draining board.

Billie watched transfixed as Kelly dug her hands inside and rummaged for a second before pulling out a carrier bag, sending white powder everywhere. From the bag Kelly removed a package and Billie knew instantly what it was, even before it had been slapped onto the kitchen table.

'There, satisfied? Fifteen grand, give or take a few hundred quid that I've already spent. So now do you believe me?'

Kelly looked triumphantly down at Billie who was completely lost for words. Euphoric but speechless. When she managed to form a sentence and her brain had re-engaged, Billie placed her hand over her mouth, this time not faking the shock she felt.

'Oh my God, oh my God, Kelly! Where the– I honestly thought you were joking but you're not.' Billie looked away from the huge wedge of notes and over to Kelly who was now seated at the table and pouring herself another drink, looking immensely pleased with herself.

'So now you believe me, can we cut the crap and get on with having some bloody fun in our lives or shall I ring for a taxi and you can go home to dear old Davey?'

Billie laughed out loud, and that wasn't fake either because she'd only bloody gone and done it, found physical proof that Kelly was a bona fide blackmailer. All she had to do now was put the last piece of the puzzle into place.

'No way am I going anywhere, and you can pour me one of those. My headache has suddenly disappeared, in fact, I think it's party time.' No sooner had she said the words than Kelly had poured some wine into a glass and passed it over.

When they clinked glasses, Kelly looked extremely pleased with herself as she downed her drink in one. Billie did the same, if only to steady her nerves because it wasn't quite over, not yet. There were two more items on the agenda: the identity of the poor sod who'd handed over the money, and a black iPhone that was literally inches away. Billie intended to get them both.

37

They were both a teeny bit merry now, Kelly more than Billie who had been sipping rather than glugging in between taking selfies of themselves for the album they were going to post on Facebook. Billie had also managed to take some of the pile of money, the shot had Kelly in the background, her back turned, filling the kettle.

Kelly was literally jabbering away now, showing Billie photos of where she wanted to go on her iPad in between filling the coffee pot. 'We could even go backpacking, you know, do the whole Australia and the Far East thing. How fab would that be? What do you reckon?'

Billie was uploading a selfie to Facebook and tagged Kelly in it, knowing that Aiden would also see it and hopefully get the hint from the big thumbs-up she was doing in the photo.

'Oi, what are you doing now? Will you put that bloody phone away and pay attention!'

Kelly's tone made Billie jump so doing as she was told, she placed her phone back into her top pocket and then accepted the mug of coffee she was offered. 'I've posted a photo of us, to show Davey I'm out and having fun, and that I mean business.

He won't like it but I really don't care anymore. We're over. It's the end of that sad little story.'

'Hallelujah to that. So we need to go to yours one day this week and get your stuff, preferably when he's out.'

'Mmm, that might be tricky, but we can sort that out tomorrow, I'm more interested in where you got this money from. So come on, who's this bloke? You can't only tell me half a story, not now we're flatmates *and* best friends of course...' Billie was expecting the usual resistance but this time, Kelly didn't miss a beat.

'Oh him, the loser. He works for Stan, or used to. I bumped into him one night in the boozer on the corner, near the plumbing yard. I was looking for Stan so stayed and had a few drinks with Eddie who was drowning his sorrows, big time. Biscuits, that's what we need, do you want one? I've got some Penguins.' Kelly then stood up and went to fetch some.

Billie knew she was trembling on the inside and prayed it wouldn't show on the outside, so clung onto her mug in case her hands gave her away. Eddie... It was Eddie. Good guy Eddie who'd worked for Stan, the man he'd trusted the firm to while he was inside, who he'd probably confided in about Billie and their split. They worked side by side and had been mates as well as colleagues. It was all making sense now, how pillow talk had been stored up and used by Kelly when she needed it. By the time the biscuits were on the table, Billie had got her act together.

'But how did you manage to get all of this out of him... surely a few nude photos didn't do it?'

Kelly huffed. 'The man is a complete mess, sex-starved, stressed out and once I had the photos, he was desperate and shitting himself.'

'I don't get it.' Billie played dumb.

Kelly rolled her eyes. 'While he was knocking back the

scotch, he told me all about the IVF his wife was having and that he was on rations in the bedroom department... They save the sperm up or something? The details were a bit boring to be honest. Anyway, one thing led to another and we ended up in a taxi and then in bed. I have to tell you, though, all that stored up testosterone or whatever it is led to a very satisfactory session. He's quite cute, for an older guy, not like that knackered-looking thing of yours, and we hooked up a few more times. Like I said, I could tell Stan was losing interest and I suspected he was cheating so I thought, *Sod it*. Eddie was good in the sack and it was fun. He also had loose lips and told me all sorts about Stan, you know, about his perfect ex and why she dumped him. Then his wife *actually* managed to get pregnant and he wanted to call it a day but no way was I letting him get away with that. It was bad enough that Stan had cooled off so some old fart wasn't going to do the same. That's when I told him I wanted the money, otherwise I'd tell his wife *and* Stan, then he'd lose his family and his job.'

'So where did he get the money from?'

'I reckon he had his hand in the till. I really don't care. It's so not my problem. Luckily, I managed to get three lots of five grand out of him before he lost the plot and went on the sick so there's no point hassling him for more. Well, for the time being anyway.'

Billie's stomach was swirling, nerves causing havoc with her insides. It was like all the most terrifying, gut-clenching experiences rolled into one, but now she had a name, so almost pooing her pants would be worth it.

'Surely he'll get caught though, by his firm when they notice the money and stuff is missing.'

Kelly tutted before she replied. 'Like I said, there's absolutely nothing to tie me to him so even if he did mention my name I'd deny it but I doubt he's that stupid, do you? His wife will find out he's a cheat and an embezzler so it'll be bye-bye Daddy Eddie.' Kelly made a sad face, sticking out her bottom lip as she waved goodbye.

'Well remind me never to mess with you. I'm glad you've not got a chest freezer, because it would be full of the bodies of all your dead lovers. I wouldn't put it past you.' Billie took the jokey route as she checked the time. Forty minutes before they needed to head out so surely Kelly would go and get changed soon, then Billie could grab that phone and clear off.

'Ha, no dead bodies, not yet, which reminds me. We need to take some photos of your bruises in case Davey becomes a problem and we need to get rid of him.'

Billie laughed nervously, not quite sure what Kelly meant. 'I thought you said no bodies. But you're right, he might be hard to shake off and that's a worry. He's not going to like being dumped and he scares the crap out of me. The more I think about it the more I get cold feet.'

'Don't you dare chicken out now. Anyway, if he proves to be a problem I know how to get him out of the way, at least until we can bugger off abroad. It's not like he can track us down in Thailand, is it.'

There was something about what Kelly said that made Billie's skin prickle, and when the question popped into her head for a millisecond she was too scared to ask it, then her lips took over. 'What do you mean, "get him out of the way"?'

Kelly hesitated, and her expression was a bit sheepish then she looked away while she answered. 'Nothing, forget I said it, I was joking.'

But Billie couldn't let it drop and instinctively placed her hand on Kelly's arm and said the first thing that pinged into her head. 'No, I mean it, Kelly. I've taken enough good hidings from Davey so if you know a way to keep him away or teach him a lesson, I want to hear it. Or are you exaggerating?'

'You thought that about the money and I proved you wrong so it's about time you started believing me, don't you think?' Kelly looked annoyed and met Billie's eyes. It was more of a challenge than a question.

'Yeah, I do believe you but sometimes you make me edgy and I don't know where I am with you. All this time we've been mates I never knew I was hanging out with the demon blackmailer of Manchester and look, I'm still here. And I'm going to share a flat with you so I'd like to know who I'll be living with *and* most important, if you can keep me safe from Davey. Otherwise I might as well go home now.' Billie's mouth was dry and she really was getting a headache now. The pressure of all the new information was building in her temples and she wouldn't have been surprised if steam was escaping from her ears.

Kelly checked her watch and sighed. Okay, okay, you win but what I'm going to tell you now is our secret and I swear if you repeat it...' Kelly paused as if choosing her words carefully. 'Well I'll deny every single word, okay?'

Billie nodded, relieved that Kelly hadn't threatened murder because going on what she'd already confessed to, body parts in the freezer wasn't that far-fetched. 'I swear I won't tell anyone. It's between you and me.' She crossed her heart.

Kelly raised an eyebrow. 'What I meant was that if Davey turns out to be a pain, it's easy enough to get him into trouble, especially if we have photographic evidence of your injuries to back it up.'

'Yeah, I get that but photos don't prove he did it, do they? It could be anyone.'

Kelly did her exasperated face again and when she spoke sounded the same. 'Yes, which is why we have to set him up, so he attacks you again. Then we ring the police and have him arrested, plus we can tell them he's done it before. Believe me, it'll be easy.'

'What do you mean? Have you done it before? You know, set someone up?'

'Duh, yes of course I have, with Stan, you know the one I said raped me. He ended up doing a nice stretch so perhaps we should consider doing something similar to Davey. It'd serve him right. They might even end up cellmates, now that *would* be ironic.'

Billie's heart was going to explode and there was a whooshing sound in her ears but before she could even stutter a few words, Kelly jumped in. 'You look like you've seen a ghost. Are you really that shocked? It's just a suggestion so don't get your knickers in a twist. We might not even have to go that far.' Kelly turned away and began to apply lipstick, totally absorbed in what she was doing.

All Billie could think was, *She's a psycho, a cold-hearted psycho.* And without thinking, she mumbled a question, one more for her brain to log and store, the thing was, in her heart she already knew the answer. 'So you weren't actually raped then? You made it all up?' Billie could taste the bile in her throat and wasn't sure if she was going to cry or scream or punch Kelly in the face if she said yes. She had to keep control, breathe, in and out, stay calm.

'Not all of it... Well some of it, but the whole thing got out of hand and then there was no turning back and he ended up inside. Like I said, he was a cheat and deserved it, just like Davey does.'

38

Billie slumped into her chair. Kelly calmly squirted perfume onto her neck. Billie wanted to wrap her hands around it and squeeze and squeeze until she was dead in a heap on the floor.

Instead, she sucked in air through her nose and as silently as possible exhaled slowly. *Think Billie, think, don't bottle it now.*

'Well say something. Don't sit there looking shocked. I know you want to ask me why I did it and shit like that. So go on, get it off your chest then we can move on.' Kelly sounded like she'd confessed to pinching a lipstick from Boots, not framing an innocent man for rape.

'Sorry, sorry... I'm trying to get my head round it. So what do you mean, it "got out of hand"?'

'For fuck's sake, Agatha... do I have to spell it out? Seriously, Beth, you need to toughen up and wise up if you want to survive because there's a big bad world out there.'

'I know, I'm gobsmacked, that's all.' To Billie, that was the understatement of her whole life.

In response, Kelly rolled her eyes and began to pack away her make-up. 'Chill out, it's not like I've killed anyone, is it? Right, here it is in a nutshell.'

Billie couldn't even summon a response because she was on the verge of tears.

When Kelly noticed, she apologised. 'Sorry, that was harsh and I know you've had a crappy Christmas. I didn't mean to upset you and I can be a ratty cow sometimes. This is a lot to take in and my acid gob doesn't help. Right, are you sitting comfortably? Let Aunty Kelly tell you a story.'

There it was again, the switch from one to another, the critical to contrite, aggressive to slightly patronising but whichever personality Kelly adopted, right there and then Billie was too appalled to speak so instead she nodded quickly.

'I'd gone round there to get my stuff but was having second thoughts about binning Stan off completely. I thought maybe I could keep him on a hook, to amuse myself with I suppose, and what better way than through sex. I'm really good at it so knew I could persuade him. I'd had a key cut yonks before: I like to make contingency plans. It's wise, staying one step ahead of the game, so I let myself in and waited for him upstairs. It was all too easy, getting him into bed and afterwards he didn't ask me to leave so I stayed put and fell asleep.

'When I woke up and went downstairs he was out of it on the sofa and his phone lit up and I saw the message on the screen, from fucking Billie, his perfect ex. I told you about it, asking to go for chips. Anyway, I saw red and gave him a slap. I was so mad. We'd had sex and I felt used because the text confirmed my suspicions that she was coming home and they were getting back together.

'I lost the plot and went upstairs to get my things, but he followed me and the more he told me to calm down the angrier I got. I was punching him and then he slapped me really hard so I grabbed a statue, we struggled and I fell. It didn't last long, and once I'd stopped fighting back he let me go and went downstairs.

'I knew that was it, we were really over. I just wanted revenge and knew how to do it when I felt the cut on my head. It was so easy. I grabbed my clothes and ripped them up, put my coat on and crept downstairs. I could hear him in the loo so ran past and managed to get to the front door as he came out, then ran as fast as I could to the house across the street. They called the police and Stan was arrested. Boom!'

Billie's hands were clasped together, her armpits were dripping with sweat, her whole body was on fire because a pot of anger was bubbling deep inside, spreading through her veins, pulsing in her brain that wanted to know just one thing.

'But why did you carry on, you know, let them charge him and send him to prison? You could have stopped it, but you didn't.'

'It had gone too far. Simple as that. I'd done a video interview, had the examinations and then there were my parents to consider. I couldn't go back on it then, not when everyone knew. I'd have been the one in trouble not him and no way was I going to let that happen, no chance.'

'Don't you feel bad that a man is in prison because you lied?' Billie's voice was barely a whisper.

'No, I don't. He was a cheat and used me so he deserved it. Now is that it? We can't stand here talking about the past all day. We've got to get ready and you can't turn up looking like that. Do you want to borrow something of mine? Come on, the saddos will be waiting for their star turn to arrive.'

Billie felt physically sick, dazed and now, even more confused. 'Sorry, who do you mean, what saddos?'

'The whiners, you know, Jude and her little gang of downtrodden women who haven't got the sense to get out of their miserable little lives. And while we're there you need to take a good look around and be grateful you met me otherwise that's how you could've ended up. Now come on, get a wiggle on.'

Kelly had turned again, cocky as hell, and grabbed Billie's arm as if to guide her from the room and hurry her along.

Billie yanked it away, couldn't bear to be touched, and now, the anger she'd held in for so long was evident in her voice when she rounded on Kelly. 'Seriously, is that how you think of them? Is that how you think of me? All those women are there for a reason: they need help and support because they are trapped, or hurting and damaged. I can't believe you'd say that after you've listened to their stories and they listened to yours. You sat there, Kelly, you held their hands, helped them out. They think you're their friend and now you're mocking them and me.'

Billie noticed that Kelly just about managed to cover her smirk but the exasperated sigh escaped and when she spoke, her voice was laced with sarcasm, harsh too. 'Oh stop being mard. I'm only speaking the truth. Once today's over I'd already decided I'm not going back. They've served their purpose and I can't be arsed with it and anyway, we'll be jetting off to the sun soon and I don't need that lot making me feel miserable. Now come on, look, we're going to be late.'

Billie couldn't take any more. She had to get out of there and see Aiden. She was losing it, barely hanging onto her temper but she still hadn't got the phone. Maybe they didn't need it. It could be useless anyway, and Eddie might confess. *What to do, what to do?* Panic was washing over her as she tried to focus and think. 'I'm not coming. You can go by yourself. I don't feel up to it.'

Kelly began gathering her things from the table and her head snapped around when she heard, then came the cajoling tone. 'Oh don't be like that. I want you to come and support me in case I get nervous. That's what besties are for.'

'I said I'm not coming.' Billie grabbed her coat from the chair and as she did, her phone began to ring but in her haste, before she had time to even see who was calling, it flipped from the top pocket and crashed to the floor before skidding across the tiles. The ringing stopped as Billie scooped it up and saw the screen was smashed and black. 'Fuck, that's all I need.'

Kelly was blocking the door and looked angry. 'Hey, what's wrong? Okay, look, I'm sorry if I offended you about the group, you know me – a spade's a spade – but I was only messing about. I got carried away so let's start again and I promise, I'll be really nice to them when I get there. Is that a deal? Do you forgive me?'

Dear God, thought Billie as she squared up to Kelly in the doorway, *she really is like fucking Jekyll and Hyde.* She had to play this carefully. She risked arousing Kelly' suspicions or starting a full-on row.

'Yes I forgive you and I'm sorry for being a touchy cow but seriously, I need to go outside. I feel sick and my head is pounding so a bit of fresh air will do me good.'

A whiny voice cut through the tension. 'Are you sure that's all that's wrong? And you can't bail on me now, not after I've bared my soul to you. Please Beth, don't be like this.'

'Like I said, I don't feel well. It's the wine and the chocolate biscuits, and the pills, that's all.' There was a voice inside Billie's head screaming *GET OUT* and it provoked a knee-jerk reaction. Panic, desperation and rage were building by the second, like someone shaking a bottle of pop then taking off the lid. When it exploded, Kelly would have felt the full force of Billie's strength as she pushed her aside, ramming her back into the door jamb. With lemonade fizzing through her veins Billie almost ran to the door and pulled it open, ignoring Kelly's pleas for her to come back.

Then firm hands grabbed her coat and she was forced to stop. Billie found Kelly's face pushed against hers. Angry eyes accompanied the incredulous voice. 'Beth! What the fuck is wrong with you?'

'Kelly, let go, I want to be on my own, to think stuff through, okay? It's all been a bit much and I need to get my head straight, that's all.'

Kelly relaxed her grip. 'Straight about what? I don't understand.'

Billie said the first thing that zapped into her head. 'About Davey, and moving out. It's a big step even though he is a twat.'

Kelly squinted, eyeing Billie as she spoke. 'You won't tell anyone will you, what I said about Stan and Eddie, promise?'

'No, of course not, promise. I said I wouldn't and anyway, all that Stan stuff has got nothing to do with me. It's your business so don't worry. We're mates, our secret okay? My head's a mess so you get going to the centre. You don't really need me there.'

Kelly still had questions. 'Are you going to come back? Please don't tell me you're going home to him.'

Billie managed to twist free from Kelly's grip as she spoke and pulled her reassuring voice out of the bag, anything to get away. 'No chance. I think I'll go and see my mum, let her know I'm okay and get my pressies. I'll come back in a bit. We can get a takeaway or something, and I'll try to get my phone fixed then I can text you. You'd best hurry up or you'll be late. See you later, okay?'

Billie backed away from Kelly who looked a mixture of crest-fallen and suspicious, but maybe the thought of missing her big moment snapped her out of it because she suddenly rallied. That psycho smile was too bright, fake as fuck really, and then she began to wave Billie off.

'Okay, you do look a bit peaky... text as soon as your phone is fixed. The takeaway's on me, whatever you fancy.' Then she turned and shut the door.

Without a second's hesitation Billie took the steps three at a time before bursting through the main doors onto the street, sucking in air. Despite the tears and the angry hysterical sobs that made her gasp and struggle for breath, Billie's legs sprang into action and she ran.

People stared and one man called out and asked if she was okay as Billie raced almost blindly towards where she prayed Aiden was still waiting in his car. She thought her heart would explode but the sight of a familiar face broke through the panic, he was there, Aiden, running towards her, his arms outstretched. When their bodies collided Billie collapsed into him, crying and gulping her apologies, ignoring his pleas for her to shush as he frantically wiped tears from her face.

'I'm sorry, I'm sorry, it's no good, Aiden, she told me, she admitted it, she said it to my face that she lied but we have no proof, I should have recorded her... why didn't I record her? And I couldn't get the phone but we can get Doog to break in and pinch it, yes, that's what we'll do. But it was Eddie, she got the money from him. Let's go and see him right now, make him go to the police and tell them. That'll work, won't it? Stan can't stay there anymore. He didn't do it, Aiden. My Stan told the truth, he didn't do it...' Billie was now a gibbering wreck but responded when she felt Aiden shake her hard.

He was almost shouting in her face. 'Billie, STOP! Listen, Billie, just shush. It's okay, I know, I saw it all, everything that Kelly said. It's going to be okay now, I promise.'

Aiden fixed Billie with his grey eyes, waiting until her breathing slowed and she could take in what he was saying.

'Now listen to me, Billie. I don't know how the hell you did it, because knowing you it was a fluke, but, somehow, after you posted a selfie of you and Kelly, you hit the going live button and everything that happened in that kitchen has been shared on Facebook. Do you understand?'

Billie shook her head, still confused.

'You were live on Facebook. Me and Tom, and whoever is on

your friends list, saw it too. Tom's making a record of it right now. Do you understand what I'm saying, Billie?'

When Billie looked at Aiden with a dazed expression he spelled it out for her. 'She confessed, Billie. I saw it and so did everyone else. We have proof. You did it, sweetheart, you proved Stan is innocent and now we can get him out. Billie, do you understand what I'm saying? Stan's coming home.'

When the words finally broke through her hiccups and tears and parted the fog in her brain, Billie's eyes widened as they began to make sense and just when she'd managed to get a grip, relief engulfed her followed by another wave of emotion that teetered on the brink of rapture and hysteria. As she rested her head on Aiden's shoulder and let it all out, he smiled into her hair, nodding and winking at the passers-by who looked on with curiosity.

Once she was able, he steered her back towards the car. There was somewhere they needed to be, and someone they both wanted to see.

39

Kelly was in a flap, pulling up her suit trousers and shoving on her shoes when her mobile trilled into life again, and the name Jude appeared on the screen. In no mood for being mithered, Kelly grabbed the phone and disconnected the call, because chatting would only slow her down. She'd drunk far too much wine so after she'd stashed the money, this time in the Crunchy Nut Cornflakes box, she ordered a taxi that was now waiting outside. Checking herself in the mirror as she pulled on her jacket Kelly thought she looked okay. She smoothed down her hair and then rushed along the hall, throwing her mobile into her bag and locking the door.

Inside the taxi, Kelly searched her bag for some chewing gum – chardonnay breath wasn't appropriate and if she'd had time, another cup of coffee would have gone down a treat because she still felt slightly tipsy. It was all bloody Beth's fault, coming round in a state, asking for help then going all weird when Kelly had told her exactly how to sort her life out. *And I can't believe how she stormed off like that when we were supposed to be going to the centre together. That's what you got for trying to help someone and cheer them up.*

Now, thanks to Beth's phone getting smashed she couldn't even ring and ask her if she was okay.

On top of that, there was this nagging feeling that Kelly was finding hard to ignore, despite the excitement of her impending telly interview. Kelly half wished she hadn't been so forthcoming about Stan. She always talked too much when she'd had a few. *But I trust Beth. Of course I do, after all, we're going to be flatmates. Just like I planned all along.* Surely Beth wouldn't turn down the chance of free lodgings *and* a holiday to boot, not for that scumbag Davey or because Kelly's confession had shocked her. *Christ, people do worse things every day of the week. All you had to do was watch the news to see that.*

The traffic was a nightmare and the taxi driver obviously wasn't inclined to take a diversion or put his foot down and Kelly was considering walking when her phone vibrated in her bag. Tutting, she saw two more missed calls from Jude and one from Lynda – *Probably trying to cadge a lift to the centre*, thought Kelly – and one from Adele, another of the regulars. All of them must be wondering where she was.

After firing off the same text to each, saying she was in a taxi and five minutes away, Kelly checked her make-up and went over all the things she wanted to say in the interview. Once she'd had her five minutes of fame it was *adios, amigos*. Like she'd said to Beth, her days of listening to that lot at the centre drone on were coming to an end because there was only so much she could take. Now that travelling with Beth was on the cards maybe it was time to ditch the counselling idea and focus on having a good time and living the life.

There it was again, that voice in her head casting doubt, leaving her with an uneasy feeling about Beth because her reaction wasn't what she'd expected. Instead of admiration for how Kelly had dealt with Stan and the possibility of getting rid of Davey the same way, she'd gone all righteous and acted like she was disappointed, especially when she mentioned the women at the group. Still, it was a lot to get her head around and she'd had a rough Christmas, but surely Beth respected Kelly for sharing her secret... that's what best friends do.

Then again, what if Beth *was* actually the same as all the women she'd met lately, who still loved the bloke who treated them like dirt, and deep down, she had no intention of leaving Davey? Perhaps her flit was merely to teach him a lesson? Beth probably thought a couple of nights away would bring Davey to his knees. *Yeah, like that ever worked!*

Kelly rarely cried but the thought that she'd lost Beth caused a lump in her throat that she quickly swallowed, forcing back tears that were misting her vision of the community centre as it came into sight. But there was no time to worry about that now, and as the taxi slowed, Kelly told herself that Beth would come round and be glad to move out of those grotty flats and into a nice new-build block. Beth wasn't a grass: her type hated the law and anyway, who would believe her? Who would she even tell?

After paying the driver, Kelly raced up the concrete ramp towards the entrance, passing the white car emblazoned with the local radio logo, parked next to the regional news van. A smile played on Kelly's lips as she thought of them all waiting inside, checking their watches, eager for their star guest to arrive. Sandra, who worked on reception, raised her hand and looked like she wanted to say something as Kelly breezed past the glass panel but there was no time to chat. Instead, she made for the meeting room, slightly nervous but more in anticipation than anything so before she pushed open the door, she took a deep breath and then entered.

On first glance, Kelly thought there'd been a poor turnout because the chairs were empty; but there was a buzz of conversation to her right which drew her attention. There, she saw a crowd of regulars, plus a few strangers, obviously the reporters and dignitaries. She had imagined that Jude would greet her first and then introduce her to the others. They'd spend a few moments making small talk and then the filming would begin, Kelly at the centre of it all. What she hadn't envisaged was the hush that fell over the room when everyone turned to face her, so quiet that you could hear the teacups clinking against saucers. Someone coughed, and there were whispers too. For a moment Kelly was taken aback but rather chuffed they were all staring and then as expected, Jude began to make her way over. There was urgency in her stride and a very cold look on her face.

Shit, thought Kelly, *I must be really late.*

When Jude reached Kelly's side she took her by the arm and steered her towards the door which she opened with one hand as she spoke. 'Kelly, would you mind stepping outside for a moment, I need to talk to you about something? I've been waiting at the entrance for you for ages. I think it's best you don't speak to the others so–'

Jude didn't get a chance to finish because before they'd made it into the corridor another voice cut through the mutterings in the room.

It was Adele. 'Oi, I want a word with you.' Adele was marching towards Kelly, much faster than Jude had. Her face was etched with anger, her jaw set firm and her eyes squinted.

Kelly placed a nervous hand on her chest, confused and slightly embarrassed because the whole room was focusing on her and not in a good way. Eyes glared, hands were on hips, faces set like stone. 'Me... why, what's the matter?'

Jude sighed and tried again to pull Kelly towards the door but Adele was too quick. 'This is what's the matter, you spiteful lying cow!'

Adele held up her mobile and held it towards Kelly who stared at the screen, trying to make sense of what she was seeing. It couldn't be but it was, a video of her, and at the top of the screen it said Beth Daley was live. Kelly swallowed down dread as she watched the scene in horror. She was in her kitchen putting on make-up and on the table in plain view was the money... and *Oh dear God, no*, she was telling Beth about Eddie.

Blood does actually drain from your body. Kelly could feel it happening to her, like sand running through an hourglass, and it made her body feel cold. Or was that fear? And now her lips felt funny and her mouth had gone dry, preventing words, but she didn't have any because her brain wasn't working properly.

'Come on, gobshite, explain this to all us saddos! You know, the ones you've been taking the piss out of behind our backs, we'd love to know what you really think of us, wouldn't we, ladies?' Adele turned to the other women who were now crowding around Kelly.

Andi spoke next. 'Yeah, we don't take kindly to being called miserable, downtrodden whiners by some slag who set her boyfriend up and sent him to jail.'

Kelly felt her legs go and Jude grip her arm. *They know, they know about Stan*, she realised. And then the blood that had drained from her body suddenly returned in a whoosh of panic, causing her head to spin and her cheeks to flush. Now she really did want to leave the room. She had to get out, she had to run.

Whipping around, ignoring the taunts and Jude's requests for calm, Kelly pushed her out of the way and began to run towards the entrance that was now a haze of blue flashing lights and black-clad figures. Halting, Kelly looked over her shoulder but her way was blocked by Adele, Jude and the rest of the women. Looking towards reception she saw Sandra, arms crossed, impassive. Kelly was trapped, there was nowhere to go. The police were in the building now, approaching slowly and it was then that she saw her, Beth the Traitor.

After that, so many things happened at once, the police asking her to accompany them to the station, like it was a date or something. Then she was led away but managed to keep her head held high as they walked down the ramp, past Beth who was standing next to that scumbag Davey. It seemed he scrubbed up well in a smart suit under a grey overcoat and his arm was wrapped protectively around her shoulder. *Probably been to a funeral, or court, the druggie scumbag.* The thought caused her to grimace.

Beth didn't say a word, but she did smile as they passed. *Or was it a smirk? The bitch.* At the car, the policewoman placed her hand on Kelly's head and guided her into the back seat, and then the door slammed shut. As they drove away from the community centre Kelly turned her head slightly, just enough to see a bank of mobile phones trained on her, and further back a man with a large video camera perched on his shoulder. At this Kelly smiled and rested back in her seat. It looked like she was going to make it onto the telly after all.

40

Stan and Billie huddled together and watched the murky waves roll onto the beach as the wind blew in from the Irish Sea, making the windmill that was wedged into Iris's pushchair spin like crazy, keeping her occupied and giggling. It was freezing on the promenade yet there were plenty of other tourists, dog walkers and joggers who thought that Blackpool in February was the place to be.

It was the norm for Stan to lapse into long periods of quiet, where he would just stare, his dark eyes fixed and sometimes tearful, lost in a place only he could visit. Billie knew it was best to leave him there for a while. He always returned to her when he'd got it out of his system. It was his way of dealing with what he'd been through but sometimes she wondered if the anger over what he'd endured would ever fade because the nightmares didn't seem to. That's when she could help, hold him close and remind him he was safe at home, with her and Iris.

He didn't bottle everything up though. He did talk it through with her. They'd learned their lesson and vowed not to make the mistakes of the past. But perhaps that was because Stan got it now, what it felt like to be trapped in your own head and tormented by the demons that lived there. On the positive side he loved life, wanted to live every moment of every day to the full and saw the wonder in the smallest of things that she took for granted, like privacy and fresh air, proper knives and forks, Heinz beans, Sky telly, freedom.

And he was a brilliant dad and seemed intent on making up for lost time which included getting up for Iris if she cried in the night, no matter how many times. He'd watched all the videos of her since the day she was born, over and over. He even changed nappies albeit with a tea towel wrapped around his face so he looked like a retching bandit, much to his mum's disgust.

A huge seagull swooped low, searching for a morsel of food and then landed by the pushchair, pecking hopefully at the pavement. Billie peeped at Iris who was sucking on her dummy, eyelids drooping, mesmerised by the kaleidoscope of windmill colours. Then she risked a glance at Stan who was still wandering through his garden of memories. She hoped some of them were better than others.

Like the day he walked out of the prison gates and they were all waiting for him.

Billie had cried so much, happy, angry, relieved tears. While she sat in Aiden's car and listened as he rang one of his contacts on the force and in a voice that could barely contain his determination, he more or less demanded then begged to have Kelly arrested immediately. He was even more forthright with Stan's solicitor who he told to get his finger out and down to the police station where they would produce the evidence.

Next, Billie had attempted to tell Sue and Darren but couldn't get the words out so Aiden took over and they both listened on speakerphone as mother and brother started screaming and cheering like crazy people, and then made Iris cry. Again that night on the phone when Stan called, and during the hours and hours that stretched while they waited for an emergency hearing and the judge to agree to bail.

Since then it had been a time of adjustment for the whole family. Because Kelly had been totally discredited and her testimony was wholly unreliable, after a short court hearing with the legal teams on both sides the CPS offered no evidence and the judge ordered that Stan be acquitted of all offences. Once the news came in, they had held a small family celebration, plus Aiden and Jed and later that evening Doog and his girlfriend Holly. Even Billie's mum and dad showed willing, much to everyone's surprise.

They all still had their moments though, mostly in the form of fickle friends and hurtful memories. Stan was adamant there would be no second chances and he'd drawn a red line under the word *disloyal*.

At least now Sue could walk down the street with her head held high but Billie knew she would never forget being shunned and whispered about. Sue would always remember the day her son was convicted and imprisoned, the hours of worry she endured, wondering what was happening to him behind bars.

The same went for Darren too. His life was back on track but amidst his successes and sunny disposition, now and then a hint of bitterness seeped through. Maybe injustice would always blight him, even in his subconscious. Billie hoped not.

There was still more to face. Kelly's trial was looming, another hurdle to leap but they would do it together, all of them on team Stan the Man. Kelly had eventually been charged with wasting police time, perjury, perverting the course of justice and blackmail. She was looking at a lengthy prison sentence if found guilty. Billie had to believe in the same justice system that had wrongly convicted Stan but after that, she had no space in her head for thoughts of Kelly. She refused to allow her mind to ponder the psycho's fate, because as far as she was concerned Kelly could rot. She'd ruined enough lives, not just Stan's and his family, but Eddie's too. Because of his affair with Kelly, Eddie's life was in tatters and once he'd faced his hearing to answer charges of embezzlement and theft, how he would repair his marriage was anybody's guess.

Then there was Kelly's parents who had no doubt been shamed and shocked by their daughter's crimes, not to mention the trouble she'd caused before she even met Stan.

But all that belonged in the past and now, Billie wasn't going to allow Kelly to taint the future. As far as she was concerned, the future started in Kelly's kitchen when instead of tapping the photo icon on her phone and uploading another damning selfie, she'd absentmindedly pressed the one next to it, Live. Unwittingly, she'd broadcast Kelly's frank confession to all of their Facebook friends, including the secret group containing the women from the community centre. It had turned into a joke now, whenever she took a photo but Billie didn't care because it was the best mistake she'd ever made.

Feeling movement from Stan beside her she smiled to welcome him back from his thoughts. He tucked Iris in, covering her gloved hands with the blanket then turned her pram away from the sea. When he finished, he wrapped his arm around Billie's shoulder and pulled her close. 'I think she's had enough sea breeze for one day. That windmill was three quid well spent. Who said kids today aren't easily pleased?' Stan flicked the hood of his parka over his head then dragged Billie's bobble hat over her eyes, one of his favourite annoying tricks.

'Oi, pack it in.' Billie rearranged her hat and snuggled closer.

Stan seemed in the mood to chat. 'So, what is it you wanted to talk to me about? Your big idea? I've been really patient up to now but my arse is getting numb and I'm starving so go on, I'm all ears.'

Billie had mentioned she had stuff to discuss but at home with Iris and with Stan getting stuck in at the firm, there never seemed to be a quiet moment. But now felt like a good time. 'Promise you won't laugh and hear me out.'

'Promise, plumber's honour.' Stan made a weird hand signal that looked very rude.

Ignoring the gesture, Billie took a breath and went for it. 'I've been making some enquiries and decided I want to go to university, in Manchester obviously, to study law. It was Carol who suggested it and ever since my head has been buzzing with ideas and plans for the future. But you might think I'm completely mad, or a dreamer if I tell you what they are.'

'Babe, whatever you want to do is fine by me. I'll pay the fees. I don't want you being a poor starving student.' Stan kissed the top of her head.

'Well that's very nice of you but I might even qualify for a student loan. Anyway, I've bagged myself a part-time job so I can save up.' Billie was enjoying the look of surprise on Stan's face.

'You really have been busy haven't you – but you don't need a job. I can look after you and anyway, where is it at, this job? And what about Iris, and my bloody tea that I expect on the table every night when I get home?' Stan was teasing as usual but got a dig in the ribs for his trouble.

'Just listen and I'll explain. I didn't want to say anything until I was sure but I am now, and with your support it will all work out fine, for everyone. So is your numb bum sitting comfortably?' Billie got the thumbs-up from Stan, who also made the zipped lips signal but she didn't expect it to last. Everyone knew he was a terrible interrupter. 'Then I shall begin.'

Once the shock and awe of Stan's release and Kelly's arrest died down and everyone settled into a new and much happier routine, Billie began to think about her own future and role in life. They were due to move into a new house, and Stan was back at work full time aided by his new right-hand man and head of security, Doog. It was him that unearthed the scam that Eddie had run to pilfer and pay his blackmailer, and he discovered a stash of stolen plumbing equipment stored in, of all places, a lock-up in Stan's storage facility. Billie had already worked out that the bond Stan and Doog had formed inside continued on the outside. And then there was Quentin. Stan had promised him a job as soon as he was released; doing what she had no idea. But Billie suspected that it made Stan feel safe, having Doog around, and eventually Quentin, and that's all she cared about.

The thing was, during the day, in between caring for Iris, her mind and heart was drawn back to the women at the community centre and that yearning to do something constructive turned into an urge. They had got under her skin. She felt a bond that was probably borne from being a victim of a violent assault, whatever, their faces and their plights still haunted Billie. So did the lies she'd told.

It wasn't lost on Billie that to expose Kelly, she herself had become a liar. Not only that, she'd adopted another persona, become duplicitous, hiding her activities from her own family, spent time with women who trusted her, and it didn't sit well.

For this reason she had been back to see the women in the group and explained everything because she felt she owed them that. The humility and understanding they showed her in return for honesty simply overwhelmed her, as did the wider picture, the enormity of the situation so many women found themselves in. The incidences of domestic violence and rape were on the increase, juxtaposed to the rates of reported incidents and the help available to all victims of violence, resources were under great pressure which was a cause for concern.

Billie had no intention or desire to fight crime as she had done before, but she did have a smouldering need to make a difference, to tackle injustices in the law and society, to fight for change and the resources that were so lacking. But how?

It was Carol who gave her the notion that studying law might be a start. It would be a long road but along the way Billie could still volunteer and gain experience. And now Billie could think of nothing else. In the space of a week, she had set the wheels in motion and if all went well at her interview, and she was offered a place at Manchester University, she would accept the offer of a part-time job from Aiden. Sue and her mum would share childcare and Stan could make his own bloody tea.

Billie had studied Stan's face throughout her well-rehearsed explanation and now, she was eager to hear what he thought. 'So, go on, what do you think? And don't dick about. Be sensible and honest, I mean it.'

Stan cowered dramatically then pulled her close and landed a kiss on her forehead. 'I think it's a brilliant idea and I'm with you all the way. I've never seen you fired up like this and I can tell how much you want to do it. I'm proud of you, babe, and that's even before you've put pen to paper because I know you'll smash uni. I'm a bit worried about you working for Aiden. You won't be doing anything dangerous, will you?'

Billie shook her head. 'No, not at all, I already made that clear. No way do I want to be in a situation that's remotely life-threatening or scary. I've had enough of that to last a lifetime. It's more research or sitting in a car taking photographs of cheating husbands, or wives. Nosy parker stuff like that. I'll flippin' love it.'

They were both laughing now but then, Billie took a serious tone. 'I really do want to make a difference though, Stan, for women like Adele and Lynda, and all the faceless women who haven't got a voice and are too scared to speak out and ask for help, or who get let down by the system or slip through the net. I'm talking about everything here, physical and mental cruelty, sexual assault, domestic violence. And not only women: it happens to men too. Once they've found the courage to speak out, they need their voice to be heard. But there's another type of victim, the one nobody believes, who is accused of something they didn't do and as a consequence they lose their liberty.'

'Like me you mean?'

'Yes, Like you. Do you remember what you said to me that day when I came to visit? You were so angry because nobody was speaking out for you, your voice wasn't being heard, you said, "I never gave any thought what it must be like to be at the receiving end of injustice, how it feels when nobody believes you and nobody listens. Well now I do because it's happened to me too."' At this, Billie saw a shadow cross Stan's face so carried on, hoping to convince him of her aim.

'I've not been able to get it out of my head especially because the Me Too movement is all over the news. But I think it applies to everyone, to many, many situations. How many times have you heard someone say, "yeah, it happened to me too?" Lives are being wrecked by violence in the home. The ripple effect touches everyone, rips families apart, as do horrific attacks on women and men. But false accusations do terrible damage of their own and make everyone's job harder, and it's a slap in the face for real victims. If I can make a difference, do something to help every type of victim, then I don't care how long the road is, at least I had a go.'

Stan remained silent so Billie soldiered on. 'Perhaps it starts with education, in schools and the home, making sure that boys and girls understand that no means no. And that they should respect each other and themselves, and their bodies. Nobody should use sex as a weapon to control or have power over someone, and definitely not use it for revenge. It's like kids are losing their way, and these kids grow into adults and it scares me so one way or another I'm determined to do something, whatever it takes.

'I think it's time men and women stood together instead of letting sex tear them apart. We shouldn't let a phrase come between us, it should empower us all, encourage us to join hands because the word "me" is universal, genderless. Me is everyone.'

Despite the bitter wind Billie's cheeks were hot and her heart was bursting with something she could only describe as passion. She believed she could do it, she really did but she wanted Stan to believe in her too, like she had him.

In answer to her question, he puffed his cheeks out and made a whistling noise. 'Well all I can say is God help anyone who gets in your way because it sounds like you've made your mind up and I wouldn't want to cross you, that's for sure.'

'So you're with me then?'

Stan smiled. 'One hundred per cent.'

Billie was awash with relief and happiness and now she'd got everything off her chest she didn't want the day to descend into gloom, so gave him a peck on the cheek and left things there.

Stan returned it with a hug. 'Now you've sorted the next three years of our lives out I think we need to go and celebrate cos from what I remember I promised you fish, chips and mushy peas.'

Billie laughed. 'And two rounds of bread and butter and a pot of tea. And treacle sponge and custard.'

Standing, Stan held out his hand. 'Whatever madam desires,

because you know what, Billie, I bloody love you, and I always will.'

Taking his hand, Billie felt him heave her upwards and as he began to push Iris towards the restaurant, she linked his arm and squeezed it tight. 'And I bloody love you, Stan, always have and always will.'

EPILOGUE

Five Years Later

The screams woke him first, the men in other cells, crying and yelling, then the unmistakeable sound of the key in the lock that they wiggled from side to side to open the stubborn catch. Next, the creak of the door and the smell of stale prison air, cabbage and sweat that gushed in and mingled with that on the inside: a shared toilet and smelly socks. He never opened his eyes until the last minute, when the shuffling feet were by his bed and the dark figures were on him, a razor blade glinted and he waited for the slash, then the pain. Their rancid breath lingered on his face and hateful words touched his ear causing him to shrink away. Then he would start to scream for help but no sound came out, no matter how hard he tried and the muscles in his neck strained and stretched, he was mute. Then hands on his chest, his face, a voice, one he recognised, not cruel, but kind and soothing, bringing him home, out of the dark.

Stan gasped and struggled for breath as Billie told him where he was, that he was safe, it was a dream... and soon his heartbeat returned to normal and his eyes focused on the room, in the villa, in Votsi.

Billie's hand remained on his chest that was drenched with sweat and as always she remained silent while he gathered his wits and the recurring nightmare faded. It was their routine and it worked.

Patting her hand in the half-darkness, Stan spoke softly so not to wake the kids. 'I'm okay now, you go back to sleep. I'll go and get some water. Sorry, Bill.'

He kissed her head and waited until she'd turned on her side and drifted off. No need for words because she understood. Stan dragged off his T-shirt then padded along the tiled hallway in bare feet and checked on Iris and Ernie.

His long-legged daughter with the sun-kissed arms and bleached hair looked more like her mermaid mum with every day, while their two-year-old terror was the image of Daddy Stan, all gypsy curls and broody eyes. Both had kicked off their sheets but slept soundly after a day on the beach that bordered their holiday home, Billie's favourite place in the world and somewhere they bolted to at every opportunity, her busy job in the city permitting.

Continuing on to the kitchen, Stan took a bottle of ice-cold water from the fridge and glugged it down while watching the lights flickering along the harbour wall in the distance. Replacing the bottle he then made his way back to the bedroom and checked his phone, not particularly expecting a message but noting the time, 4am which meant it was 2am in Manchester.

Climbing into bed, calm now, he allowed himself a wry smile. It was also one of contentment and satisfaction. While he lay in his villa, next to his beautiful wife and his gorgeous children sleeping next door, Stan relaxed in the knowledge that two thousand miles away, his trusted workforce would be keeping the home fires burning and the cogs of his little empire turning, and making sure the specific instructions he'd left were carried out. Doog was good like that.

Yawning, Stan turned on his side and slipped his arm over Billie, pulling her close, then closed his eyes and let sleep take him.

~

PC Gibson and Ward were having a cheeky break, keeping their heads down in a side street while they ate their burgers, when the shout came over the radio. Gibson knew they'd have to respond but was in no rush, not for this one anyway.

'Finish your brew then we'll get going. That woman's a pain in the arse and I've been round there about five times in the last few weeks. The community bobby is sick of her too.'

Ward yawned and blew on his coffee that was miles too hot to drink. 'Why, who is she?'

'An ex-con, remember her? Might be a bit before your time though. She's the one who framed her boyfriend and got him locked up for rape. Poor sod managed to prove he was innocent in the end but he still did time. She's out now and insists she's being stalked and never off the bloody phone. I reckon she's got a screw loose or one of those attention disorders, but whatever it is we've got better things to do.' Gibson scrunched his wrapper.

'Attention disorder? What's one of those?'

Gibson tutted. 'You know, when they make stuff up so they are the centre of attention, the clue's in the title. What the hell do they teach you lot these days?'

Ward looked thoughtful, then the light dawned. 'Ah, I know who you mean now, but we have to check though. What if it's real and someone is after her? We'll all be in the shit then.'

'Or she could be crying wolf.'

'What's that?' Ward spoke with his mouth full.

Gibson looked incredulous. 'Are you taking the piss or what?' When Ward shrugged Gibson shook his head and started the engine. 'Come on then, let's get it over with but I'm warning you, she's a nutter, and on the way, I'll tell you a nice story about a nasty wolf and a fibber.' Gibson huffed and headed towards the estate, in no mood for gormless newbies, time-wasters and ex-cons, especially someone like Kelly Langton.

Kelly gripped the phone as she peeped through the cracks in the curtain and scanned the street below. Everything looked the same along the row of houses opposite. The same unkempt gardens, second-hand cars and dog-fouled streets that showed no signs of lurking yobbos or careless drunks who were looking for a wheelie bin to piss up or deposit their tray of chips and curry. That was a ridiculous notion anyway because round there it was more likely to end up splattered across the pavement or left on your wall, along with an empty can of Stella.

There had definitely been someone outside though. She heard the side gate creak but this time, the front one was closed shut. At least whoever was tormenting her hadn't tipped the green bin over again because she was sick of scraping up the contents in the morning, just like she was getting tired of having flat tyres and her windscreen wipers bent backwards. And now she was paranoid about her brakes being tampered with. Kelly was actually getting paranoid about everything, if she was honest.

Where the hell are the police? She'd rung them over forty-five minutes ago and still nothing. They should be here checking she was okay and there wasn't an intruder in the garden. So much for visible policing. Her dad wasn't picking up either so in temper, she rang the landline. Surely he'd hear that.

A sleepy voice answered but Kelly didn't give it time to continue. 'Mum, put Dad on quickly, I need him to come round. I think there's someone in the backyard. I keep hearing noises.'

When she finally got a word in her mother's voice sounded vexed. 'Kelly, it's the middle of the night and this is the second time this week. It's probably just a cat or a fox. We hear them all the time here–'

'No Mum, it isn't a bloody fox. Why don't you believe me? I'm telling you someone is stalking me and I need Dad to come round and check because the police can't be arsed. I rang ages ago and they're still not here.'

'Don't you swear at me, Kelly, and I'll thank you to watch your tone.' With that there was a muffled conversation and the phone passed over.

'Kelly.'

'Dad, at last, can you come round quick as you can?'

A loud sigh was audible, then the terse reply. 'No Kelly, I'm not coming round. Your flat is secure and the extra locks I put on the back door would keep an army out so I want you to stop this. It's making your mum ill again. It was your choice to get a flat when you could have stayed here with us but no, you had to have your own way and we've helped you all we could–'

Kelly didn't give him time to finish, her short fuse lit instantly by his attitude. 'Oh yeah, and bring shame to your door! You hated it when I came out of prison and only let me stay because the halfway house was a shithole. You couldn't wait to see the back of me and I'm sure your stuck-up neighbours felt the same. So don't make out you gave me the deposit out of the goodness of your hearts, you pair of hypocrites!'

'Right, Kelly, that's it, I'm putting the phone down and I'll ring you in the morning when you've calmed down and have a civil tongue in your head. Your mum's upset now so I'm going. Goodnight.' And with that the line went dead.

Kelly threw her mobile onto the bed and pulled the curtains shut. How dare they treat her like this, their only child? She was sick of them feeling sorry for themselves when it was her that had been banged up for five years, not them. It was the same when they came to visit – when they could be bothered and her mum wasn't having another sodding nervous breakdown. The look of shame on their faces, her bloody mother weeping into her tissue, her dad giving her lectures about keeping her head down and behaving, then she might get out early. *God, he was a patronising pillock sometimes.*

You'd have thought they'd bought her a swanky pad in Salford Quays the way they went on, not given her the bond for a shitty ground-floor flat on a dead-end estate.

And she wasn't making it up either because someone was stalking her, making her life hell especially at night, so much so she sometimes thought it'd be easier back in jail. At least there she had her little crew around her. It hadn't been easy at first but she'd soon identified the winners and losers and Kelly sought to ingratiate herself with the former. After that, she'd had a pretty easy ride in return for doing their bidding. She couldn't wait for them to be released then they could have some fun. She'd already promised Julie the boxroom.

There it was again, a creaky sound. She definitely heard it. Taking another peep through the windows Kelly knew she wouldn't sleep tonight so decided to make a brew, and put all the lights on and the telly. *That'd tell a prowler I'm up and awake, might scare them off.*

Taking her phone and opening the bedroom door she flicked on the hall light. On her way to the kitchen she paused in the small lounge to press the TV remote and relaxed slightly when the news came on. It was company at least.

The second she pushed down on the handle and opened the kitchen door she knew something was wrong: the cold blast of air first, then her feet were wet and there was a sound, running water. Instinct forced her to switch on the light, but nothing happened even when she flicked it on and off a few times.

Dragging her phone from her dressing-gown pocket she turned on the torch and immediately saw the cause of the flood, water pouring over the edge of the sink. Aiming the phone at the back door she let out a sigh of relief. It remained firmly bolted.

Scanning to the right and following the source of the cold air, Kelly spotted the opening light on the window that was hanging loose. Stepping forward warily, her socks and hem of her pyjamas wet through, she could tell that the hinges had been prised open and splintered wood was scattered on the windowsill. Panic-stricken, Kelly turned off the taps and removed the plug.

No way had she left them on. Or had she? She'd drunk quite a bit of wine earlier, easily a bottle and a half, yes that was it, she'd been pissed up and careless. Or could someone have got in and done it? It might be kids playing pranks, or worst case, burglars who got skinny runts to squeeze through the narrowest openings. She'd learned that in prison, along with other tricks of the trade but her own speciality was how to intimidate other women, and worse. If she got her hands on the little shit that'd done this he'd be sorry. But for now she had to work out what the hell to do with a broken window. Her mind was scrambled, and she was desperate to find an innocent reason for the state of the kitchen. Still, no way could she ring her dad until morning and then she'd have to eat humble pie, which was so fucking annoying.

Maybe the police, whenever they finally arrived, would have

the number of a boarding-up service, or she might be able to flutter her eyes and flash some boob and get them to help her out. Didn't matter to her if it was a bloke or a woman, either would do these days.

All she could do now was stay in the kitchen till they got here and if anyone tried to get in again, she'd stick a carving knife in their hand.

No more late-night booze, she thought. She couldn't really afford it, not on her shitty wage from the meat-packing factory. Then she remembered the light. Why wasn't it working? Surely that was just a coincidence. Mere minutes had passed since she'd entered the kitchen but it seemed like hours, waiting to hear the sound of a police siren coming to her rescue. Trying to be brave, all the time listening for noises and keeping an eye on the window, Kelly trained her phone on the lampshade in the centre of the ceiling. Sure enough, the bulb was missing. Where the hell was it?

Every single sense was on red alert as reality dawned and her brain screamed the truth. *Someone's been in. Fuck, someone's definitely been in! Get out! You've got to get out, now.*

The words fuelled the terror that was building as Kelly darted for the hall but as she did, her torch lit up the back-kitchen wall and something caught her eye. Dread ran through her veins and her legs shook slightly but she forced herself to look, training the beam, her bowels churning.

There, scrawled across the white wall, written in red paint that dripped like fresh blood, were words she didn't understand at first, until a distant memory was triggered and the meaning filtered through. In an instant she knew exactly what they meant, why she was being targeted and who by.

This was revenge, this was Stan. Two more thoughts, in rapid succession caused her breathing to shallow – where would it stop, how far would he go? Every single hair on the back of

Kelly's neck stood on end and goosebumps prickled her arms as she mouthed the same cruel words that she'd once used to taunt and punish Stan.

BECAUSE I CAN

The End

ACKNOWLEDGMENTS

I hope you enjoyed #MeToo.

This book is very dear to me because of the issues raised within it.

Whilst purely a work of fiction, the story was written from the heart and comes from a good place. By speaking out, and to some extent laying bare elements of my own life, the hope was to send a message to men and women alike.

Instead of tearing each other apart, setting one against the other, maybe one day we can come together and support each other through education, respect and understanding.

The ripple effect, as mentioned in the book, touches the families and friends of victims. It ruins lives, while trauma and stigma linger, mental and physical scars sometimes never truly heal.

The subjects of sexual assault, domestic violence and false accusation are deeply disturbing and complex. This book was written after drawing on my personal experiences of each.

In addition, throughout the research process I also sought the advice and opinions of various individuals in a professional capacity and those affected by, or with personal experiences similar to the characters in my story. Some prefer to remain anonymous but I would still like to acknowledge them.

I'll begin with the men and women who have messaged me privately and shared their experiences. I am humbled and honoured that you trusted and confided in me. I hope I did your stories justice.

To those determined and brave individuals who are rebuilding their lives and gave their time to explain how group meetings and counselling has helped them, I applaud you. Despite your own predicaments and heartache your under-standing of my reasons for writing this book touched me deeply, as did your honesty and encouragement.

From the bottom of my heart, thank you all.

One person whose opinion meant a great deal to me is Adele Shea. You're a wonderful friend, an inspiration and a survivor. Thank you for your insight and advice. You read the book first and I held my breath waiting for your verdict. That's how much it meant to me, and how much you mean to me.

Next, to someone I am immensely proud to call my friend, who has been there for me ever since the days of Over My Shoulder, and helped me survive them. She was a serving police officer of 25 years, a Public Protection Investigator Specialising in Sexual Offences and now, works as a Civilian Police Investigator in the same field. With her wealth of knowledge and expertise she cast an eye over the contents of this book. Rita Farnan, thank you for your time, advice and support. Most of all thank you for your steadfast friendship.

At the time of writing this, during lockdown, another of my friends has been extremely busy, working in her professional capacity with victims of domestic violence which sadly, has surged during this crisis. I admire her for many reasons, our connection is precious. Her opinion of this story mattered greatly to me. Mikayla Lloyd-Richards, diolch, fy ffrind. Keep doing what you do, you're an amazing lady.

To the probation officers and offender managers who gave me an insight into the workings of HMP Manchester (Strangeways) and to the ex-prisoners who shared their memories and experiences of being inside, thank you.

As I said earlier, some of the people who assisted me with this book prefer to remain anonymous but they will always be part of this story and I will be forever grateful.

Those that can be named, also deserve a huge thank you.

Aiden Joseph Mulligan, I always said I'd put you in a book and here you are. Not only did I use you as inspiration for Doog, I thought I'd turn you into a detective. At least I didn't kill you! This time.

Anita Waller, what can I say? You should know how special you are to me, my writing buddy, my guiding light, my grumpy mood alleviator and perfectionist personified. Thank you for being my mate.

Keri Beevis, you are an absolute star and my respect for you as a fellow author is immense, so the hours awaiting your judgement seemed like forever. Receiving your message was a very special moment. Thank you for the tweaks and everything you've done behind the scenes to support me. I treasure your friendship.

To my super ARC group who not only read early copies of my books and diligently report back, you are also my loyal cheerleaders and valued friends. You were so brilliant when you received your copy of this book, a tricky ask which you handled so well. Then you went the extra mile and helped with publicity, it was fun and I'm glad you came along for the ride. I will be forever in your debt.

To Nicki Murphy, my favourite blogger, confidante and

trusted friend. You get me. I get you. That's all I need to say apart from thank you.

Now to the superstars at Bloodhound Books, Alexina, Tara, Heather, Fred. You are a dream team and the whole process is made so much more enjoyable and perfect by having you guys on board from start to finish, and then so much more.

To Clare Law and Ian Skewis for your respective editing and proofreading skills. I really enjoyed working with you. Thanks also to the publicity team who do their magic behind the scenes.

Before I started to write #MeToo, I talked the idea through with my husband and children. To have their blessing was important, they come first always. I should have known they would support me, but on this project their understanding and encouragement meant everything. To my super six, I love you.

Finally, there is one very special lady I have to thank, the wonderful Betsy Freeman Reavley.

It is always with trepidation that I send in a manuscript so when I received her email and subsequent phone call saying she loved the book and was behind it all the way, I felt great relief and yes, euphoria. I am immensely proud and honoured to be published by Bloodhound Books, but this is eclipsed by having someone I admire and respect endorse my writing.

You know how much you mean to me. Thank you awesome woman, boss and friend.

That's it. Apart from thanking you, the reader, for choosing my book and even sticking with me right to the last line of these acknowledgments. Please take care of yourself and your loved ones, and stay safe because we never know who's around the next corner, if life is going to throw a curved ball, or our world is about to implode.

Most of all, please remember, what happened to me, could happen to #YouToo.

Printed in Poland
by Amazon Fulfillment
Poland Sp. z o.o., Wrocław

59938863R00186